THE HOWL OF THE WOLF

Hong Ke (the pen-name of Yang Hongke) first came to public attention in 2000 when his breakthrough story 'Blowing Smoke' won the Lu Xun National Excellent Short Story Award and he was recognised as a Most Promising Newcomer by the Feng Mu Prize.

The author, who was born in Qishan County on the Zhou Plateau in 1962, received his higher education in Baoji and spent a decade (1986-96) teaching and carrying out cultural research in Xinjiang, a geographically and ethnically diverse region stretching for more than 1.6 million km². On returning to his home province, he taught at Shaanxi Normal University, while continuing to evoke the vast northwest in his magic realism-suffused stories, novellas and novels. His longer works include *Rider to the West*, *Tiger! Tiger!*, *One Hundred Birds Worship the Phoenix*, and the Mao Dun Prize shortlisted *Kalabu Sandstorm*.

Hong Ke passed away in Xi'an shortly after the 2018 Spring Festival. His short stories and novellas were posthumously added to the prestigious China Classics International list as selected by the state.

This book is part of *Shaanxi Stories*, a series of translated works by acclaimed authors from the Shaanxi province of China, produced by Valley Press in collaboration with Northwest University, Xi'an. The series editors are Hu Zongfeng and Robin Gilbank. Books in the series so far include:

#1 MOUNTAIN STORIES, YE GUANGQIN
#2 HOW OLD DAN BECAME A TREE, YANG ZHENGGUANG
#3 THE EARTHEN GATE, JIA PINGWA
#4 THE HOWL OF THE WOLF, HONG KE
#5 THE BLOOD RED SUN, WU KEJING

The Howl of the Wolf

Hong Ke

Valley Press

First published in 2019 by Valley Press
Woodend, The Crescent, Scarborough, YO11 2PW
www.valleypressuk.com

ISBN 978-1-912436-16-3
Cat. no. VP0136

Copyright © Hong Ke 2019

The right of Hong Ke to be identified as the
author of this work has been asserted in accordance with
the Copyright, Designs and Patents Act 1988.

All rights reserved. No part of this publication may be
reproduced, stored in or introduced into a retrieval system,
or transmitted in any form, by any means (electronic,
mechanical, photocopying, recording or otherwise) without
prior written permission from the rights holders.

A CIP record for this book is available from the British Library.

Cover design by Jamie McGarry. Text design by Jo Haywood.
Cover photograph by Tambako.

Contents

The Howl of the Wolf — 7
Blowing Smoke — 32
Sweetness Setting In — 46
Passing the Winter — 63
Golden Altay — 74
The Tears of the Trees — 137
Snowbird — 151
Hometown — 171

Acknowledgements — 224
Endnotes — 225

The Howl of the Wolf

A LONE WOLF'S howl descends from the skies, puncturing the depths of the wilderness where the withered autumn grass stands tawny yet erect. The beast bounds and leaps as vigorously as molten lava spurting out from beneath the ground – so agile and so fierce that it is dazzling to behold. The wild grass and assorted trees retain the last verdure of autumn, which is scattered into the air like mauve smoke given off by the pyroclastic flow. The wolf springs onto a greyish rock, wherein is preserved the passions of the lava. His wiry, forceful legs become riveted to the spot. Such is the pressure exerted by the boulder and the wolf that the earth begins to pant breathlessly. From the bowels of the land, there rises a feminine sort of moaning.

"What can you hear?"

"It sounds like a woman's voice."

"You are a queer lass. You're the one who's on top of me, but you insist that someone else is making a racket."

The woman is indeed mounted on top of her partner. Taking hold of his head, she kisses him once and then again as though gnawing on a huge watermelon. The man, perhaps exhausted, feels too sluggish to perk up. She jumps down off the bed, fetches a packet of Ashima cigarettes from the tea table, strikes a match and lights one for him.

When they first grew acquainted, she had lit a cigarette for him in just this way. Back then, Red Snow Lotus was his brand. This particular gesture of hers never fails to draw his fancy. A woman who can blend her own being with cigarettes should prove irresistible to the opposite sex.

The man's eyes narrow and he sucks on the fag as if he is drawing a deep breath. The glowing end hisses like a patch of arid land as it is drowned by waves. His self-control is quite something. The cigarette tip burns merrily and brightly without a flicker of flame; the fire has ducked its head to dive into the core of the tobacco and is doing its utmost to hide in the billow of smoke. As he inhales, the fragrant cloud swirls within him like an eagle hovering above the steppes. The man seems rangy and splendid – he lies prostrate on the bed, his chin jutting out high, casting a shadow over his entire face. He has a black stubbly face. The cigarette protrudes from the midst of his beard, blazing for a moment and then falling dim. Black smoke spews relentlessly from his nostrils and freezes in suspension above his facial hair after the fashion of a mist hanging over a forest canopy.

It is a fine cigarette. After finishing, his palate feels parched. He craves something to drink, but instead he hauls the woman over and plants her on that dry, bitter and wide mouth. He might as well be a herdsman driving his flock to green pastures. Her moist red lips peck cautiously at his stubbly mouth and then sink all the way down to the root of his tongue before landing finally on his Adam's apple as it bobs up and down. She lets out a fierce, strangulated *wu wu*, her legs kicking out for all she is worth. Those thrashing limbs are gaunt, long and vehement.

Her mouth is agape. Whether she is breathing laboriously or shouting it is impossible to tell.

The stiff ears of that distant wolf now prick up. Birdlike and with a *whoosh*, his lobes take wing and within a split second have flown past the Altay Mountains, the Alatao Mountains, the Tarbagatai Mountains and the Genghis Khan Mountains.

The sound the wolf's ears are trying to locate originates in an oasis encircled by rolling mountains, steppes and deserts. Right now, numerous men are thrusting their way into women's soft warm bodies. Life stands at that chaotic primordial state. The wolf's ears can only catch the buzzing noise from electric wires.

Roadside poles leading across the wasteland into the oasis resemble musical instruments – *rubabs* and *dobros*, to be specific.[a] A flock of sparrows lands on the overhead cables. Mistaking them for twigs and the electrical currents for the romantic charms of the earth, they skitter to their hearts' content until the fatal zap.

Sparks cascade. They shriek as they are nuked into crumbs that patter down.

The wolf finds himself transfixed. Without opening their beaks, the birds have made a kind of music of their own.

The creature suddenly lets loose a long-drawn-out howl aimed at the wilderness below the rocks. He gives the impression of spitting out a sabre embedded in his chest cavity. The blade duly pierces the abdomen of the wilderness. The limbs and trunk of the wilderness – the rolling mountains, deserts and steppes – start to twitch and tremble.

The man hears it clearly this time. He puts on his clothes and stands in front of the mirror to shave his beard – he even shears away his sideburns.

"This doesn't look good on you," the woman comments. "Bonny like a baby."

With a faraway expression, he gazes at his face, which has been harvested too hard.

The man stands with his back to the window. It is preternaturally bright outside. A kind of golden yellow entity – too searing to be taken in – lingers in the air. It is the Genghis Khan Mountains spreading themselves out along the horizon.

The woman's reflections do not, it must be said, gravitate towards the Genghis Khan peaks. The mountains, which owe their fame to that great man, are in reality a mass of greyish blue rocks and gravel pits without a single blade of grass. The place she remembers lies to the north of that range and is called Altay. Here one can find rolling mountains keeping company with plateaux and pasturelands.

The woman babbles on while the man holds his tongue, his broad, substantial back still directed towards the window. Outside on the taupe rocks at the edge of the sprawling wasteland, there is another fellow his equal in strength. His tail pokes out bolt straight as if he wants to pound the stones broken. The man is looking without looking, his back turned to the window. There are few things that he wants to watch with his back. Through the course of his life, he cannot recall whom he has gazed at with his wide, thick back. He really cannot. He knows that this is the first time, as if he had not really been born to face this strange world. He is already in his thirties and is quite familiar with the planet. However, with his back he sees a brand new world; the view so accurate and meticulous. "He is here to look for you," he cannot help blurting out.

"Who is looking for me? Who are you talking about?"

"Him. Who else would I be talking about?"

The man is magnanimous and holds his adversary in high regard. He regards the wolf as a fellow human being without any hesitation.

"You know each other. He's come to look for you in such a hurry, but you don't know?"

The woman has been divorced more than once. Each of her ex-husbands shouldered a painful sense of embarrassment that could never be expressed out loud. She happened to bump into this man; he is her latest. "Don't get any wild thoughts. Allah gives every woman only one man. I have neither cause nor need to leave you." She leans against him and gives him a bear hug, her hands clamped precisely and seemingly ready to block the eyes on his back.

"I won't sleep with a man out of wedlock. I'd never go to bed with a bloke before we'd tied the knot. Do you hate the fact that I am a divorcee?"

"Are you truly satisfied with me?"

"You are the best man I have ever met."

"You are not exactly flattering me."

"I meant what I said. You are really very good."

The woman's nimble and mighty hands grope their way up from the man's waist to his chest, back, shoulders and arms until they slide finally across his gallantly round mandible.

"Such a handsome chin," she murmurs. "Like the rocks." Her fingers scratch his solid jaw. Her fair-skinned digits are like white sheep, the ones that are hypnotic to look at. They gorge on the grass that grows out of the fissures in the rocks. They turn their heads away from the wormwood that carpets the marshy lowlands yet have taken a liking to the vegetation on the rocky highlands. The grass is short and tough like gold that is as yellow as yellow can be.

"You don't need to search," he says. "I know everything now."

"I don't know what you mean. If you have anything to say, spit it out. Why do you behave like this?" she quizzes.

"I don't know why I've come over like this."

The man starts to look for something and the woman is keen to help. He doesn't let her. He wants to do it himself. It must be something that belongs to him. He delves into all the cabinets and even digs about upstairs. Dog-tired, he slumps onto the sofa lost in a trance. But he is unwilling to quit. He must find the item he's looking for.

"Let me help you," the woman insists.

He casts a glance at her but is tongue-tied. A woman is a woman after all. She raises the cushion and yanks at the boards of the sofa bed for all she is worth. Two big coffers are stashed beneath it. The pair put their backs into it and together prize the lid off one of them with a bang. A hunting rifle rests inside just as a beast lurks in its den. The barrel is oily black and shiny. He wasn't expecting that she would take hold of the weapon before him. A woman is a woman after all. She doesn't grab at the butt, instead grappling with the barrel. The dark, heavy tube slides to and fro in her tender, fair-skinned hands like the flailing of a listless submarine. As he watches her proceed in an experienced, calm-minded, steady and imposing manner, he doesn't know why, but his mind wanders back to how they had disported around in bed.

Come what may, he will never be a match for that gun. No man is a match for a hunting rifle fully loaded with bullets. Forged from top-grade steel, the powder in the cartridge cases is peerless and even the butt was turned from date wood. He is only too familiar with this gun – he once used it to rip the top off a black bear's skull. When she has it in her grasp, she considers aiming it at herself, so she might peer with child-like curiosity into the hollow interior. He senses danger, but before he can cry out, the gun has already barked loudly, striking terror into both of them.

The discharging lead bullet lodges itself in the wall, which now looks like it might tumble down at any time. Bit by bit, her face emerges from behind the powder smoke, looking simultaneously terrified and excited as if she is playing a perilous game.

"It never occurred to me it might be loaded. I was scared stiff."

He warns her that this is a hunter's habit – a hunter always leaves the last bullet in the chamber of the gun and won't fire it until his next hunting trip.

"I got it," she says. "A hunter never spends his last round."

"Bullets are a kind of symbol. Having bullets in there means the hunter is still alive."

"A gun without ammo is a pitiable thing."

"A gun without ammo is less use than a fire poker."

"Do you still have bullets?"

"Of course I do, stupid woman. How could I not have bullets?"

"Honey, I've gotten on your nerves again. I didn't mean to. I didn't know what to say. Don't be cross with me."

The man does not utter a word, but his hands are still livid, as are his spine and back and his shoulders. No longer does he need to forage around in the boxes and chests. He drags open a drawer. It is chock-full of gleaming ammunition. He retrieves a handful and holds them out in front of the woman. "I have bullets. Tons of them."

"Don't act like this," she pleads. "You had me scared stiff. If there weren't any bullets, we could go and buy some."

He gives his head a clout. "What is wrong with me? Nothing serious. Why have I come over like this?"

He slowly calms down and helps her pick up the bullets from the floor. She likes the bullets very much. All of them were wrought from brass instead of having iron casings.

"I'm hungry," he declares.

She asks him what he fancies. Shredded noodle dough and veggies or wheat flour noodles?

"Take it easy. Anything will do." He puts away his rifle.

"Don't play around with it," she warns from inside the kitchen. "It is loaded."

He did not spot her loading the gun. But a bullet is already there, rammed into the chamber. What is more, judging from the tone of her voice, you would assume that the gun is hers. He feels annoyed. He had never felt like this before. You could say that no man in Xinjiang is as irascible as he is today. He begins to doubt whether he is a Xinjiang guy after all. Thinking about his foul temper fills him with revulsion. She calls for him to come and have his meal. He nearly slaps himself across his face before hesitating and laughing out loud. She asks him what is so funny.

"Just now I was pissed off with you, but ended up being angry with myself," he explains.

She gives him a slap. "This is what a man should look like."

After he has dined and drunk to his heart's content, he drags on a cigarette as he listens to her scrubbing and rinsing the bowls and chopsticks. She reminds him that there is a premier league football match on. He switches on the TV. The shouts and cries and goal shooting on the screen bring on an insufferable nausea in him. *Bang* – one time; *bang* – another time. The players' feet have metamorphosed into bombs ready to be let off. They detonate among the crowd. The goals are a couple of bomb craters left behind by the explosions. The frenzied spectators need them. They have worked themselves into a delirium over the striking and the explosions. They squeeze into the stadium simply to experience this.

The man clicks off the telly. After standing in front of the set for a while, he starts to pack – he loads up all the implements he needs for the wilderness, finally trussing up his gun and ammunition. He is tentative about telling the woman that he wants to go hunting. He doesn't know why he has adopted such a tone of voice. He had hoped that she would put her foot down or else be indecisive. He never expected to receive her resolute support.

"Maybe you can bag a bear. There are black bears in Altay."

"I won't go to the mountains. I want to go to the steppes."

"Then you can only bring home some hares and maybe some Mongolian gazelles."

The man doesn't mention the wolf. He shoulders a grudge against the beast. If he hates something, he won't enunciate it in advance. He has thought it over beforehand. The wolf's pelt will be utilised as a coverlet and the tail fashioned into a scarf to be draped around the woman's neck. The head, meanwhile, will be stewed for one day and one night in a cauldron with lye. As a work of art, it will take its place on the back wall where it will cover the bullet hole. The shot that struck that wall made the house as unsightly as an animal maimed by gunfire. He has to attack poison with poison by using a wolf's head to decorate the wall. The woman wants to paper over the bullet hole. He will not permit that.

"You are still angry with me. I'll make up for my mistake," she implores.

"You did nothing wrong."

"What on earth do you want me to do?"

"Really, you did nothing wrong. I want to hang something artistic there."

"No matter what is hung there, the wall shouldn't be left with a hole in it." She now cottons on. "I am powerless to stop you. You go it alone."

He straps on the hunting gun and clutches her against his chest for a long time.

"When will you come back?"

"It won't be long." Pausing for a second, he cannot find it in his heart to see her so worried and frightened. "This time I shall definitely bring home a work of art."

Her guess is a deer or a Mongolian gazelle. She requests that he bring back a decent deer or gazelle horn.

How could an antler do? he thinks. *It is too sharp. Why didn't you think of an animal's head? Animals are like humans. Each of them has a big useful head, where all their strength and wisdom is stored.*

The moment he ponders the animal's wisdom, he becomes vexed. It will be a bugger if his mind keeps on wandering like this.

When he leaves the house, she is still pondering the bullet hole. The bullet head might pass for the pupil of an eye. She is utterly obsessed with matters of lead and brass. Without murmuring the least sound, he strides out of the courtyard with the long gun.

狼

The city is small with outlying belts of trees and arable fields beyond the urban area. Further abroad are assorted trees and wastelands rank with weeds. Many rocks crouch among the grasses and trees. The stones are all flat-topped without any expression or with only one expression – the result of exposure to the weather. Some boulders occupy the tops of the earthen hillocks with the posture of predatory beasts. The wind has to surrender in front of these fellows. The boulders will sooner peel away than allow themselves to become flat and round. A few vultures perch there regularly. The wolf that poses a dire threat to the man is now crouching on a boulder. This much the man can sense even from within the confines of the small city.

The man traverses the croplands and belts of trees at a rapid pace. However, caution sets in on the wasteland as if he has breached a minefield. In fact, only dusky white stones deck the prairie, their docility in contrast to the unfathomable nature of the strands sprouting from their cracks. The grass is like a woman. When a windstorm whips up without warning, it grins and bears the devastation. When sheep and goats come to graze, it becomes amiable, beautiful and coquettish; when it encounters vultures and wolves, it rears up like the hair of a hot-blooded woman in a fury – pointing straight to the desolate cloudy sky.

The man and his hunting rifle catch a whiff of the desolate atmosphere.

Above the wasteland, the sun beats very bright; bright as virginal pupils. The sun is mantled in an unadulterated clean blue without one wisp of cloud. If a vulture were to wheel in at this moment, it would have no trouble in pecking out the pupils from the sun's eyes. The vulture could then use its own light to illuminate the sky. But, at the moment, there are no vultures. Birds of prey brood over the Altay Mountains. This expanse of wasteland has been left to the wolves.

The man wants to fire a few volleys. But, on second thoughts, he puts away his weapon. He knows that a wolf is hiding among the motley trees and tall weeds. If it hears the bark of the rifle, the creature will pounce in his direction. A rattled wolf is habitually ferocious beyond description. He can't afford to underestimate it. He is familiar with the predator, but the predator is not familiar with him. If the beast knew that he had come, he would have pounced this way long before. A wolf is not like a man. A wolf has nothing on his mind. If you challenge him, he will hurl himself into the fray without deliberation. A wolf presents a threat to the whole of mankind. He stands as only one man among countless others. He is unable to muster any menace against the wolf. This makes him indignant – as it surely would all other men. Still, indignation is indignation. In the face of the wolf's inimitable magnificence, he must remain cool-minded nonetheless. He should adjust his mood as the situation dictates, relax his sinews and bones, breathe deeply and then sup a little liquor and check over his gun carefully – especially the chamber and the bullets. He has changed the bullets three times. Despite being identical, he still views these rounds with suspicion. He weighs every one of them repeatedly in the hope of singling out any that is heavier than the rest – like a leader selecting and choosing his successor, always fearful that somebody might betray him. When he presses one bullet into the chamber, he drums into it the command: "You must bang." How nice it would be if a bullet were a man's fist. He would fire his fist into the predator's body. A fist would do the job better than a bullet.

His gun fills him with regret. What is more regrettable still is that the weapon itself has sweated profusely from the barrel to the butt and now trembles in fear. Believing that an earthquake has struck, he scans all around and then looks at himself. Nothing has stirred. He blames his rifle. The weapon's confidence duly abandons it and it becomes chicken-hearted. He cannot bring himself to tote the gun, so it lies there in rascally fashion, unwilling to move even if the threat of death were to rear its head.

It suddenly dawns on him that the wolf is right in front of him. The rifle has worked that out already, hence its petrified state. He inspects himself. Sweat had started to pour off him long before.

What is more, it is a cold sweat. Even his bum crack is drenched in perspiration. His groin feels chilly as though a stream is rushing over it. Sweat seeps out of his every last pore. The only shred of fortune is that his brain is not in disorder. He relays commands to himself. According to these, the gun must be fully-functioning and primed to engage in combat at any time. His shuddering hand, dripping as it is with sweat, reaches out to move the rifle, which is likewise shuddering and shedding sweat. This time, he doesn't give the orders, but rather implores the gun to stay tough, display a little bravery and brace its spirit.

The mouth of the barrel flashes towards him as if giving him a dirty look and regarding his word as hot air. He wants to say more but finds that his mouth won't toe the line. His mouth is duping him by going through the motions. The lips quiver but no sound is produced. He can merely murmur in his mind, not even able to blabber to himself out loud. Throughout his whole body only his brain is operating, though in a very abnormal manner. The gun and his own limbs have all betrayed him. These deserters quit before the beginning of the war to listen to the enemy's dispatches.

His huge adversary – the wolf – appears. He doesn't approach. The man looks through the assorted trees and sods and spots the greyish-white boulder. He catches sight of the beast. The wolf is gazing somewhere else as if in deep meditation. Wolves can, in fact, think. The wolf is unable to see him. He can only catch the smell of a pile of food. Out of instinct, he charges towards the man. Without thinking, the huntsman plunges down and holds his breath. He is in suspended animation. Still his brain doesn't fail him. It remains loyal and uncomplaining. What is more, it reminds him that it is not good to play dead. This trick may dupe a black bear but not a wolf.

The beast's tongue is already hanging out. Its tip scratches several times and then retracts. Its mouth must be dozens of times bigger than the mouth of a gun barrel – big enough to rival that of an artillery piece. The wolf directs its massive maw at him. He almost jumps to kneel and kowtow to the wolf as if he were his grandpa. Actually, he springs to his feet without dropping to his knees. He is a Xinjiang man. No matter how shiftless he might be, he won't kneel and kowtow. If it comes to the crunch, he won't stoop to that even if it means being eaten up by the wolf. No matter how much he shivers and how much his bones perspire, he must hold on.

The wolf doesn't pounce. The creature must have seen through his scheme, or else is full to his throat to start with and needs no further sustenance. In other words, he is acting out of character. He takes one step forward to put pressure on his opponent, who responds by taking one step in retreat. The process is repeated. The man frequently stumbles, but crawls to his feet and continues his backwards course. Finally, he brings himself under control. He is now in a position to turn and flee. He doesn't do so, apparently complying with the wolf's posturing on purpose.

The wolf forces the huntsman all the way out of the wasteland to the suburban belts of trees and arable fields, where some farmhands are toiling. On hearing their shouts and cries, excitement sets in. He has ceased to perspire profusely and his flesh has stopped shivering. The wolf pays no attention to the war cries around him. Many people draw near wielding farm tools. He brushes them away. He wants to drive out the man who has encroached on the wasteland like a bodyguard deals with an intruder.

The wolf charges out of the wasteland and enters the belts of trees, which are suffused with human odour. So many staffs and guns and bullets assail him. He dodges them all and continues his advance. Even the vast belts of trees step backwards. The wolf has thus enlarged his turf in one forceful circuit. His torso starts to stiffen under the mad attack of the cudgels and guns and bullets. In his state of satisfaction, he regains his wanderlust. Luckily, he has a head of iron. The cunning humans know this, so they don't aim their sticks and guns and bullets at his head but rather his torso, which is beaten into a mush and, finally, oblivion. His eyes perceive a huge ball of fire, a roaring raging fire capable of consuming the wasteland. He too howls.

Like air blasting up from the depths of the earth, the howl throws everyone to the ground. But as the wolf is already dead, none of them experiences a twinge of anger. They toss his iron head back on to the wasteland – where it should stay.

They then crowd around the man who had been pursued by the wolf, blaming him for going out empty-handed and bare-fisted. He should have had a gun – or at least a blade – about him. The man hasn't yet regained his addled soul. Staring at the group, he holds his tongue. In his innermost heart, he wants to tell them that he had a gun, but he just can't spit it out.

He returns home. The woman already knows what has happened. She is extremely conscientious and never utters a single word about the wolf. In fact, from then on they have never mentioned the wolf and have never even talked about it, despite it being a colossal entity. They don't have to discuss it, sidestepping any number of embarrassing situations.

She strains her nerves to cook all sorts of delicious food. He gains weight and his face becomes ruddy. He naturally puts forward a certain request. She cooperates harmoniously and lies down docilely like a tree with a sort of obeisant clamour. His hands rapidly untie her rustling belts and bands. Soon, he can touch her body. She too senses his strength and cannot help but reach out her hands to fondle his waist and back.

It would have been OK if she had just kept on caressing him like this. She never suspected she harboured such a flow of dormant strength within her or that it might burst forth through her arms and hands. Her fair-skinned limbs are like a rapid torrent. Both break free from their former bonds and acquire a new, strange and horrible power. With a nasty look on his face, the man bares his teeth, crooks his mouth and lets out a howl like a predatory beast. He then digs his teeth into her neck. At this moment, a vast desolate wilderness stretches out before her eyes. A game animal with its neck gripped between the teeth of a wolf is always hauled to the depths of the wilderness in this way, its blood sprinkling across the weeds and gravels. She sticks her mouth to his ear and whispers: "Take me out, take me out." He reminds her that it is inconvenient to go outside. She is exceedingly stubborn and unreasonable, insisting on going out in the glaring daylight. He reminds her once again: "We don't have a stitch on. We are naked."

"I don't care. I want you to take me to the wilderness."

"Why would you think of such a place?"

"I like it."

A number of years previously, the man had driven to Altay and bumped into the woman at Hoxtolgay. She was trudging along the one-thousand-mile-long wilderness alone. Her red windcheater stood out against the dull khaki background. Many drivers honked their horns, stopped their vehicles in front of her and invited her to get in, but she gave them the cold shoulder, ignoring their pleas as if she was deaf.

The motorists left disappointed.

He was the most patient among the drivers and tailed her wherever she roamed. She quit the road in favour of an abandoned beach until she finally reached a gravel pit. The booming vehicle pitched down and the man was flung several dozen feet away. Infuriated, he leaped forward, grabbed her and gave her the full treatment irrespective of the blood all over his face. She was so badly beaten she cried out.

"Why did you pester me?"

"I was afraid you might be eaten by a wolf."

"That is exactly what I want."

She was clearly insane.

He trussed her up with a tarred rope, tossed her into his vehicle and brought her back to Altay. She knew what she had to do. When he untied the rope, she was as docile as a lamb. The tarred rope was as thick as a wrist and she appeared much smaller without it. He undid the rope, hefted her down and growled: "Clear off!" She left timidly while constantly glancing back. He was busy under the vehicle and ignored her.

When he left Altay, she was waiting for him on the big bridge. His anger had already subsided. He pulled the door open and allowed her to hop up. The vehicle streaked off along the River Kelan. He asked her what was up with her on the day they had met. She explained that a driver she had hitched a ride with had tried to rape her. When she spurned him, he left her at the mercy of the Gobi Desert.

"After that, you hated all the drivers."

"Can you guarantee that you would never do the same?"

"Girls have only ever done it with me of their own free will. I've never forced myself on them."

"Then you are a good man."

"I would never do such a thing in the Gobi Desert. Altay boasts such beautiful pastures. Why cast a woman away in the Gobi Desert?"

They had already gone past the elegant steppes. He showed no intention of laying a finger on her. They duly reached the Gobi Desert, where she had suffered her misfortune. She never anticipated that her heart might be swayed again. She nudged the man with her hand, but received no response. He was in rapt concentration. This was the most perilous leg between the great Gobi Desert and the Genghis Khan Mountains. Vehicles frequently overturned into gravel pits. Her heart was already being swayed and her body seized by a kind of transparent fire, which incinerated her clothes and extended outwards. Her hands reached out of the inferno but felt cool and refreshing as ice. Like a shivering tongue, they touched him and sucked him and kissed his arms. In a trance, his hands left the steering wheel and started to steer her. The vehicle broke off from the road and bounced along the Gobi Desert as far as the rocks, which barred its way.

He couldn't remember now if it was her bosom or her neck that he grabbed between his teeth. Anyhow, it was a graceful part of her body. Through his throat rolled the kind of growl let out by a predatory beast. He hauled her forcefully to the gravel pit behind the rocks. The wilted yellow weeds inside squeaked as they pressed down on them, and they were soon buried within. Her pale legs and feet rose and fell like the pure blue flames in the furnace a Taoist priest uses to refine longevity pills. The gravel pit had become a crucible, which burned violently in the bright and clean sunshine.

"I see the light of the world. That is the sunlight."

"No, that is the light we are giving off."

"No doubt about it."

Their clothes were strewn about the gravel in a disorderly fashion like the ashes of a fire. The light was bursting out of their bones.

When he started the ignition again, he felt a sudden jerk from the oil tank. Petrol rushed into the air cylinder together with the spark and spurred the wheels to leap onto the road. His free hand couldn't help but clutch at her waist. She stared at him, motionless.

"The best fuel in this world is coursing through our bodies," he told her.

"You mean our blood."

"Yeah, that's the stuff."

She knew about blood and she knew about life, but she didn't know a thing about vehicles. Now, she had taken a liking to them. She appreciated his imagination too and associated the oil tank of the vehicle with her heart. He told her how the transmission shaft converted the power of the petrol to the wheels so the vehicle could fly. It was the thick long steel shaft beneath the undercarriage.

"It grows out of the vehicle's waist," she said.

"Yeah, yeah, it grows out of the vehicle's waist. You are so smart."

"It is so capable when it spins. It can seize the four wheels so they turn smoothly."

"It is the transmission shaft. A transmission shaft spins."

"I like the way it *spins*."

Not until later was he aware of the overtones of this word. By then, their relationship was already steady. When they joined together to form a single body, he could hear the crackling, burning sound of his own blood. Next, a stream of miraculous strength started to swirl from his chest to his abdomen as far as his thighs, spinning heroically in her body like the steel transmission shaft beneath the vehicle.

"I like the way you *spin*."

She is downright stubborn and insists on going into the wilderness. The gravel pit and the tufts of wilted yellow grass have branded too deep an impression on her. Steeped completely in the story of how they met, she even recalls some details she couldn't remember clearly back then. She swears blind that he pinched her neck between his teeth. "Here, right here." She points at her fair-skinned throat, showing it to him. "You dug your teeth into my throat. Your mouth let out a sound like a wolf does."

"What did you say?"

"I said you were like a wolf."

Sure enough, the wolf blows in. It is her words that have made it appear.

The man and woman gape at each other and then turn their heads to look at the expanse of wasteland and the solitary wolf.

"Didn't you beat that wolf to death?"

"His head was still left behind."

"He didn't want to eat you, only drive you out of the wasteland."

"A Xinjiang man can't surrender his wasteland."

"But he really doesn't want to eat you."

"Do you think that being buried in the pit of a wolf's stomach is the worst thing imaginable?"

"I like the way you spin. You not spinning any more is the worst thing imaginable."

"I'd never expected I'd be so bad today."

"You've been very good today."

"It seems as if I'm no good, in spite of what you say."

"You are always good. I meant what I said."

"Don't hoodwink me. I know how bad I am."

"What on earth has happened to you?"

"Not to me but to both of us. From the very beginning there's been this mysterious voice."

"I love nobody apart from you."

"If it were a man, I could challenge him to a duel. But these few years it's been a kind of mysterious power I've been up against."

"What makes you say that? You beat him to death, didn't you?"

"His head is made of iron, and his spirit still looms above the wasteland."

Their house is like a wartime blockhouse standing guard against the boundless wasteland where the wolf dominates the miscellaneous trees, weeds, gravel, sand and earth. They hide in their home.

"I surely wasn't the first one to shoot him," he remarks.

"All the men who ever had anything to do with me hated the wolf. Each of them went out with a gun to take him on."

"And they all lost."

"I like the way you spin. They could only thrust in and slide out. They didn't know it was possible for a man to spin. Men who can spin are an endangered species. I must watch over you. I won't let you loose."

"You told them the story of the wolf, but you refuse to share it with me."

"In all honesty, I have never told it to anyone."

"But the story has unfolded."

"I am really stupid."

"You were not wrong."

"It wasn't my intention to get acquainted with the wolf."

"It could be seen as a kind of good luck – a challenge presented to all the men. What a pity they all lost."

"I never expected that they would be screwed over."

"We can only say that this has given us an opportunity – an opportunity to hold our heads high and let out a long breath. You're not the slightest bit to blame."

Exhausted, the man falls fast asleep the moment he collapses on the bed and the woman dozes beside him. He dreams of the Genghis Khan Mountains and the Altay Mountains and of the vast wasteland, the countless gravel pits and hard sundry trees and wild grasses between the two. Later, the wolf turns up like a tongue of flame soaring out of the tufts of grass.

The woman leaves him now.

He is dreaming. He doesn't know how she loves him. She kisses and nibbles at him repeatedly, but he is none the wiser. He even dreams of her packing up her things, but fails to wake up. He thinks that it is only a dream. A dream is not true. It is the complete opposite of reality. He needs the woman in real life, though not in his dreams. Therefore, he doesn't expend much thought on the matter, continuing instead to indulge in his reverie, like a rider giving free rein to his steed. Subsequently, he observes how she hunts out the Mongolian sword from the drawer. Many years ago, he had regularly strapped that blade to his waist. Sometimes he slid it into his boot as if his shin were in want of a bone and he became as stout as stout could be. She picks up the knife and inserts it into her right boot. A man sets greatest store by the left while a woman favours the right.[b] Whatever would a woman look like with a knife stuck by her calf?

He is in a dead sleep yet sees everything. His gaze follows her out of the house, through the city and into the unending wilderness.

The wolf's head had been discarded where the wasteland met the oasis. A stream of power that would never dissipate gathers together slowly and spirals around the cranium. When she steps close, a whole wolf materialises. The wolf is not even remotely on his guard. Eye-catching as it is, the creature still doesn't spy the hilt of the knife poking out of her boot. He darts straight at her. Blood surges and her face turns rosy. She reminds herself of the proverb that *one should never follow the tracks of an overturned chariot*, but still falls into the trap. The wolf lunges at her chest in an adept, easy and indefatigable manner. All she can do is reach out her arms and wrap them tightly around his neck. The wasteland is gone. The earth and the skies are gone. Only the wolf's fervent breathing and boorish howls are left behind.

Everything happens out of the blue, just as it had many years before. Back then, she was only sixteen. She went out into the wilderness to paint from nature – heaven only knows why such a bizarre idea would leap into her mind. She painted the eagles, the stampeding horses and the grassland. Heaven only knows why she would also paint the gravel pits, which looked as if they had been pecked out by bombs. The edges of one pit were very sharply defined despite the pit itself being rough and deep. Her paintbrush bestowed a kind of light on it out of the ether. The gravel pit became infused with vitality; an eye via which the earth could directly scrutinise the firmament. She realised that this was the most outstanding picture in her portfolio. She had apprenticed herself to her art for many years. Not until this day, however, had the passions of her life genuinely been projected onto a new continent – her own world. She had mingled not only into the gravel but also into the entire wasteland and earth.

On the spur of the moment, before she had time to put away her sketch-board and paintbrush, she ambled down to the bottom of the gravel pit. Gripping the rocks, she slid down cautiously. Her feet had barely made contact with the ground when the wolf shot out of the blond grass. Her soul soaring away and her spirits dispersing, she had never expected that a predatory beast could make its lair inside the gravel pit that was so pleasing to the eye. At first, she thought her imagination could compensate for a lack of familiarity with the bottom of the gravel pit. She took the light on the painting as the miraculous strokes wrought by her own paintbrush. She didn't know that the gravel pit could give out light by itself – the light of the wolf's life. Her inspiration, passions and imagination had become one with the wolf.

She remembers how her mouth was wide open. She also remembers that her mouth did not make a sound, that it was her hands and feet that hauled her out of the pit, and that she fled in desperation after reaching the level ground. The wolf was in hot pursuit. She was as speedy as a horse but still couldn't shake off the beast. The whole wasteland was his kingdom. She quickly reached the oasis, but the wolf still caught up with her. He leapt forward, floored her and grabbed her neck between his fangs. Like all the victims who had fallen prey to a wolf, she wrapped her arms tightly around his neck and fell into a trance. Later, she was surprised she could hear the rustling sound of the grass. Her body woke up too. What she clutched to her chest was a rough round head of hair.

A callow young man who learned painting with her in the small city had once kissed her. He was slippery as oil. After kissing her lips, he wanted to peck at her neck and came close to divesting her of her virginity. They had known each other for barely a month, but he had pressurised her as far as her last line of defence. She swore an oath that she must hold back. It was OK to kiss her lips, but not her neck. Nevertheless, she found herself helpless when ambushed by that bearded mouth. She sank into a deathlike state. So awful for a girl to lose consciousness.

Of all the parts the wolf could seize in his mouth, he went for her neck. At the base of her neck adjacent to the snow-white creamy bosom upon which the young man wanted to release his passions and schemes, the wolf withdrew his sharp fangs but kept her immobilised with his lips, clamped like the jaws of a vice. She came back fully to herself. The wolf zipped away across the limitless dark wasteland as if he was flying. She had ridden in trucks and on horses, but only noble steeds and wolves can attune themselves to the vastness of Xinjiang. One old Kazakh man told her: "Horses reign over the steppes just as tigers rule the mountains." What about the wastelands? Xinjiang boasts so many wastelands. "Wolves are the kings of the wastelands." The old man's face was inscribed all over with admiration. "You Han Chinese hate the wolves, but we people of the steppes regard them as the heroes of the animal world. Only horses are on a par with them." She still retained an equine scent and energy, yet she wanted to grow acquainted with the wolves.

The wolf reached the spot she had been painting with her still dangling from his mouth. He then foisted her into the gravel pit. In her passionate imagination, the gravel pit became the eye of the earth. The wolf dropped her on the pupil and crouched down alongside her until dawn. With a long howl, he bounded out of the gravel pit and rushed off. Her narrow escape from death shocked the small city. Her mother ran her hands over her from her head to foot and still couldn't believe it was true. Her father used to be a soldier. He came over to check out her neck. Her neck was uninjured apart from two rows of tooth marks.

"The wolf was not hungry," her father surmised. "Only a ravenous wolf will eat a man. He was only teasing you."

"How could a beast play around like this? It's enough to scare a big man to death," her mother complained.

"Wolves are not as bad as they have been painted. Isn't the child still alive and kicking? Child, you bumped into a chivalrous wolf. That is never easily done," her father concluded.

He poured half a bottle of hard liquor down his throat.

There was that slippery-as-oil young man as well. He was so experienced and dexterous. She actually thought she was his first and obeyed him like a silly girl. An audacious idea even flashed through her mind. She hoped he would grab her between his teeth. In the depths of her heart, she yelled time and time again. The young man had already entered her body. It was impossible for him to take an interest in her neck. She no longer felt ashamed. She had already made that great transition from girl to woman. Feverish was his excitement, as feverish as a little fighting rooster. She forced his head to her neck. His fuzzy mouth clutched at her snow-white neck. In the past, he had always liked digging his teeth into this spot. But this time he wanted to avoid it. The girl had survived the snout of a wolf. He didn't have the guts to release his passions on a spot at which a wolf had gnawed. And yet, he had no route of retreat. The girl had guided him here to be the wolf's rival. The moment his lips made contact with that place he felt a current of agile and fierce force coming over from the wasteland. The small house couldn't withstand it; an eggshell-like young man like him couldn't withstand it either.

He had gone to bed with many girls and kept mature women company. Even so, his sexual history could do nothing to save him. He struggled recklessly for once. Emboldened by his nugget of pitiable dignity, he forced out a roar and wanted to charge over and then sound a hasty retreat after a temporary orgasm. However, his bark aroused a more imposing and long-drawn-out howl. From the apex of the skies to the heart of the earth, the wolf's howl burst out. The young man's hair stood on end. His little pecker retreated like a startled snake. Cramps struck his lower abdomen. His proud seminal boast spurted out all over his own body as he retreated. His cannon had fired before it stood tall, the cannonballs landing on his own battlefield and detonating.

All the men were ruined like this.

He was her first man. Others followed after him. The processes differed, though the outcome remained the same. No matter how they writhed about, the agile and fierce smell left on her by the wolf always drowned them. Without the least scrap of strength to fight back, they all shrivelled.

Then, her latest man came along. He gave her a good hiding in Altay and struck fear into her. The wild wolf's smell about her person evaporated. Their romance wore on smoothly. For the first time, she felt the strength of a man and her life as a woman truly began. She no longer related the story of her bizarre, thrilling experience and no longer talked about the wolf because this agile, fierce man and the wolf were of a piece. She couldn't distinguish one from the other. Moreover, she could never tolerate it when her man slipped into despondency. She was duty-bound to help him.

She thus has her own dreams.

狼

She strides out of his dreamland, treading onto the wasteland. She perceives with her own eyes how the wolf has reconstituted his vital essence to resume his former shape. He then pounces on her. He surpasses his previous frenzy and ferocity and his life advances into a sacred realm. Precisely as he had done many years ago, he takes hold of her throat with his lips but not his fangs. Like a true gentleman, he allows her to feel his agility and fierce might as well as the splendour of the wasteland.

He conveys her to the enormous-mouthed, smooth and boldly-edged gravel pit in the depths of the wasteland. The yellowed grass is shivering. He lunges on her without stopping to suck at her round, snow-white, smooth-skinned neck. His blood and energy stampeding and surging, he can't help letting out a mad howl, which pierces the zenith of the skies and the core of the earth.

The man in the small city immediately sits up. He has shaken off his dreamland completely. Bracing himself with both hands planted on the bed, he fixes his eyes on the breathtaking scene that is unfolding on the wasteland. The gravel pit is so marvellous and fascinating. Its shape is similar to a woman's vulva cleft into the fissures of the rock. What a miraculous portal to life has been flung open amid the stones! Like a naïve piece of ancient pottery, it forms the crucible for the flame of life. He discerns the woman's pale, bright arms and legs, bosom and neck. A hyper-masculine mouth is clamped to her neck. It is sucking for all it is worth, as if it wants to suck the round earth dry. Such is his excitement and stimulation that he feels he is at one with that mouth. He even cries out, "Water. Water. Hurry. Water!", as he is being scorched by a lustful fire, the flames upon his body, but his body also full of water. The interweaving of *yin* and *yang* and wind and fire was also the symbiosis of water and fire between the heavens and the earth in the universe.

In the depths of the distant, vast, serene wasteland there exists a miraculous stone pit. A place of which there can be no doubt.

The man regains his miraculous power. A shaft of masculine power spins between his abdomen and buttocks like the steel transition shaft on the undercarriage of a vehicle. He wants to howl – to let out a long howl. He really does howl. He doesn't care about his neighbours' protests and curses. When he was in Karamay, he saw with his own eyes how the mud, sand and crude oil burst out from the innards of the earth like fury, tossing the drilling platform and workers into mid-air. He howls so sharply and ferociously, the others curse him for being an animal. Nonetheless, their curses are music to his ears. Later, he sobs because the one that flashed the fire of life in the gravel pit had not been him. Truly, it was not him.

It is the woman who has come to his rescue.

She hasn't forgotten the despondent man in the small city.

Taking advantage of the wolf's senseless mania, she plugs the knife into his belly. The blade immediately goes to work like a stampeding Mongolian horse.

I like the way you *spin*.

The knife starts to swirl as well.

The giant wolf tumbles down, his iron head rent apart. The wasteland relaxes.

She doesn't care about this. She doesn't give a damn about anything. She returns to the man. His face is deathly pale and every inch of him is trembling.

"Who am I?" he asks her.

"You are my man."

Blowing Smoke

They are downing the opening round of drinks. Before picking up their chopsticks, everybody is meant to polish off the trio of shots standing in front of them. Someone calls from outside. He is mounted on a horse, the hooves of which can be heard churning up the earth. The incomer announces: "Your old pal, Ma Jielong, is calling for you."

"What for?"

"To come and blow some smoke up his … "

The fellow exits on his beast.

Ma Jielong's pasture is dozens of miles away from the town. Everyone shouts boisterously: "Drink the wine. Go on, drink. Put that off until tomorrow."

The man sinks the opening round easily but does not lift his chopsticks.

They are all displeased: "He can pull over any old grandma and blow smoke with her. Why must you go now?"

Ma Jielong has reared a large herd of cattle. The man loves Ma Jielong's cattle as much as their master does.

"Sorry, I must go."

While everybody is in a state of bewilderment, he makes his exit.

Mounting his mare and shaking the reins, he trots along the road. As he reaches the outskirts of town, he turns back and rides the entire length of the street again, entering the general store, where he draws right up to the counter. The people in the shop all raise their heads and look at him. His horse snorts repeatedly.

The shopkeeper asks what he wants. From high atop the steed, he points here and there. Soon the counter is piled with Greenland sugar cubes, Yunnan brick tea and four bottles of Ili liquor. The owner asks him what else he requires. His eyes scan for a while and then he spies peanuts and broad beans. He says that he wants some of these and is doled out a few packets of each.

Again, the proprietor asks the customer what further items he requires from the many wonderful perishables in the shop. Two cartons of Red Snow Lotus cigarettes are offered up and accepted, then two bags of Afanti washing powder are brought out. The man lets out a *humph* and his face grows sullen. The owner becomes very embarrassed.

The bystanders laugh: "Only women buy washing powder. He's not a woman."

He points at the goods on the counter: "Pack them for me."

The shopkeeper finds a hessian bag and stuffs the brick tea and sugar cubes into it. When he is about to add the Ili liquor, the guy snatches it from him. The horse cranes its head over the counter and nearly knocks the owner down. He stumbles back against the shelves behind him. The man slips the bottles of Ili liquor into his pockets, one by one until both sides of his torso bulge as if fistfuls of knives are concealed there. He fastens the hessian bag to the saddle. With a shake of the reins, he departs.

Once he has left the town, the horse slows its pace, its trots growing gentler and shorter. The horse knows how his master adores this. The master's back is straight, but his head droops down, the collar of his corduroy overcoat brushing against his cheeks. His eyes squint narrowly. With the swaying of the horse's back, a ray of light appears in his eyes like water is seeping from them.

The steed gallops up a long slope. From the edge of the precipice, there extends a range of miniature hills. Each of the hills is russet-coloured like sand and stone. Vegetation cannot survive here. Grasses and alhagi have become scarcer and scarcer. Further on still, the alhagi disappears altogether. By now, the man is fast asleep.

Possessed as he is of the kung-fu that engenders balance, the rider is able to slumber on horseback. Once he has reached the sandy and stony area, he starts to doze. Like the vegetation, he can derive no hope from these sands and stones. The wind lifts up his hair, curling the strands. Sandy dust falls on his hair and soon becomes invisible, the particles having sunk down onto his scalp. His hair remains dark. The grains continue to sink down. The larger ones are like worms, keen to burrow into his skin. He has already become accustomed to their nip. They are itchy as lice. He does feel an itching. He now begins to snore – something that has earned him notoriety.

When he snores in bed, his wife tips water into his mouth. Even water cannot bring his magnificent snoring to a halt. It percolates like boiling tea and his sleep grows even mellower. At this point, his wife will start to cry, causing him to wake up straightaway. His snoring ceases. His wife's cry is thus very effective. Other women cry out because they are being beaten, but his wife cries because she is assaulted by snores. He has never lifted a hand to her. "How can any man beat his wife?" he asks brutish guys. "Real men are born with a dick. Why resort to using a hand? Your hand should be reserved for fighting with other men."

Others ask him about his tricks for taming women. *Snoring* is his reply. His wife loves him and his snoring as well. Although his snores make her cry, the snoring also tempers his wild, bull-like nature. His wife keeps their home neat and organised. She waits upon him attentively. After a meal of fine food and drink, he lies down on the bed and then the large bomber takes off. He compares his snoring to the sound of a massive, powerful military aircraft. For him, sleeping is not a pause, but the beginning of a new world. There are beautiful dreams to be had while snoring. How splendid it is.

Ma Jielong is his bosom friend. He always has a kind of splendid sensation when he goes to Ma Jielong's home. He can even sleep on horseback, his snores so resonant that mountains quiver and waves whip up in the oceans.

He and his horse now walk through a series of undulating hills. When they go up, his body leans back then pitches forward on the descent. He never falls to the ground, however, only sashaying back and forth and never to the left and right. Were he to sashay in those directions he would be sure to dismount.

Sometimes the path is extremely narrow. Stones are scattered about the road. The horse jumps up and almost wakes him in a sweat. His sleep is close to being broken. His head is not a balloon, but it can grow to envelop the hardships of sleep. When his head swells, all the hills are smoothed out and become soft, cushioned as they are beneath the steady hooves of his horse. He and his head stand tall in the saddle. What could pass over his crown except for the sun and an eagle?

Green light rises in the sky. The grassland appears on the horizon. The horse lets out a succession of happy snorts. He too wakes up within this strong green hue. He spies herds of cattle on the grassland. They are all prolific dairy cows; piebald like a collage. Ma Jielong's cattle are more remarkable than this. As he and his horse pass through the animals, the cowherd greets him and tosses him a cigarette. He tosses him another back. He is known to all the people on the pastureland. He is Ma Jielong's pal.

Ma Jielong's cattle pen is empty. His wife is shovelling cow dung. When she catches sight of the liquor bottles in his pockets, she starts to nag. Every time he comes, he gets drunk and so does Ma Jielong. The two macho men always become a little wild for a while and her home looks like it has been looted. The woman is not afraid of their drunkenness, but is apprehensive about them causing real trouble. Sometimes their drinking is very elegant and they blow smoke up each other's … as they drink. The woman serves up countless dishes. She is fond of listening to their bragging about their proudest moments.

They would never cause serious trouble, no matter how strong the liquor was. Their bodies are as sturdy as the mountain. What is liquor? It is just water that flows with a babbling sound. The man is a good drinker, though no match for Ma Jielong. He is always the first to get squiffy, so Ma Jielong has to allow himself to become intoxicated too. Otherwise, he would not be a good friend. Every time they drink, the woman gazes at her husband's "elder brother", making him feel ill at ease.

"Sister-in-law,[c] why this look?"

"Your sister-in-law is afraid that you will get plastered."

"Is my brother plastered too?"

He is a little tipsy. He must beat Ma Jielong down. "Brother Ma, you are still steady – *humph*, *humph*, I shall make you sway."

Ma Jielong smiles. She comments: "Brother, you are too silly. You have come here from a long way off, while he has been resting here waiting for your arrival. If you want to beat him down, you need to rest for the night first."

In this way, he has cultivated the habit of sleeping on horseback in order that he can set himself on an equal footing with Ma Jielong. A refined atmosphere takes hold now. When the pair reach a stalemate, they start to boast without limits. After all, the pastureland is a backwater. Ma Jielong is always willing to yield when it comes to bragging. Ma Jielong is fond of blowing smoke up others' … and everybody on the pastureland appreciates his talent. His bragging begins with small towns and then spreads to middle-sized cities like Kuitun, Shihezi and Changji, ending up with the provincial capital Urümqi. These are all the big cities he has visited.

They are becoming drunk less and less frequently these days. His sister-in-law still nags all the same, so he starts to make fun of this comely woman. "Sister-in-law, please have mercy on us. Your brothers haven't been drunk for nearly half a year."

"Your sister-in-law doesn't want to see you looking like a drunken ghost."

The woman really is growing angry.

He squeezes out the bottles of liquor for her to take a look. "Not so many bottles. No reason to worry."

"I wouldn't worry, even if you moved the distillery in here. I have driven him out."

"Sister-in-law, your heart really is cruel."

He dumps his hessian bag in the courtyard. Pressing his legs against the horse's side, his mount dashes out. The woman shouts: "You must fetch him back. You can drink at home. I will cook meat for you."

He hums happily. He already feels an unusual kind of sensation. No matter how crazily one drinks on the infinite grasslands, there is no need to worry about knocking over tables, chairs and trestles. He and his horse dash like a gust of wind. When they jump over the hills, it seems as though, at that moment, the ground is gulping something down. He rushes into the forest. The leaves on the trees flutter noisily as if the trees themselves have just stood up straight.

The grassland gradually broadens out. No more short hills and sparse forests are in view. The space is wide and wild. The sun stands alone in the sky and he looks exclusively at that. The sun is sure to know his friend Ma Jielong. Jielong is right here on this grassland. Even if Jielong were to run away to Russia, the sun would still be able to see him.

Up on horseback, he raises his head and stares at the sun. One of the countless beams emanating from it lengthens and thickens. Its spearhead points in the direction of Ma Jielong. He gives the reins a swish and hastens over there.

He cruises through the purple alfalfa and the blue forget-me-nots. Huge patches of grassland daisies flash before him.

His chum Ma Jielong is sitting in the golden land of the daisies. He is smiling. His smile looks like it has come into blossom together with the flowers. Ma Jielong is cross-legged on the carpet of blooms. According to legend, the Khan of the Kazakhs sat on a white blanket in the same way surveying the stunning grassland through squinting eyes.

Ma Jielong tweaks his black beard and says: "Hello, my good pal." Jielong's big hand beckons and the man follows his gesture to be seated. His buttocks can feel the bumps of the grassland daisies. His hands can detect them too. The flowers have the texture of silk and satin. Four bottles of Ili liquor squat beneath Ma Jielong's feet like a pack of hunting dogs. The man still has his own four bottles of the same brew, concealed like knives in his pockets.

Ma Jielong says: "Take your bottles back. Are you afraid that I can't afford such booze? I have crates aplenty at home."

"I love to drink your liquor."

He whips out the broad beans and peanuts. There is no container for them. He simply tears open the bags and picks them out to eat. Ma Jielong scrabbles for some broad beans as well. Both of them, bottle in hand, realise the broad beans taste too salty.

Ma Jielong exclaims: "You can eat this." He then plucks one of the blooms from the masses of grassland daisies and tosses it into his mouth. His friend plucks one too and chews on it. The taste tingles and the grassy aroma is pungent. Even so, once it has been swallowed, there is a clean and fresh aftertaste. The fragrance spreads out from one's nose.

"What a tangy flower," he remarks. "It sinks right down to your lungs."

Ma explains that he has grown accustomed to eating it and so can no longer appreciate the taste. He advises him to chew slowly. Ma Jielong chews steadily and with care as though he is savouring cheese. A kind of sweet aroma emanates from his nose. He lets out a shrill sneeze. Ma Jielong takes a sip and he does likewise.

Jielong says, "I want to sneeze some more," then swallows down a grassland daisy and follows it up with a sneeze. "I'm so cosy I could die. I have never experienced a feeling of comfort like this."

"This is known as 'snuff'."

Ma Jielong's eyes widen. The liquor bottles in his hand leap up and down giving off a bright light. He continues: "The princes and aristocrats of the Qing Dynasty smoked this. They put it into carved jade bottles and inhaled it through their noses."

"They didn't use their mouths?"

"Didn't use their mouths."

"The tobacco must be grown on the grassland."

"They are grassland daisies." He plucks one of the daisies. "The ancestors of the Qing Dynasty came from the grasslands of the north. When they came to Beijing, they missed the local flavour of their homeland, so they processed this treasure of the grassland into tobacco. They didn't use their mouth to imbibe it, but used their noses to inhale it. All of the taste is to be had in one sniff."

"The mystery of the grassland is to be found in this smell?"

"Including the sneeze."

"The sneeze is truly wonderful."

He lets one out and Ma Jielong follows suit.

Ma Jielong comments: "You sneeze only when you think of a woman. How can this small thingummy cause people to sneeze?"

Jielong rubs one of the grassland daisies between his palms and the released petals swirl around. He proceeds to pat the man on the shoulder, saying: "Good brother, I love to listen to you blowing smoke … Come on, let's down the last drop like we are blowing on bugles."

The two uncap their bottles with their teeth and swill down the contents as if they are riders sounding instruments fashioned from a bull's horn. After finishing that one, both let out a long *Ahhh* and open the next. They bite open the covers and the aroma of the liquor surges out like a demon from an enchanted bottle, hightailing into the grassland in every direction.

Ma Jielong says: "I'm in a bit of a trance."

"Me too."

"Here is my true brother. Together we will bother the demon."

They rest their liquor bottles and then hold them up against the sun. Ma Jielong observes: "The sun has turned into a woman. The sun is wearing a red cummerbund."

He perceives the red waistband of the sun as well. The magnificent muscles of the sun reveal themselves from beneath the tight wrapping. He tears away the red garment. Actually, the beautiful design is but a label. The label of the Ili liquor is red and fits over the sun rather well.

He shouts: "Ah, the sun is naked now."

Jielong screams too: "The sun is a woman."

"Let's be civilised now. The woman is looking at us."

He sits up straight and Ma Jielong raises his chest too.

Ma Jielong surmises: "Your sister-in-law is just such a person. She nags, but in reality she enjoys our drinking and she enjoys your bragging too."

"My sister-in-law is a good sort. Let's have a toast to her."

The two bottles clink.

They are drinking their fill. They toast the sun and murmur about how it could be that the sun does not hear one iota yet sees everything. They toast the sun and the sun draws over. The sun walks up to them. They belch from all the wine while continuing to sit up straight.

Jielong declares: "My good wife, today we will not eat vegetables and meat, only drink pure liquor."

The sun is empty-handed; she carries nothing. The sun strides elegantly towards them.

Ma Jielong clasps his hands and proposes: "My good wife, sit down."

His friend clasps his hands likewise and echoes: "My elder sister-in-law, please take a seat."

The face of the sun suddenly turns red.

"Oh, my brother," Ma Jielong demurs. "Your sister-in-law is not old. When you said the word 'elder' your sister-in-law got annoyed."

"My sister-in-law is still quite young."

"Then how can you say she is old?"

"Old means 'good'. We are Chinese, when we want to show respect to somebody we call them 'old so-and-so'."

Ma Jielong is elated. "My good brother, I do enjoy listening to you blowing smoke."

Jielong glances at the sun. "Wife. I shall not call you a 'good wife'. The word 'good' is not as fine as the word 'old', so from now I shall call you 'old wife'."

Ma Jielong addresses the sun as 'old wife', though this friend addresses her as 'sister-in-law'.

The sun is dignified and stately. She lifts up the hem of her golden skirt and flounces away.

"That's your sister-in-law to a tee. I didn't ask her to prepare dishes, though she insisted on doing so."

The sun squats on the green grassland. The entire grassland is shining intensely. All the women on the grassland cook like this. They build a fire using dried dung and boil tea and meat.

"It is not easy for women to live on the grassland. At home, they must wait upon their man. When their man goes out, they have to follow after the herds and live in tents."

"My sister-in-law has followed you all over the grasslands."

"If you want to raise calves to be big you must find the best pasture, but once they have grown up they turn into this."

Ma Jielong removes several pieces of paper from his chest and rustles them noisily. "Here is a cheque issued by a food processing plant in Kuitun. The figure on it is 125,000 RMB."

"My brother, you have made a fortune. So, why are you still complaining about it?"

"A big herd of cattle is transformed into big heap of Arabic numbers. Whatever can you say about this?"

"This is a headache to be sure."

"As your older brother, I feel that headache. Your sister-in-law feels it too."

"She's fine. When I came over, she was shovelling the muck from the cattle pen. She is working gladly."

The sun is collecting cowpats from the grassland. The sun piles the dried cakes into a steeple.

"That's your sister-in-law to a tee. She never spares any effort in her work. There is enough dung to use in the cattle pen, but she still goes outside to collect more and piles it up as high as a mountain or a hill."

The sun sets the cow dung alight. The flame rises fiercely and gives off a roaring sound.

"That's my cattle lowing." Ma Jielong wipes his face and his tears disappear, saying: "I'm alright."

Ma Jielong shoots his pal a glance, maintaining adamantly: "I really *am* alright. I have left a few head of cattle for your sister-in-law. She has a tender heart. To begin with, we planned to keep two calves. She nagged so I left two extra big ones. They are the father and mother of those calves."

"I've seen them."

"You've seen them?"

"In the pen. Quite nice."

"You think they are quite nice too?"

"They are Ma Jielong's cattle. Ma Jielong always has the best cattle on the grassland."

"But my cattle have been driven away by them."

"Whoah, my brother, you sold them, didn't you? The price you were offered was pretty fair?"

"The price was fair, yes, but I could not bear this. I even went out with a storm lantern in the middle of the night to sprinkle more feed for them. The cattle pen was empty, however. I suddenly became vexed by a demon. I picked up my rifle and mounted my horse. I sped across the grassland for that entire night, spending all of my cartridges. When I reached Kuitun, my heart became heavy. There was no grass there. My cattle would have been very hungry. No matter, I had to drive them back, drive them back to the grassland. The people in the processing plant did not listen to me and said that I was being irrational, stirring up trouble. I didn't care what they had to say as far as my stock were concerned. I told them that this was not the place for cows to stay. Cows should be on the grassland. The head of the plant became sullen: 'If you welsh on the deal you will be penalised.' I said: 'I don't care. You can fine me in whatever way you see fit. I only want my cows back.' The head made a call to the factory floor. The head said: 'It is too late for you to renege. All of them have been slaughtered.' I shouted: 'Two hundred cows?' The head replied: 'We are a mechanised plant. We have a processing line.' The workers shouted too: 'Don't mention about there being two hundred! Even if there were two thousand we could still have them sorted in the blink of an eye.' I asked them why they had killed the cows. Did they have a score to settle with them? They said that I was a lunatic. They had nothing more to say to a lunatic."

"You really are a little crazy."

"Tell me, will my cows come back?"

"They can come back."

"In that case, you can brag to me about how my cows could come back."

"One of them is already over there." He points at the sun on the grassland and tells Ma Jielong: "My sister-in-law is milking."

Jielong squints and takes a look. His eyes remain fixed on the spot even while he is drinking.

The golden skirt of the sun droops down onto the land. The hands of the sun are golden too. On the daisies of the grassland lies a gleaming red cow's teat. The golden hands of the sun squeeze the teat tightly and a white ray spurts out.

Ma Jielong gapes directly at the beautiful sun. He even forgets about his liquor. The man gives him a nudge and Ma Jielong follows him robotically. His friend understands him. He also understands his marriage.

He puts a head of grassland daisy into Ma Jielong's mouth and whispers: "This is the cow's teat."

Ma Jielong's cheek twitches. He sucks noisily at the daisy. Jielong has already tasted the sweetness of the cow's teat.

He whispers: "Do you still remember that grassland? I am sure you do." Ma Jielong, the best rider on the grassland, has covered a journey of hundreds of miles. He has become unbearably thirsty. He grabs a cow and bites and sucks at its teat to take his fill. He continues until the teat is withered.

"It is withered now." Ma Jielong swallows the daisy; then another daisy is placed in his mouth.

Ma Jielong adds: "Right, quite right. There are two. Cows have two teats."

"You have a good memory. There should be two teats. You have driven away your thirst and now you go away on your horse. When you wake up, the cow will be lying outside your tent. The cow has been munching on grass the whole night long. Its teat has grown swollen. You come over so happy. The cow wants you to suck again; not only once, it will let you suck every day until you have had your fill. You are twitching with excitement, but this time we haven't sucked out milk. You've sucked hard for a while, but not even one drop of milk has come out. How bright that cow's big pair of eyes are; they have been watching you like the sun. You are moved to tears. You have surely heard what the cow said to you."

"Did the cow really say something?"

"Sure. How else could you – Ma Jielong – have been moved to tears? How else could you – Ma Jielong – have grown so bold? You sucked their milk and, what is more, took away their girl."

Ma Jielong drinks mouthful after mouthful and is so nervous.

Ma grabs the man by the hands: "My brother, my good brother." His voice is very low, almost a murmur. "That cow is sure to have a guardian. These animals, having as they do a knowing god within them, are able to speak and point out the right path for people who get lost. The cow told you that if you want to become the happiest of men you should invite its master. The hands of the master would make the cow's teat run like a never-ending fountain. On your wedding night, you took your bride as a cow. You didn't call her names. What you shouted was: 'Oh cow, my cow'."

"Did I shout like this?"

"Sure, you shouted like that. You bit your bride's nipple too."

"Is that so?"

"That is so. The gods were watching you from up in the sky. You didn't suck out any milk, right?"

"Yes, that is so."

"You didn't suck the nipple until it was withered."

"Yes, that is so."

"The more you suck the bigger it becomes."

"Yeah, that's true."

"All of the cows on the grassland combined are no match for that small pair of nipples."

Ma Jielong has downed all of the spirits and sprawls out on the ground. He chomps the golden grassland daisies. "Oh, my tiny nipple, my cow." Ma Jielong's neck stretches upwards and the whole ground stretches up. Ma Jielong bites the nipple of the earth. With his head wobbling to the left and to the right he sucks for a long, long time. He then raises his head and lets out a long breath.

"My cow has come back!"

Ma Jielong looks at him again and then confirms: "Brother, my cow has come back."

"My cow has come back too."

There is a clarion call resounding in his brain. He cannot control himself. He pulls out the last bottle of Ili liquor from his pocket, rips off the cap with his teeth and begins to blow the bugle, his mouth clamped against the glass neck. The sound of drinking is like the powerful and plaintive call of a bugle fashioned from a bull's horn. This time, he does not glimpse the red cummerbund of the sun. He does not tear the label from the bottle. The sun requires no clothing and has no need to be somebody's wife. The sun appears rude and fierce. Upon its great head there are two horns. The sun charges over with a jolt.

He says: "The cow has come."

Jielong hollers: "That's my cow."

"That's mine. It is a bull. You see, it has no teats."

The two argue maniacally.

Ma Jielong says to himself: "Old wife, sorry. I have to act crazy."

He says to himself: "Old sister-in-law, sorry. I have to act crazy."

Their heads butt into one another with a *pam*. Then another *pam* as they butt into one another again.

Horns appear on their heads. The two grin.

"Cow's horns, cow's horns, cow's horns. You have a pair and so do I."

They prang into one another with even greater gusto and the cow's horns on their heads grow larger and larger. They are overcome with surprise. How can cow's horns behave like women's nipples, swelling bigger and bigger? Both of them touch their heads and find that there are in fact cow's horns on them.

They stop butting one another and start to walk back. Approaching the gate of the house, the woman screams: "What's the matter with your heads?"

"Been butted by a cow," they answer in unison.

Sweetness Setting In

It is a truth universally acknowledged that any long-distance haulage mission requires two drivers. This much was emphasised emphatically by the captain when assigning tasks.

The younger man's close relationship with White Cloud is the stuff of common knowledge. Early August has come around, though in the Dzungar Basin in northern Xinjiang it has been sweltering since the end of April. The sun has drawn close to the earth and is now pouring forth continuously its passion and might onto the land. Nevertheless, the Gobi Desert remains still, as do the other sandy wastes. But, all the oases, like archipelagos scattered across the barrenness, seem to be illuminated and seared by the sun, making every scrap of vegetation on the desert a paragon of arrogance.

When August takes hold, melons and fruit begin to poke out from beneath the leaves, like black cannons directing their mouths towards the sun. They are the offspring of the sun, thriving while their parent shrivels. The autumn sun is lazy and spiritless. Still grasses, trees, crops, ripe melons and fruit cannot survive without it. They depend on it for growth.

As he is leaving, the captain cracks a joke in front of his junior: "Don't worry, your White Cloud won't run away while you're gone. I'll take care of her on your behalf." The captain receives a playful punch to his body, but still feels contented since the tasks have been assigned.

The apprentice is heading out of town on a long-distance haulage trip with his master, an experienced driver. The older man is over forty, married and with a brood of kids. Past the age of forty, husbands are not inclined to stay with their wives all day long. So, embarking on a long trip he has the air of an old lag being let out of his cell for respite. In his jolliness, he begins to hum a ditty.

The apprentice and his girlfriend, on the other hand, are loath to be parted. Not being attentive to the younger folk's infatuation, the master starts to honk the horn. He has no choice but to stop them. By now they have been walking together for miles and reached the suburbs. Still the couple have not bade farewell. Will they have to go even deeper into the desert – as far as the rose willows or the sandbags – before they can bring themselves to say goodbye? The courting couple is torn cruelly asunder by the blaring of the horn. The girl is left waving her hands in the distance.

The apprentice angrily grinds his teeth. He doesn't say a word to his master for quite a while. His master ignores him too. The master is the master; he shows his dignity by keeping a straight face, but deep down is kind-hearted.

"Have you done anything yet?"

"Done anything of what?" The apprentice asks in return in a cold and unfriendly voice, pretending to fumble out a spanner to work.

The master cannot contain his temper anymore, reaching out one of his hands to jab the apprentice's waist, while keeping hold of the steering wheel with the other. "This part, does this part feel hot? Don't you understand? Silly boy, have you girded your strength?"

The apprentice's innocent response demonstrates how truly clueless he is about what the master means. He now has to rephrase it in a very direct way: "Have you done the deed with White Cloud?"

Once again, he finds himself taken aback. The apprentice believes his master is referring to obtaining a marriage licence, so laughs with his mouth agog: "Why hurry? I am not in a hurry."

The apprentice is very proud and confident about his relationship with White Cloud, so his mood is extremely cheerful. He helps his master light a cigarette and assumes the steering wheel. Now the master can relax and unwind for the rest of the journey. After smoking and drinking his tea, the master is refreshed and has collected his spirits again. Now he begins to cajole the boy into spilling the beans.

The giddy, incautious apprentice lets slip nothing special save for how he and White Cloud have hugged behind sandbags and smooched among the rose willow.

Even such a tiny piece of information, so painstakingly extricated by the older man, raises the apprentice's guard.

"Master, did you 'do the deed' before applying for your marriage certificate?"

"Watch it or I'll rip out your tongue."

"Joke, joke, just a joke."

"You cannot tell such a joke to your master."

"Just pretending to be decent," the apprentice whispers.

"What did you say?"

"Isn't it you who started the topic?"

The master opens his mouth but says nothing. With greater agony than an inveterate stutterer, he merely swallows his saliva.

There then follows a rather protracted period of silence diluted only by the diminishing hum of the lorry in which they are travelling. Other cars keep overtaking them. A large cloud casts its shadow onto the ground, and the dark shape lurches forward at almost the same speed as the lorry. It practically becomes an umbrella shielding the vehicle. It's so weird to hear how the sound of the two wings of the animated cloud is audible as it moves together with the lorry towards the middle of northern Xinjiang. There can be no mistaking how the sky is pitching closer and closer to the ground. Perhaps since the truck is passenger-less, the huge cloud wishes to hitch a ride?

The apprentice appears to be able to hear the cloud wheeze. As he accelerates to 120 miles per hour, the lorry starts to break free a little, but the cloud gathers pace too.

Actually, the explanation for all this is quite simple. The deeper the vehicle penetrates the basin, the broader the motorist's line of vision becomes, making the sky seem less elevated and the clouds resemble a mass of vapour exhaled from the mouth of the sky. What about the lorry then? The lorry, like an insect, is propelled upwards by the vapour so that it does, indeed, levitate.

The master cannot sit still, so reaches out his hand to reclaim the steering wheel as the truck leaves the road. Unfortunately, it is too late. Like a cardboard box thrown from a car, the truck grinds to a halt quietly against a bank of sandbags. The saxaul trees along the barrier teeter gently in the wind.

In effect, the vehicle has cut loose and rushed off the highway, growling like a lion. The surface of the road is just 30 centimetres above the desert floor, so the truck cannot career too far, only stalling once or twice as it hits the desert and before the engine dies. At the very moment the lorry came off track, the master had managed to prize the apprentice away from the wheel, which he seized tightly, then slammed on the brakes.

This is nothing catastrophic; a common mishap in Xinjiang. When a driver is drowsy or absent-minded, they veer off the road. The motorist is naturally startled, though no harm befalls anyone or any vehicle. All they need to do is to grapple hold of the vehicle, like tugging an obstinate beast, to get back onto the asphalt and resume their journey.

After twisting over a few times in the sand, the apprentice gets back to his feet. Rather than inspecting what might have gone awry with the truck, he once more becomes aware of that huge cloud, stalking overhead like a gigantic bomber aircraft, sweeping them aside to pursue the other cars ahead.

There is the lightest smattering of traffic on the road. Once every half hour or so, some vehicle will pass by. Nearing the hinterland of the Dzungar Basin, fewer cars are to be seen. That big shining asphalt serpent of a road prostrates itself along the ground. From being the prey of the huge cloud, it seems to have been slain as its victim. The cloud begins to shake like a lion.

The lorry is back on the road. The apprentice cranes his neck to watch the regal-looking cloud and carries on watching it after clambering into the cab. The master forbids him from driving anymore. Insist as he might that he wants to do it again, it is to no avail.

"You might think you are very capable at driving. Go and be a pilot and fly a plane if you want to drive."

"Don't provoke me like that. I am not capable of flying a plane, but in the future my son might."

"Fine, fine, sounds good. Then you should hurry. Hurry and make White Cloud's belly plump so she can have a little pilot for you."

"You've got a crow mouth; a smelly mouth."

The apprentice trembles with anger, while the master hoots with laughter.

All men have to endure this. When jesting about what goes on between the sexes, sooner or later their woman will be the butt of the joke.

The master proceeds to enlighten his apprentice: "You are a decent young lad who knows little about what goes on between men and women. White Cloud is as innocent as you are. A good girl!"

The apprentice is as antagonised as a black bear that has been shot in a vital organ and is now groaning to release the pain.

White Cloud was recruited from Kuitun, a small city near the mining district. She is very simple but favours the trendiest apparel. Since she got to know the apprentice and struck up a relationship with him, she applies herself to anything to which he introduces her, whether playing video games or dancing. During his absences – lasting ten days or a fortnight – she swears off any invitation other young men give to go out with them. It has been no more than a month since she first met the apprentice. The other boys insist over and over again that they only ask her out because there are not enough girls in the mining district. They simply want to hang out, without any other wicked purpose. It is no use explaining. Contrarily, their words put her on even stronger alert and she vows to keep away from single men altogether.

She is trendily attired as usual. She has a vivacious personality like a bird and dwells a little bit farther from the ground than other "birds". She is entwined with a big tree. The big tree is the lorry driver. She is a bird as long as she is in his company. She is inclined to stay quiet for a long time – at least as long as he is absent.

Family men tell the bachelors that there will be no laughing and singing in the unit after she has gotten married. She will store up her merriment for the home. "What a good woman; the model of a good woman."

All this is the fruit of experience and can only be understood by men who've set up a household of their own. Bachelors don't think in this way. Reckless words spew out of their mouths before they give them a second thought and these are met with smiles of solicitude, the type of smile children are shown by their elders. This makes the bachelors even more insufferable.

There is no way to alter the girl's love for the young man. People do not understand what it was that helped the chap to win the girl's heart so that she would commit herself desperately to him. Actually, he has given her nothing tangible. When other men were doing their damnedest to please and woo her, he sent her his clothes to wash. Stupefied for a second, the girl nevertheless rinsed them in the pool under the tap.

As she was washing her own handkerchief, this shameless fellow came over and plonked a pile of dirty clothes before her. The girl was stunned.

Then the voice of the shameless fellow chimed in, "I can't go out of town on a haulage job in these stinking togs. Do me a favour, please. My master is honking the horn for me."

The girl has had her eye on the young man since then. He was really busy, driving out on business almost every day. When they came back, the master would take a rest, but the apprentice had to hose down the truck. Although this troublesome boy claimed he was incapable of washing clothes, he could clean the vehicle until it gleamed. This made his leader very satisfied, and he said: "Your good upkeep should make it run seven or eight years beyond the normal lifespan."

With one eye on his clothes, the girl chuckled as she scrubbed. For the first time she realised how dirty men are! It took her two and a half hours to finish washing the soiled garments, which she hung out on the iron line. She still needed to put them away before he came back after work, fold them up and pile one on top of another. When they were presented to him, they would carry with them the aroma of sunshine. Nothing could make him as excited as this.

"Oh, my, I haven't worn such clean clothes for a long time."

His parents live in Ili; he seldom goes back there.

"Every time I go back and visit, my ma complains that I've crept out of a pigsty."

The girl smiled and asked how he used to do his laundry.

He answered frankly, "Tip some washing powder into some water, then throw the clothes into it and leave them for the whole day, rubbing them for a while, before finally taking them out and slapping off the bubbles."

"You're kidding. Tell me the truth."

"You want to know more, but that is the truth." His voice became firm when he put on airs. "You have done me a good turn. So how do you want me to thank you?"

The girl was annoyed and ignored him.

Thereafter, he lowered himself to the level of a pack animal, keeping on the same clothes for a fortnight without changing them. One day, when there was no one else around, she couldn't resist splashing a basin of water over him. Immediately shocked, he received the order: "Take off your clothes! Do you hear me?" He went back to his room obediently and peeled off the wet and dirty items, flinging them out of his room one by one. He spent the whole day in bed wrapped in a quilt, his uniform having been confiscated by the girl.

In the blink of an eye, the arid climate of Xinjiang dried the laundry out. The quilt-coddled man heard the girl's footsteps coming towards his room. Although carefree in manner, in this instance he was extremely scrupulous. He could discern the sound of the girl's walk from the noise of poplar leaves. He even made out the girl's clothes and hair being blown by the desert wind, which reminded him of feathers being ruffled. He had driven to many places over the years and seen mountains, deserts, oases and prairies. Above all, what obsessed him the most were the flocks of migrating birds. They soared across the horizon, like clouds eclipsing the sky and the sun. He would, at that juncture, stop driving and lean out of the car to clearly see the soft, fine feathers on the convex bellies of the birds.

His behaviour caused the master to sigh: "Take your time and have a good look. Silly boy, look on and on then you will see a girl's flowery dress and two hot 'breads'!"

"You are so shameless!" Aggravated, he nonetheless tried to restrain himself and not fight against his master.

He was almost afraid of him. Alas, an old timer with experience can always stir a young man's heart. He sensed the downy, fine feathers almost upon him, virtually tickling his face. He could indeed hear the girl's footsteps. She folded his clothes and laid them at his door on a piece of paper, and then left.

The girl hadn't said hello, yet the pleasant sunshine smell from the clothes and the desert wind wafted into his room. He took his time to get down from the bed, reaching his hand through the crack in the door to retrieve his clothes one by one. He then put them on, transforming himself instantly from a troglodyte to a man of today. He was now as handsome a young man as he used to be.

With his eyes kindled, he surveyed himself in the mirror, feeling like a colt in the wild. Since the girl had washed every garment he owned, he now had numerous changes of clothing to hand. It is said that a stallion moults several times in the process of growing up. So too does a man. This was his conclusion that Sunday afternoon as he looked at himself in the mirror with fresh gear on.

No longer did he wear grubby clothes, making sure instead that he was neatly turned out no matter how busy and how tired he was. Marks such as oil stains, sweat patches and even stray beads of alcohol left over after a bender played their part in strengthening their relationship step by step. They had no commitment and no bond of promise though and could only be counted as "comrade" friends. Any single man was still liable to chase after the girl.

As a matter of fact, the bachelors in the unit had been eyeing her covetously since she began working here. They laughed at the apprentice's stupidity when he asked the girl to wash his dirty clothes. Of course, they didn't count him as a rival suitor. For in their minds, asking the girl to wash for him was bound to drive her away instead of enticing her.

What the other men were not aware of is just how many times he requested her laundry skills. After witnessing his brazenness a couple of times, the puzzlement of his married colleagues could be read not so much on their faces and lips, but in the looks they cast.

The lad felt not an iota of strangeness or shame, nor did the girl. Every time he beseeched her for help, she would wash for him.

The word "shameless" reared its head when they learned that the apprentice and the girl were going to apply for their marriage licence. They all felt it at the same time, but as a cry kept in their hearts, it remained inaudible to others. This issue could be discussed later on.

They are now unknowingly entering a very subtle stage, seldom realised by young men. The family men cast their eyes on them and calm down all of a sudden. No one would like to break the rule to tell the truth that most single men are apprentices, learning a trade from their master, who might go on to care about the apprentice's matrimonial affairs. However, this rule cannot be divulged – even though everyone knows it. No wonder people are nervous and discreet about it, since it is a matter of the masters' decency.

It is not until many years later that the apprentice comes to know how much care and thought his master gave him. During those most "nervous" days before his marriage, his master behaved so enigmatically that he nearly fell out with him. The master is like an old fox, whose teasing leaves him half-dead. When returning to the unit after a long-distance trip, he will "torture" the good-natured girl with his smelly dirty clothes.

He is not a lump of wood, so he knows that many of his colleagues are chasing the girl. His heart beat like a wild horse's hooves when the girl sent back clean clothes to him the second and third time. In his mind, it was too late for him to realise his love for her. He had left a bad impression on her by always asking her to wash his dirty clothes. Worse still, his shameless master, the old bugger, knew everything but without telling him anything. He even concluded at one point that his master had a psychopathic bent. His wife was garrulous and a bellyacher, as if the whole world ill-treated her. The master, unwilling to go home, would rather hang out with his apprentice after work.

That is what he is thinking at this precise moment: how desperate he is to have a crush on the girl. He is not a lump of wood and so quickly perceived how obsessed the girl was with him.

This he attributed to her kind heart. His hate towards his master has lasted intractably. In the master's mind, there's plenty of time ahead of them. The apprentice will grasp the truth sooner or later. Thus, he keeps on treating him shabbily as usual, teasing and annoying him in his own way.

The master raises the topic of the huge white cloud again. Disliking the tardy manner in which his master drives, the apprentice takes over the steering wheel. While he is in control, the master likens his driving after a huge white cloud to a toad wanting to eat swan meat. Although he doesn't spit out the word "toad", he feels as if he were a toad, because he has failed to catch up with the huge white cloud. No matter how loud the lorry roars or how fast it runs, it is to no avail. The cloud has disappeared behind the sandbars. The horizon is now clear without a bit of cloud. The sky has turned watery, blue and deep.

The master speaks in a very low voice, "How nice it would be if it was autumn."

"It is already autumn," he responds in a cold tone.

The master continues in a light manner: "I mean late autumn when white swans fly over. As old Kazakhs are fond of saying – 'swans used to be white clouds'."

"What I've been wanting to tell you is that as soon as I get back we're going to apply for a marriage licence."

"You need a license before you can be legally married, just as you need a driving license before you can get behind the wheel!"

The master dares not continue with the topic after the lorry has gone off course a few times. He closes his mouth and is quiet for a long time. Then they spy oases. The master takes over the steering wheel. With more and more pedestrians walking along the roadside, the lorry cannot go too fast.

"Boy, you must keep your speed down." There is no response from the apprentice.

The lorry reaches a field of big watermelons. A strain of melon named Red Artillery lies on the ground like cannonballs. Around the field are poplar trees, standing with the posture of batmen ready to serve these sleeping fellows.

The master keeps a slow pace. As his eyes sweep across the melon fields he murmurs: "That melon's as long as the God of the Earth's dick.[d] No man can boast a plonker like that."

The apprentice is not angry with him anymore and begins to call him "master", suggesting: "Here's the place to buy."

Paying no attention to him, the master pushes ahead nonchalantly while praising the watermelons. He clatters on and on about how so many cars are hauled up by the roadside with hulking specimens; and about how some hawkers have halved or quartered their fruit so the flesh can be scooped out with spoons. No one can resist the temptation to stop and buy some. Unable to stomach the apprentice's constant nagging, the master stops at a melon stand. Stretching behind the stand-holder are hundreds of acres of melon field, so it is small beer to supply dozens of truckloads of watermelons.

Anyhow, the master just craves one melon; yes, only one. The owner singles out one of the finest. It really is a dandy melon, which splits open the moment the blade makes contact. A wet and sweet wave spurts out, nearly splashing their faces. The master only takes a few mouthfuls and then stops. While the younger man is happily having his fill, he is the spitting image of a dog nibbling on a bone. Before long, half has gone, and there follows a succession of hiccups. The master asks him whether he's had enough, only to be greeted with a smirk and the question: "Should we move on?"

The master fires up the ignition and is keen to know, "Why do you think the melon is so good?"

"Sweet, very sweet."

"It's not just the sweetness that makes a melon good, daft boy."

The vehicle continues at a slow lick, with the master scanning the melon fields they pass until one finally takes his fancy. Four or five trucks are parked on the edge of the woods, and the drivers are smoking and making small talk with the landowner.

The master walks over to them and hands one of his Red Icefollies cigarettes to the owner, lighting it up for him. He immediately senses how abnormal it is for five or six drivers to be encompassing such an upstart farmer. He tramps into the melon field. Might there be golden eggs growing there?

The master jumps over a surface water channel, with his eyes fixed on the melons. Florid-skinned melons are showing off their round bellies like babies do. It is hard to tell them apart from the melons in other fields. They were actually the same variety, the well-known Red Artillery. He squats down and pats the melons, banging them a few times. Each melon is as loud and clear as a copper gong.

Suddenly, he is stunned, and little by little he retreats from the melon field, as if a rising tide is forcing him back. That is a mere hallucination. The truth is that he found that the five or six hundred acres of melons have been left dry for at least a day. The vines remain green, but the leaves are less verdant than usual. As he walks towards the crowd, he hears a novel expression, "sweetness is setting in".

They lodge in a motel – the sort of spot where melon hauliers always choose to stay for a couple of days.

Just as they are settling down, he asks the master what "sweetness is setting in" means.

"Haven't you understood the concept, even after visiting the melon fields?"

"The field is dry."

No more questions seem necessary. He suddenly catches the meaning. He knew it when he was in that field. He had cottoned onto the reason why his master didn't buy the melons that he thought were good. Generally, melons are picked and sold in the market when they are ripe. But when he was in the melon field, the ground was wet, which meant that the owner wanted to increase the weight of the melons!

Lying on the bed, he finds himself grappling with a question, which in his mind is necessary and not redundant.

"How many days does it take for melons to grow sweet?"

"Three to five days, depending on the weather conditions."

When melons are ripe but there is no more irrigation water at hand, farmers are left to imagine how sweet they will grow. The melons no longer depend on being watered to swell but rely instead on the moisture within their vines and leaves, which function like a magic green processing plant, squeezing all the juice they can muster into the fruit to ensure they are as sweet as possible.

The night is silent, except for the noise of the woods and the twitching sound of vines and leaves in the melon fields. They are distending their bodies like earthworms, gasping and moaning, to siphon their juice into the melons.

In his dreams, the sleeping boy keeps stretching his arms and trying to grab something in the air. Fortunately, they are sleeping on two beds; otherwise, the apprentice would surely mistake the master for someone else. Jokes of this kind do the rounds in the mining district. When married men work in the fields without going home and end up bunking down with colleagues, someone will always mistake the fellow next to him for his other half and embrace him in his dream. Of course, this only happens when a chap is dreaming.

The master – the fox-like know-it-all – lies on his bed, eyes wide-open and smoking after the light has gone out. The moon is as bright as daytime. He observes every aspect of his apprentice's dream and how his body contorts during it. His mouth goes numb, but he continues smoking. Nearly all men his age have a heap of troubles of various sorts. People even directed their mockery at him when his apprentice won the girl's heart.

His own story is known to almost everyone in the mining district. Some time ago, he gave the daughter of his general manager a lift to Urümqi, and the girl developed a fixation with him. He felt he had become another person in front of the girl during the journey, as if he was possessed by something diabolical.

In those days, the road surface was mediocre, so it took them a whole day to get to Urümqi City, during which time they had to pass through five or six counties via oases – sprawling and small – through the Gobi Desert, and share two meals. The trip, like a stage big enough to perform on, was lengthy enough for the man to express what was in his heart. The details of the journey are not important. The point is that in her short life the general manager's daughter had never seen a man so witty and wise. Under the illuminations of the evening, they arrived at the metropolis of Urümqi. The master had become, in the girl eyes, her Mr Right on the Central Asian hinterland.

The outcome of the story can be imagined. The girl's family was strongly opposed and the two of them couldn't get married without the approval of her parents. The master refused to accept it and hatched a plan to sleep with the girl. The general manager had no choice but to accept the result. From then on, he became very cruel and began to treat the abhorrent man coldly. Many years passed, his wife's sisters and brothers lived decent lives, receiving compassion and support from their father. The master and his family were exiled to a postage stamp of a house on the remote Gobi Desert. Their life was impossibly hard.

The master's wife began to mither and nag. She would nevertheless still do as much housework as other wives once she had got the mithering and nagging out of her system. She was basically a hard-working woman. The master had no means of changing her. Workers' wives always act like that. So, whenever the opportunity arose to go on out-of-town business trips, he would snap them up. And, away from home, he would smoke.

After three days, they come back to the unit with a truckload of watermelons.

The moment they climb into the vehicle to start the journey back, the master asks his apprentice: "Are you anxious to return?"

The apprentice tells him the truth: "Sure. I have promised the girl that I will meet her on the first night home."

Before, they used to leave in the morning and go back to the unit in the evening. The one-day trip made it hard for masters to get to know their apprentices. But this apprentice talks and laughs all the way, informing his master how in his dream he had been teleported back and the girl named White Cloud was waiting for him on top of a sandbag two kilometres away. Neither the master nor the apprentice pays too much attention to this little episode.

Back at the unit, everyone busies themselves distributing watermelons. The young man is not anxious about the fruit, nor is White Cloud.

Reunited for the first time since their long separation, the girl says, without waiting for him to speak: "You came back halfway through to see me – so unexpected. I thought you'd forgotten about me before that."

He is stupefied for a moment. It then occurs to him that when he was dreaming he genuinely believed he had come back. He then smiles and caresses her hair, as if perhaps thinking again about those flocks of birds soaring over the sky with their fine and soft plumages. He relates to her his experience of chasing after the clouds in the sky, omitting the part where the truck pitched over onto the sand dunes. He sets about kissing her – so far, the only intimate thing he has done with her. A mild frenzy grips him, which comes across as slightly scary. She nibbles his ear to tell him to kiss her tenderly.

"You hurt me the day before yesterday when you kissed me."

He is shocked again to notice the love bite on her neck. Taken aback for a second, he follows the girl's directions. She does not know that in his heart he is contemplating doing more than kissing. She only observes his meekness and calmness, so kneads his hair with a smile.

"What a fool you are; a coward. You bit me and hurt me and sped away like a rabbit at the sound of a horn. In fact, I was going to let you take advantage of me that day, but – fool that you are – you missed your chance. I don't think you are stupid; you should know how to sneak back to see me in a friend's car. A wooden-top has finally had his eyes opened. You should know not to ask for help from colleagues who will gossip about us. Ask your master for help? No. Even he is your master. You are so smart to ask your friend – one of your classmates in Karamay – to help you to drive you back to see me. You are so smart!"

The waves in his mind slowly subside. He can take a breath now. He drinks the tea that the girl has brewed for him. It is sweetened with sugar.

The girl constantly dabs his face with a towel. When everything is done, she takes a few steps back and looks at him repeatedly with a smile.

"You're tired out, you idiot, aren't you."

"Nope."

"I know you are completely knackered! Don't try pulling my leg! All that direct sunshine has scorched you as dizzy as a drunk. You stumbled all the way back through the Gobi Desert to kiss me and then ran away afterwards without saying a word. What a poor sod!"

She takes the initiative to kiss him this time. The other day, he heard someone gossiping and hid behind a tree to listen for a while. The day the girl waited for him beside the sand jujube copse two kilometres away from the mining district, a stranger was seen getting down off a lorry. The man walked over to her from the Gobi Desert road.

Nobody can deny that on the days when both trucks and people are made to feel dizzy, hallucinations will happen. The stranger thought he had arrived home, so he got out of the truck and ran over to the girl he was convinced was his woman. Believing he was her man as well, the two hugged each other tightly. The honking of a horn made him snap out of his stupor and realise his mistake. The girl, meanwhile, was caught up in the vertigo of happiness and remained insensible to the truth.

He could not continue to stand by and eavesdrop on the tittle tattle. He coughed and walked up to the gossips, wearing a very serious expression.

"Listen, the man you are talking about was me and nobody else. Ask the master if you don't believe me." The master is well-known far and wide for being a fox-smart man. To ask him something means to ask for trouble.

Shortly after they tie the knot, the apprentice and his bride relocate to a more remote mining district.

His wife is none the wiser about that minor episode. She still cherishes the moment when, stricken with love, he sneaked back to see her and smothered her in frantic kisses.

She is apt to relate this story while chatting with the woman next door. "What a poor sod a man is when he is scorched by the sun!"

She also adds how happy she is to be hitched to her husband

– the only man she ever dated. Conversing with others never distracts her from the work at hand; in this case, ironing a garment of clothing. The fabric is so fine that the iron has smoothed out all the creases.

It is indeed a remote place, with only five or six households nearby. In the gardens around his house, he manages after years of trial and error to grow vegetables, then watermelons. The melons are nothing remarkable – football-sized at best – but grow well. When they are ripe, the irrigation is curtailed and the melon fields are left to dry for a couple of days, three at most, since the oasis is surrounded by desert. This is enough for sweetness to accumulate.

This is the first time his wife is able to witness the wonder of sweetness setting in. After all, she grew up in Kuitun City. He then explains to her this wonder of the melon fields in an earnest way.

Passing the Winter

ALONG THE BROAD, expansive terrain on the other side of the Kuitun River Valley runs a highway resembling a black river. This channel advances until it enters the depths of the Dzungar Basin. The river valley then suddenly contracts upon reaching the flat ground, and the highway follows its example. With water being in short supply this season, the river channel seems to strain like a squinting eyeball. Gone are the days when waves would jaunt their way forth. A single storey house happens to stand in the space between the river channel and the highway, and since the trees in the forest belt have finished shedding their leaves, no shelter is offered from the strong seasonal winds.

The old chap has been housebound here for a long while. The moment the strong gale abates, he walks out with a large broom on his shoulder. The broom, which accompanies him whenever he goes outside, is especially big when the bristles are outspread – like the great tail of a dog. The blue cast iron gate produces an echoing creak as the old chap passes through it, exerting himself as he drags the broom out. Gradually, he sweeps the vacant lot at the mouth of the gate, as if he is writing out Chinese characters with his brush. Together with the old man's footsteps, the clear and graceful brush marks on the ground advance ever so steadily towards the junction. He has soon stroked a clean path to where the roads intersect.

It is several kilometres from the junction to the highway proper and the old chap squats down by a tree in the lane to roll a fag from Mohe tobacco. There is no wind now and the broad land is tranquil. He puffs rings of azure smoke gracefully out of his nostrils, giving the illusion of old trees sprouting new leaves. The road has been scoured clean by the breeze. White and bright, it has the appearance of a river running through a forest belt. The old chap had been eager to sweep everything around him, even throughout the entire wilderness, but that would be futile.

The old chap paces towards home, the big broom following after him like a dog. He then props it against the gate to guard the entrance.

A girl calls from inside: "Pa, you've swept the whole highway."

The old chap replies: "It's going to snow."

"You don't need to sweep if it's going to snow. The snow will make it tidier out there than you can."

"The ground's clean, but the snow is dirty."

"It's dirty, dirty. The snow is not a person. You come in now, Pa!"

"I'm sitting outside."

There is no sunlight. The sky is ambiguous. It is hard to tell whether it is sunny or cloudy. The old chap likes the air outside; he likes his spacious courtyard. At the front are adobe sheds for storing coal. To the rear are brick dwellings. The kitchen used to be in the front adobe shed, but was moved to the brick room, leaving a couple of rooms as bunkers. The porcelain jar which formed the kitchen chimney has been left in situ like a decommissioned cannon. The roofs of the adobe sheds are dappled with a layer of dry soil. Coal lies in abundance inside as it would in a mine. Once he went to the Four-Tree Colliery, where the coal hid itself within great buns of hills. Later, when a transportation rail had been laid, it could be hauled out easily. The coal is lucky to be so well-treated by him.

Snow now starts to fall and the old chap's eyes narrow as if he is down the Four-Tree Colliery right now. Clusters of white snow drop quietly down towards the man like paratroopers with their white chutes bulging above them. They wake him up with a start. All at once, the roofs of the rooms and the courtyard are festooned with snow. Winter in its entirety is being borne down by the snow on its white wings. Even the old chap himself is transformed into a snowman and the big broom by the entrance becomes a snow leopard. He laughs and runs outside to beat the brush against the ground. In no time at all, the blizzard has submerged it as a ship sunk in a river.

This time the old chap doesn't venture far. Rather, he stops at the junction. He sweeps all the way from the gate, believing that more snow is set to fall. Crouching down, his posterior skirts the snow, and as he sticks his rear-end up a little, his head tilts nearer to the snow on the ground. It appears that all the seeds from the crops have been buried. In fact, the seeds have been scattered all over the fields by the road. A road may be trampled and trampled by passersby, but this doesn't mean that any seeds left behind will spring into life like those in the field. The more snow that falls, however, the greater the likelihood that the seeds will lie undisturbed and thus germinate. People plant in the ground what they want to eat and wear as though it is their hopes they are sowing. However, not liking to stay in one spot, people are inclined to press forward along the road. Their continued footfall prevents the seeds from taking root and the road is left barren. The earth is fertile in a way that the road can never be. The old chap stretches out his hand into the snow to probe the surface of the road, which is as smooth and hard as stone. He hopes something might yet grow from it.

As expected, a great behemoth appears in the roadway, stumbling nearer and nearer so that it almost strikes him on the nose. The snow is crumbling into powder without melting, so the tyres are dry. It is a really good harvest when a car grows from the earth.

No cars have run along this leg of road for a long time. These days, cars opt for the Dushanzi-Karamay Highway several kilometres away. There around-the-clock, one after another they trundle along like chassis on a motor production line. From the oilfields of Karamay to the refinery at Dushanzi, traffic spews for hundreds of kilometres.

This car has come down from the Dushanzi-Karamay Highway. The old chap doesn't realise that it is his son's car until the vehicle wobbles up to his door. His son hops down from the cab and enters the gate. Meanwhile, the car pants for breath outside. The old chap runs, crunching and tumbling his way through the tons of snow, his eyebrows, beard and mouth completely white. The flakes on his mouth turn into water – the earliest melt-water of winter. The fluid smells like a daikon radish.

The vehicle is loaded with coal. Cloaked with snow, the coal underneath is black and thick like a mountain-dwelling bear. The old chap can almost hear the coal breathing. A bear which crawls about in the snowy mountains may be breathless but does not tire no matter how far he climbs.

The son comes out of the gate, asking: "Pa, where have you been in this blizzard?"

"Just strolling about on the road."

"How come I didn't spot you?"

"I was in the snow. Of course, you couldn't spot me."

They go back inside. The girl is pulling and tearing strands of noodles by hand and the smell of mutton and onions is everywhere.

The old chap asks his son: "Is everything arranged?"

He answers: "It's a good unit, located downtown. My sister can start work tomorrow."

The old chap calls to the girl, saying, "After dinner, you'll leave for work with your brother. That's a big deal."

The son responds, "Don't worry, Pa, the boss is my mate, so it doesn't matter when she begins work. Let her spend a few days with you."

Fearful of how her father may become lonely, the girl would be grateful to have a few days at home.

The old chap smiles, observing, "Your father is a bit of a bore. He has no idea what loneliness is."

The son and daughter laugh.

The son exhorts his father not to go outside and not to linger in the snow either, as it will cause him to freeze. "You can cook inside, watch TV and there will be enough food ready to eat when you want it." A few days ago, his son moved the front kitchen into his room. The cellar in the yard has sufficient fruit and vegetables in store to last the whole winter. The son promises, "In a few days I'll lug in a couple of sheep. Pa, you do live a good life. When I get my apartment allocated by the unit I'll bring you to Kuitun. Let's say goodbye to this place for good."

"I like it here. What would you do in Kuitun? Do you know

what the name Kuitun means? It's Mongolian for a 'cold place'."

The son explains, "These days a city is growing there. Your son and your daughter have found work there so it is where you must live for the rest of your life." The son continues to outline his grand plan, his mouth as restive as a croaking frog. Later he lights a cigarette, walks out at a sluggish pace and shouts for his acquaintance to follow.

The girl is elated as she tidies up, even humming a song.

The old chap asks, "You think you'd like to go there?"

She answers, "I would."

"Listen to your brother when you get there."

"Pa, I'll come to visit you often and bring you good food."

The old chap smiles, saying: "We are not in want of food and you don't need to dip into your purse."

"I'm going to buy you KFC and chocolate cake."

"I don't eat those exotic things. Mutton and onions are good enough for me."

"You've eaten those same things all your life."

"If you don't eat mutton and onions, there's nothing to live off."

"Pa, you're so funny. Really, you can't survive without mutton and onions?"

The old man doesn't realise that when he squats under the window, there are two cabbages and a pile of onions on the floor. He picks up a large one, as dark red as blood. He wipes the dirt from it, peels away a layer of skin and smells its strong, sharp tang. The old chap gives it a bite. In a few chomps he has polished off the bulb.

"Pa, I'm leaving. You'll be the only one left in the house."

"I know you're worried. I won't be alone."

"But you're the only one here."

"There are plenty of people living here. How can I be the only one?"

"You're talking about other folks. You don't have family here."

"I'm not alone," the old chap chuckles. "You'll be alone in Kuitun. You don't know anybody; only your brother. You don't know any of the buildings on the streets."

"I've seen Kuitun on the TV. That place is hopping."

"When you're young you ought to live in a bustling place."
Feeling reassured, the girl packs her suitcases in her small room.

The son has no shortage of help in offloading the coal outside. They pass the coal in through the hatch. The cobbles stack up neatly, motionless with a dusting of snow like frosted fruit. The coal nestles there as though it is back underground. The son's mates smoke the cigarettes he gives them, then leave.

The boy carries his sister's luggage over to the car. They do not want the old man to see them off, so he stands in the gateway as the vehicle disappears into the snowy pall.

The old chap knows there is a road somewhere amid the white expanse and beyond that is the city his son and daughter will reach some time in the middle of the night.

He feels a light chill, having crouched on the ground for ages, fumbling after the broom. He tugs it out of the snow and drags it back into the yard before closing the iron gate. The broom in the yard is soon immersed in snow. Nevertheless, being buried here in the yard is different from being buried outside insofar as the raw wind cannot vex it anymore.

The old chap walks to the adobe shed in the courtyard to tug a large block of fuel from the heap. Loosening his grip, the coal slips free and breaks into pieces on the ground with no more than the sound of a loose patter. It ends up in smaller fist-sized pieces, very glossy and charcoal-black. Behind the door is a leathery bucket fashioned out of tyres. He fills it with coal. A briquette falls silently onto the snow and the old chap can hear nothing save for the sound of falling flakes. The coal is crushed by the snow. He can start to make out its shadow, but more and more snow falls on the shadow, erasing it completely. The yard is totally white.

The fire in the stove leaps up like the heart of a healthy man. He is not an impatient person; he has patience in spades. The rumbling sound of the flames fades away. The hearth is quiet and so is he. Far from being weak, the stove is actually strong but has learnt to bridle itself modestly. He clanks off the lid and there is a lava-like effusion of red embers. The stove has a sturdy iron carapace to serve as a dam, holding back the waves within it when they try to roll out. In winter, the house is sustained by this stove. The old chap tries to break the embers, which within the space of a minute have become as red as an electric wire. The embers are hard like the muscles on the chest of a mare. The old man is getting on in years, though enjoys encountering things which call for muscle. He is relieved to have such a wonderful fire. He feels it is high time he adds a fresh lump of coal since the molten embers of the rock have split open, revealing gaps reminiscent of babies' mouths. He grips a piece of coal with a pair of tongs and loads it into the stove in the manner of a strong man handing over a roasted leg of mutton. The moment the coal drops into the furnace, the flames take the bait and jump up. The coal doesn't burn at once, but sticks to the embers instead, closely and tightly. The flames gush out from the midst of the coal and, with a crackling sound, gather into a blaze.

The stove has a hearty appetite, expending a bucket of coal as if it were eating fruit. The flames spring up and the old man prevents them from escaping by placing a large pot on top. The flame is pressed into the fire wall to heat every corner of the room. A chill pervades the whole winter, but cannot touch the rooms inhabited by the stove and the old chap. The stove is like his machine gun, his cannon. He once served in the Chinese People's Volunteers and fought the troops of many foreign nations. He knows all too well how a machine gun can defend a mountain outpost.

The old chap appreciates the stove, particularly the sound of roaring flames. He cannot help but rest his feet on top of it. It is like placing his feet on a beast. He used to farm the fields and graze animals. That warm feeling of livestock still entices him. A burning stove is no different from a yellow satin calf, or a white foal, or even foul-smelling pigs. When they come to rub you with their corpulent bellies, you are bound to be filled with joy.

The night is bright since the snow has a reflective quality. But the sky is blue, flat and vast. The snow falls from the sky, where it can throw off light as the stars and the moon do. When reaching the ground the stars and moon do not have to shine. This is the advantage of the winter. Although we may be cold, we do not grow tired.

The old man uses an iron dustpan to bring snow back to scatter in his room. Inside the house, it is too dry. He sprinkles the snow like tossing fertiliser, casting out one handful after another. The snow falls on the ground with the haphazardness of ducks charging in different directions.

The snow thaws with such vigour that the last moist spot retains its scent.

The old man turns off the light before going to bed and it remains alight in the darkness, recalling a black bear that is intruding in the dim woods and playing with the trees with the risk of uprooting them. The thing we call darkness has descended upon the room. Outside there is the snow, shining and exuding a pleasant and fresh aroma. The darkness that creeps out of the night secretes itself like bats in the room. Maybe the cold night is causing him to freeze too and he longs to seek refuge in the warmth. Suddenly, he is intercepted by the stove, the clumsy appearance of which belies its might. The stove catches the darkness in a firm, tight hold and drags it to its side. Slipping off its "clothes", the fire leaps out naked into the darkness.

In the old chap's dream, the stove really has become a black bear. He can hear the stove scuttling about on the floor. The dark night, like a fox, is encircling the stove, making him excited. The more excited he gets, the redder his face becomes and the brighter his pupils. He suddenly sits up, rubbing his eyes. Blue rays inch into the room. Before long, the sky is effulgent.

The old man gropes his way out of bed and pokes the stove. It blazes up despite being sleepy and he being miserly with its rations. Like a famished man, it can't be fed too much, since it would be left with a sore stomach. At the crack of dawn, he does not feel it is so charming. The stove wears a matte blue face like a newborn baby. The old chap really wants to give it a hug and sticks his hand into the chamber to let the blue flame take a suck. His hands are dry and black and scarred, but the blue flame doesn't stop and carries on sucking as if affixed to a breast. To begin with, the old chap doesn't feel much pain. He watches the flames lick his fingers and crawl along them to the back of his hand. The flame allows him to perceive the tender details on the back of his hand – such as a blood vessel. That blood vessel is still in good fettle and he knows that this unique part will die with him. Other parts of his body have broken down and are unfit to be recycled; only his blood will flow on until the end of his life. The old chap chokes with excited sobs.

A fortnight later his son returns with a deboned sheep. The son takes the fresh and succulent mutton and buries it in the yard, handing him a hatchet: "Dad, you can use this up over the winter, chopping a joint off when you need it." The old chap says: "I have a stove and I have coal; they will keep me company over winter."

The old man tells his son to listen to the fire in the stove, but the son retorts: "This isn't a tape recorder. You should be listening to the TV." The son turns on the set but finds that the father doesn't care too much for it. The elder man squats down in front of the stove in the manner of a vet examining a cow. The father is satisfied and the son slips away safely.

The old chap heaves the mutton out of the snow and, with a cracking axe, cuts away a block. He soaks it in water, which has been simmering away all morning. The meat boils through the afternoon. He carves the joint into pieces as big as his hand and cooks it in an iron pan. With ginger and salt as the only seasoning, the mutton broth tastes so pure and simple, and the meat is fresh and tender too.

Before the old chap begins his meal, he tips coal into the stove, as if he is inviting it to dine with him. When he can hear the sound of briquettes splintering, he swings his chopsticks into motion. Having a bowl of mutton to eat, his body is kept warm.

The old chap stalks into the yard to shovel some snow for the house. The aroma of the snow cannot be smelt anymore because the stench of the mutton is so sharp it floats outside and is carried far.

This is Xinjiang. One whiff of meat cooking can be detected for miles around. Especially on snowy days, the pungency of the meat proves irresistible. The old chap likes the aroma of the snow.

He tramps out of the yard and into the expansive snowfield. His mouth and gullet both relax; his tongue is thin and nimble. The bouquet of the snow is now such that he can feel it in his gut. His internal organs feel like spilled water; the tide rising in him.

The old chap stews the mutton in much the same way almost once a month. When full of food and drink, he always forgets the smell of the snow. He would invariably head far into the snowfield, breathing in the refreshing and distinct scent.

His girl has always been such a good girl and returns on her father's birthday. Her first month's salary meant she could afford KFC and chocolate cake. The old chap gnaws on a chicken leg and quaffs Kuitun liquor bought and warmed up by his daughter: "This is American chicken. It is so funny. I fought against the Americans and now we are eating Yankee chicken." The old man eats heartily. Soon the chicken has disappeared and he has downed a whole bottle of spirits. The girl wants to talk to her father. He stares distractedly at the stove. The fire has just been topped up with coal and the old chap cocks his ear to the furnace. He is intoxicated by the burning coals and doesn't hear the girl calling to him. The girl cries in a very low voice. As soon as she cries, he is roused back to life: "I have told you before that going to Kuitun will make you snivel."

"Pa, you're too lonely. Next month I'll buy you a radio."

"I don't want one. I have coal and I have a stove. I'm leading a fine life now."

The girl sees how the stove has become her father's pet. She wipes the stove up and down with a wet dishcloth. Then she goes out to the yard to shovel some white snow, which she sprinkles on the coal heap. This fuel will not catch fire for a while.

The old chap is infatuated with the winter. He has never known such a fine one. The snow is not so white. It has started to darken and in some places has become dry powder. If the world progresses like this, people will no longer rely on a stove for heating. By now, every other household has moved theirs to the adobe shed at the front, only using it for cooking. The stove will cease to be our domestic companion.

"What can I do about it? There's snow, coal and a stove. Isn't that enough?

The old man rattles on about his troubles. Everybody is conscious that he has gone too far this winter. Everyone consoles him, saying: "It will begin to turn warm after the May 1st Festival. So, you still have dozens of days to live with the stove in your room." It is early April. Winter is dragging its tail along the ground, so people dare not be presumptuous enough to take off their cotton-padded clothes and large leather caps. Whoever risks skidding on a chip of ice will feel numb in their bones and wince out tears.

At this point, the son comes over to collect his father. He has a three-bedroom apartment in Kuitun, with a living room, central heating and gas. One room has been set aside for the old chap. The son fastens the hefty lock on the gate, taking away nothing except his father.

Nonetheless, the old chap asks: "How can you live without a stove and without coal? Can the central heating be rigged up to the stove?"

His son replies: "Yes."

"So I can still burn coal for heating in that case."

"You can burn whatever you like."

"I only burn coal. It sings beautifully when alight."

In Kuitun, new apartments do not require stoves of their own. The old man listens for a long time but cannot hear the sublime berceuse of coal being consumed. A stove stands in the corridor. He squats beside it for half a day, but discerns nothing. The son has to move it to his bedside. The boy fixes castors to the bottom of the stove. When the old man goes out it booms with the noise of a fierce hunting dog.

Golden Altay

From serving as a regular field army soldier, the Battalion Commander was requisitioned to join a production and construction corps. On arriving in Altay for the first time, he found himself lost for words. Their superiors ordered each of the men to procure a spouse as quickly as quick could be. He headed back to his home village to start the search, but the magnificence of Altay continued to haunt him. He loitered for several days in the village yet had no eyes for the nattily-attired females. His vision remained transfixed by the forests, lakes and pasturelands of Altay. One couldn't blame him for being picky and choosy.

He left the village and reached the county town. The final bell had barely rung at the high school and the students were the most eye-catching figures on the street. In the 1950s, high school students were as precious as gold nuggets. A tall and slender, fair-skinned yet ruddy-faced girl materialised within the Battalion Commander's eyeline. Her visage was mashed together in a single shot with the distant scenery of Altay forming the background. His eyes distended and so too did his nostrils. His ears waggled and his Adam's apple bobbed up and down like a boulder bouncing down a mountain. He recalled how on the steppes of Altay he had heard the Kazakh people sing:

> *I rode past your home days ago.*
> *Your song pierced through the evening glow.*
> *I tumbled down off my horse*
> *And rolled to the foot of the slope below.*

His Adam's apple bobbed up and down violently. He went up to the girl student. *Ai!* He heaved a long sigh. She looked at the young officer in surprise.

"It must be a great waste for such a beautiful girl to stay here," he said.

"Then tell me where should I stay so that I am not wasting myself?" she queried.

He suggested Altay. "Altay is very beautiful. If you stay in Altay, your beauty will truly shine out; it will know no limits."

So, the girl student followed him back there.

鹿

The legendary story of the Battalion Commander unfolded like this. The Political Instructor of the Xinjiang Production and Construction Corp, Zhang Zhonghan, mentioned him by name and seconded him to go to Altay. The Battalion Commander then left in advance with various experts as his companions. Among them were those who specialised in surveying and cartography and soil science; they were all erudite people. They jostled in an American Jeep for three days before reaching Altay on the fourth.

That was in the autumn of 1958. The great steppes of Middle Asia drew into their line of sight together with the undulating mountains dripping with patrician temperament. Having toured the area on many occasions, the driver tarried in the vehicle sucking on a woodbine. He knew that this gang would be slack-jawed with wonderment for the better part of the day. The first time he came here he managed to career off-road into a grassy crater. Back then, Wang Zhen was among the crew. Like the driver, Wang was taken aback by the noble demeanour of the mountains and was to be heard mumbling to himself: "It is no wonder I am called Wang Zhen."[e]

A few members of staff poked fun at their commander-in-chief: "Chairman Mao sent you to Xinjiang exactly for this reason. He said that Bearded Wang's facial fungus was lush and that he should go to the most desolate part of the country to grow crops." The general gazed at length at the Altay Mountains with his military cap in hand. The grassland and the rolling mountains were serene. The guards, the staff members, the chauffeur and the vehicle were also quiet, as subdued, in reality, as a cluster of greenery in the abdomen of Middle Asia.

That sort of serenity remained embedded in the driver's brain. He got down and stood beside the passengers. He heard the Battalion Commander exclaim: "I have seen gold."

"'Altay' in the Mongolian language means 'gold'," the driver explained.

"I wasn't using Mongolian. What I meant was that this mountain has a golden sheen which pierces through the blueness."

"That's the vegetation. All the plants in Xinjiang take on that distinctive tinge."

"Then I have come to the right place. I am here to farm."

The fellows all imbibed the same mountain. Quite distinct from other mountains, it rose slowly from between the great North Asian steppes and the great Middle Asian grassland. All types of forage grass processed in from every side and from far away. When it reached Altay, it stood tall and lifted a palette of flowers high. The grassland flowers lined up and combined naturally to form pictures that stretched out to the highlands. Greyish blue rocks again protruded from the seas of forage grass and blossoms, linking together with the skies.

The gradient of the slopes was gentle. Livestock frequently grazed their way to the heavens. People, nonetheless, recoiled from the sight of it. While fighting to the north and to the south, the Battalion Commander had appreciated many scenes of heroism and visited numerous stately mountains. Altay was tranquil. The sedate teal mountains brightened up people's eyes and caused them to crane their necks further. A bank of haze percolated through their chest cavities and bloodstreams.

"My soul drifted out of me," muttered the Battalion Commander, a mass of mist swirling around his head.

"That is because you are too nervous. You are sweating buckets. Sweaty steam is rising off you," the driver pointed out.

The soil scientist brushed the Battalion Commander's forehead. "His body temperature is quite normal."

The cartographer lifted his eyelids to perform an inspection.

"The problem lies in here. Dreams are flashing through his eyes."

The two experts drew a unanimous conclusion: the Battalion Commander had been possessed by a devil.

They buzzed about in Altay for a number of days, dining and boarding at the Prefectural Commissioner's residence. A gold-digging brigade was there as well. The driver invited the Battalion Commander to watch them prospect. The Battalion Commander was not interested in gold; instead, the rolling mountains and pasturelands took his fancy. The Commissioner's residence stood in a small city among the sinuous mountains and hillocks. One minor branch of the River Irtysh – the River Kelan – flowed through the settlement.

Altay in 1958 had the air of a small market town. It was very easy for the Battalion Commander to wander away from the streets and into the mountain wilds. Sometimes, the day slid by without him coming back. One time, he returned sopping wet. He admitted that he had lost his footing and slipped into the Irtysh while trying to catch a fish, almost floating away to the Arctic Ocean. The staff in the Commissioner's office reminded him: "There are bandits who haunt those hills."

Guns were frequently heard barking in the depths of the mountains. The barks had a protracted whistling tail to them and sounded far from melancholy – not, in fact, unlike the chirping of the birds.

"This guy must have powers of sorcery," the driver complained. "Even those gunshots don't sound normal."

The chaps in the Prefectural Commissioner's office also felt peculiar. They had stayed here for seven or eight years. Formerly, the bandit gangs of Osman Batyr[f] had wreaked havoc in the vicinity and the residual guerrillas were still roving about the steppes and rolling mountains. Like ominous night owls, the gunfire startled people's hearts and made their gallbladders tremble. The driver consoled them: "He is a treasure dispatched here by Wang Zhen and Zhang Zhonghan. With him around, Altay will be peaceful."

With nightfall nearing, the Battalion Commander scrambled out from among the birches. His colleagues were all waiting for him. They had glimpsed a red deer entering the compound of the Commissioner's office and guessed they must be seeing things. After the red deer wove through the belts of trees, it changed into the Battalion Commander. The secret to this transformation lay in the forest, which consisted entirely of birches – birches grew on every inch of the Altay Mountains. It was indeed the Battalion Commander who went into the Commissioner's compound.

"How come you turned into a red deer?" his colleagues asked.

"The local red deer aren't afraid of strangers; they even edged towards me. One of them almost knocked me down. I dodged it, but it nudged under my crotch and lifted me up."

He had strands of the brownish hind's coat on him and carried the burning smell of red deer about his person.

His colleagues asked him if he had heard the shots. This place was crawling with bandits.

"A bomb might have dropped here and it would make no difference. All we'd be able to hear was the chirping of the birds," he replied.

He tried unsuccessfully to mimic how the birds sounded.

"Altay birds can't be imitated," he added.

His colleagues gawked at each other.

The driver was frank and mouthy. "Battalion Commander, didn't you sense something?"

"I don't know what you mean."

"You are a senior revolutionary. But why are you still like a kid?"

"Are kids not good?"

The driver hummed and hawed for half a day. "Kids are alright, kids are alright," he repeated.

Everybody stared at the Battalion Commander with strange eyes and then dispersed.

With milk tea and a naan bread in his hands, the Battalion Commander studied the clouds in the skies while setting to work on the food. The cloud vacillated – being one moment like a horse and the next like a sheep.

When the cloud swept over the river valley, he chuntered: "The cloud has let out a bang."

Sure enough, a rather large bank of cloud had knocked against the mountain with a bang and now the rocks seemed to be exhaling.

He laughed. "Ha – they are like me now."

A cloud of white mist appeared above his head.

"This is my cloud," he declared.

His colleagues were profoundly shocked.

"That's no cloud – it's his soul. Altay has shocked his soul out of his skin," the driver said.

The guys in the Commissioner's office, on the other hand, laughed at them: "You and he belong to the same gang. Why aren't you shocked too?"

"We were shocked," they retorted. "Really shocked."

"Why is there nothing above your heads then?" the office guys pried. "You are not pious enough."

They went on to complain that the Battalion Commander was fond of stealing the show and then hogging the limelight.

They wanted to go back to Urümqi. The Battalion Commander didn't want to leave.

"Defying us at every step," they moaned. "You are quite a peacock. Zhang Zhonghan will come. Will you go over there or not?"

"You go over there to report. I shall be waiting here."

"You think you are the Field Marshal?"

Severely pissed off, his colleagues went back to Urümqi by Jeep.

The guys in the Commissioner's office liked the Battalion Commander. They offered him a horse. At Altay, it was difficult for a steed-less man to move a single step. "It is like you have no legs," they mused.

When he swung into the saddle, the Battalion Commander no longer wanted to stay on the street. He galloped out of the mountains and turned the horse's head around on the level wilderness. Both he and the horse extended their necks to stare at the Altay Mountains.

He didn't hear the bark of the gun – he thought that a bird was squawking. The horse didn't register it either.

A lone bandit charged up to him, his sabre flashing in the sunlight. If he had taken the opportunity to flex the blade there and then, the Battalion Commander would have been pared in two with the halves dropping down on either side of his horse.

The Commander's pistol grunted once in the holster and the horse beneath the bandit started to bolt. The bullet ripped into the bandit's cranium leaving him dangling from the stirrups. The horse still galloped forward, the dead rider's sword mowing a swathe of ashy green forage grass as it went.

Soldier's instinct was what had caused him to fire. But then, another, more protean kind of instinct drew his eyes to the greyish-blue mountains and his hand also left the holster. He had become at one with the mountains, like a pious pilgrim at prayer. The horse too struck such a posture. The sabre and the growl of the gun failed to interrupt the animal's piety. His dripping wet eyes and their lids showed how the mountains had aroused sacred feelings within that noble steed.

Another bandit intercepted the bolting horse and unfastened his partner. He searched for a long while but failed to locate the missing half of the dead bandit's head – that half of the skull had been ground into a fleshy pulp long before. The second bandit was infuriated. He toted an American-made light machine gun, which was fully loaded with dumdum bullets. He vaulted into the saddle and galloped up the slope.

Out in the open wilderness, a rider was praying. The bandit entertained the thought of shooting the praying man. He ripped off a swaying reed, took a bite and fired a round – *bang, bang, bang*. The horse reared up. The machine gun rattled away. The dumdum bullets darted out in a fluster.

The Battalion Commander regained himself. With his body riddled with black bullet holes, he charged over. The machine gun was choked. Dumdum bullets flinched back into the magazine and never dared venture out again in spite of being threatened with death. The bandit squeezed the trigger hard but it didn't work. The Battalion Commander snatched away the weapon.

"A gift from Mackiernan?"[g] he asked the bandit.

Many years later, we are still pondering this question. The Chinese people find it hard to imagine that Irishman, Mackiernan.

Irish people's bodies and bones were said to form the sleepers of American railroads. This much was known throughout the world. Irish people were basically mostly navvies, with the remainder being literary giants such as Swift, Bernard Shaw, Joyce, Yeats and so on. Except, this Mackiernan adored machine guns. He came to China, not caring that it was 10,000 miles away from home. What is more, the place where he arrived was remotest Xinjiang. Here he tossed machine guns everywhere like broadcasting seeds.

It was impossible for the Battalion Commander to know so much about the Irish people, but he did know one or two things about that Irish-American diplomat Douglas Mackiernan. All the Xinjiang people knew of him, especially those who had suffered at the hands of the bandits. The memories he left behind must have been engraved on their bones and scratched upon their hearts.

The Battalion Commander snatched away the gun from the bandit's hand. "Brother, you'd be better off with a shepherd's crop and hoes."

The bandit's face reddened. A red-faced Han Chinese was no longer a bandit. He whipped his horse and left to look for his sheep and shepherd's crop.

The Battalion Commander had taken many bullets. Luckily, he was a man possessed by the devil. The dumdum bullets didn't explode but silted up in his body like pellets of unfermented dough. Great was his discomfort. The horse was shedding blood too. Normally, one of those cartridges was enough to decapitate a horse, yet so many were now lodged in its body. In feverish excitement, the animal flared his nostrils, but could only spit out blood. To begin with, it flowed down his legs and then dripped from his belly, splashing like water and sweeping him away. Lying on the ground, he raised his head high as if he was swimming across a roaring river of gore. An ashen-blue light was sparkling in his eyes. The Battalion Commander tilted his pistol against the beast's temple and fired. That patch of brilliant azure light vanished.

The Battalion Commander staggered forward. He was on a knife-edge. His blood was dripping and dripping and dripping incontinently. He rushed to a clump of birches on the marshy lowlands where there stood a yurt. His mangled body gave the aged Mongol woman a start.

"Old mother, please stop me bleeding," he begged. "Quickly."

The aged woman failed to staunch the flow of blood even with incense ashes. She cried. "There are so many holes, kid. Even the Lord Buddha can't save you."

"I don't want to die."

"I will beg of the Buddha and plead with him to take you in."

"Old mother, don't plead with the Buddha. I still need to farm the land."

"But that's rolling mountains and pastures. That is where the animals should stay, my kid."

"There's so, so much space between the mountains and the pastures."

"That's the wasteland."

"That is where I ought to go."

The aged woman whipped out a Mongolian knife to flay the bark from a birch. The freshly-stripped birch bark was ice-cold when it came to be applied as a poultice around the bullet holes. The Commander was stiff as a tree. She edged him back into the yurt.

"Will I die, old mother?" he implored.

"Death is very near at hand."

The Battalion Commander already spied the shadow of Death.

"A hero will face death frequently. The one that dodges is not the hero but death," the aged woman said.

"My blood's almost been drained away and my body's riddled with holes. How can I survive this?"

"The drained blood will be replenished and flesh will sprout in those holes."

When Genghis Khan was young, his mouth and throat were wounded by an arrow during a battle with the Taichiuds. He came back spent and broken with only two *noyans* – nobles – as retainers. It was snowing heavily. The *noyans* reined in their horses.

Seeing that Genghis Khan was in such a state, they seared a rock so that it glowed red and poured some melt-water onto it so that steam rose. They then positioned the Khan's mouth above the steam. Not until the exsanguinated blood in his throat had been spat out could he breathe with greater ease. Buried waist-deep in the snow, they couldn't skirt about on the spot. When day broke, they helped him to mount his horse.

Their adversaries were hunting them down in every quarter. The mountains and steppes were infested with enemy cavalry and the mountains shuddered with fear, but only the sound of the snowflakes drifting down tantalised the Khan's ears. The *noyans* arrived at this conclusion by observing his lobes, which were suspended like featherless birds.

"The snowflakes are their plumage," the Khan announced. "'Fly' in the true meaning of the word refers to this windless piety."

This was the first time the Mongols had heard the word piety.

Later on, the mounted Mongol warriors reached the four corners of the world, where there were prosperous metropolises and iridescent cultures as well as tremendous quantities of books. The books were cramped with the word piety. The Mongols told the local inhabitants that this was not piety in the proper meaning. Piety in the proper meaning is a word too sacred to be written down. The "vestige" from the Mongols' mouths referred to the words that expressed the sacred feeling "piety". The Mongols were illiterate, but they knew the skies and the earth.

The clatter of enemy hooves erupted, but the Khan had sunk into a meditation on the heavy snow, the winter, the undulating mountains and the grassland. During his tremendous meditation, he spat out only one utterance. "There shouldn't be too many noble emotions. A man has only two ears and one ear can only swallow one word." The Khan's incantation was concise. On that snowy day with dangers lurking everywhere, his word became a *yasa*. This was a law or decree by which the Mongols and the steppes and the rolling mountains should abide as well.

As laws and decrees coalesced, the enemies continued to be ferocious and cocksure. The Khan felt it ludicrous. Back then, the

Mongols were maniacal and selfish and there was no end to the dog-fights among them. The grassland was always in some kind of brouhaha.

The Khan pronounced: "The grassland must quieten down. Hope will dawn when the Mongols are as quiet as the snowflakes. Let me be the first to become quiet."

The horse read the Khan's mind before the *noyans* did and ambled through the heavy snow to a lake surrounded by trees. It was an expanse of placid water. The Khan was jubilant. "This is exactly what I want," he asserted.

The two *noyans* felt ashamed.

"Why this strangeness?" the Khan said. "You must put all your legs together to have four, but a horse has four on its own."

The *noyans* couldn't help but regard the horse with new eyes.

"He isn't just any old beast," the Khan expounded. "He is the best *nokeer* – bosom friend – bestowed upon me by Heaven. He is the most dignified *noyan*. A man is not qualified to feel ashamed in front of a horse. You will see what horses can bring to us Mongols."

At the beginning of the heroic era, Genghis Khan was so lonely and exhausted. He had only those two *noyans* and their horses. The horses were as fatigued as their masters. Their masters all collapsed on the lakeshore, but they still stood upright. From the animals, their masters discerned a kind of mysterious power.

"Let's pray," the Khan said. He untied his waistband, prostrated himself together with his two *noyans* and prayed to their horses as if they were praying to Heaven. The creatures' eyes sparkled with a brilliant marl-blue light.

On that day, horses became sacred animals dispatched down to the earth by Heaven. This word from *Tengri* – Heaven – was relayed to the Mongols through the mouth of Genghis Khan. The two *noyans* were the first Mongols to hear the oracle.

The Khan beamed: "This is the most dignified day that I – Temüjin[h] – have ever lived."

Seeing that Genghis Khan was in such a state of health, the *noyans* couldn't grasp what he meant.

The Khan enlightened them: "Men will become dignified when

they lie on the ground like the water in the lake."

The flesh on the Khan's body had all gone rank, and he extemporised: "This is rotting clean away so that I can draw close to the gods."

The *noyans* had brought with them a fishing net. They spread out the net across the lake and captured a big, fat, red fish. Lacking even the strength to haul the catch ashore, they had to leave it to swim in the water with the net in tow.

"Don't pull him in," the Khan commanded. "When a fish is brought ashore that means that you have peeled away its flesh."

"But people need to bring it ashore to eat it," the *noyans* replied.

"May the gods allow me to put on flesh," the Khan prayed. "Flesh up like the fish."

The fish struggled vehemently, but the *noyans* were unwilling to loosen their hands.

"Such a strong fish. He will take the net as a piece of clothing," the Khan surmised.

Sure enough, that net had become a garment for the fish. At the very beginning, fish scales were messy. Not until that sacred day did they assume an orderly arrangement.

Later on, Genghis Khan again spotted that huge red fish in a tremendous lake in Altay. The lake lay in the belly of the rolling mountains. The Khan called out the name of the waterway – *Kanas* – and the red fish leaped out of the depths like the sun. The fish was wearing its best finery.

Genghis Khan said to his mounted warriors: "Look what you have on." The riders studied their armour, which gave off a fish-scale-like brilliance. "With such an outfit, you can walk to the last sea," the Khan mused. The Mongols took the fish as a sacred creature because like the sun, fish also kept their eyes open during the dark night.

"If you don't feast on the fish, how can you sprout flesh?" the *noyans* queried.

The Khan seemed all too ready to be interred. It might be said that only his head protruded above ground. He was still easy and calm even though his situation was grave. "The forest will be my dwelling place and the earth my pillow. My flesh has already grown out," he pondered. The yellow earth that took in his life became fresh and alive.

"You should fashion an axe and I shall hew a handle. Let's sprout the best flesh," he continued. With these words to Mother Earth, he stood up.

The *noyans* – the firsthand witnesses to this miraculous scene – were stupefied. The earliest known name for Mongolia was *Mung-gu*, which means "the strong is budding in the weak". Genghis Khan grasped the mystery of the steppe people's life instantly.

"It was from the earth that Temüjin popped out," the Khan reasoned.

This was witnessed by the *noyans* with their own eyes.

"The grass crawls out of the earth too," the Khan continued.

This was witnessed by the *noyans* together with the people of the steppe.

The earth must have been dropping them a hint through such a plain and simple action.

"Such a plain and pious life refers to us Mongols," the Khan concluded.

On that sacred day, the Mongols moved from a budding state into their heroic age.

鹿

"Flesh has sprouted like the grass in the spring," the aged Mongolian woman shouted. She stuck her ear to the Battalion Commander's legs. "A young man's flesh first sprouts from his legs," she continued. The sound of blood flowing was soon to be heard from the Battalion Commander's body.

"Kanas, Kanas," the woman cried out. "Spring-water-like blood, please flow a little more rapidly and a little more emphatically."

Flesh was sprouting energetically and the blood flowing vigorously. The Battalion Commander sat up in one go. "Your life has come back. Your life is leaping like the red fish in the lake," the aged woman croaked loudly.

The Battalion Commander sprang to his feet.

During the days when he was still weak, the crone offered him an endless supply of milk. Having drunk so much of it, the Battalion Commander could smell a lactose odour being emitted from his body. Embarrassed, he felt just like a baby. The aged woman was beside herself with joy because she had saved a life.

"I have beaten off Death!" she yelped. "We Mongols grow up from being babies to young men within one day. We are as weak as the grass at the very beginning. Our Genghis Khan was so frail he didn't have one little scrap of good flesh, only his bones. Who can store his life in his skeleton? Genghis Khan allowed the life of us Mongols to struggle free from the cracks of his manly bones. That was how Mongolia grew so fast from weak grass into an eagle."

Now the Battalion Commander had a frame full of good sinews and flesh. Even so, the birch bark proved inextricable. Several knots had fused to his face and body.

"A young man shouldn't be too smooth-skinned. Rough skin might be better," the aged woman soothed him.

Except for those few patches of black scars, the Battalion Commander's skin had assumed the pallor of the white birch.

"You can live to be 200 years old," she commented. "Live together with a tree and you'll have a tree's lifespan. What's more, you'll have a tree's roots, which can strike anywhere into the rolling mountains and grasslands."

"I will strike my roots into the wasteland."

"Then you will have many hoops to jump through."

"I am prepared for that. I can swallow the entire wasteland."

"Then you will become an oasis."

"I *am* an oasis."

"You've received the Oracle. God has enlightened you. It is God who has dispatched you to farm the land."

A comrade from the Prefectural Commissioner's office discovered the Battalion Commander's horse on the grassland. The animal had breathed his last long before. The men then concluded that the Battalion Commander must have been slain by the bandits.

General Zhang Zhonghan went to Altay with a large gang of

people including the Head of the Infrastructure Section and the Head of the Irrigation Management Section to plan the establishment of the tenth agricultural division of the construction corps. The Battalion Commander slunk out from the depths of the wilderness. Everyone spied a tree man – a birch man to be exact. However, the General recognised his old subordinate. The Battalion Commander saluted the senior officer and his hand gave out a rustling sound like leaves.

"I have already heard the sound of a green homeland," the General declared.

"Then give a name to our hometown," the Battalion Commander echoed.

Where they stayed was a desolate place called Dorbiljin – it was here that Genghis Khan originally called the muster roll of his generals and assigned them tasks. Zhang Zhonghan was fated to be a most poetic general in the construction corps. With a flourish of his huge green hand, he said: "This is the northernmost home we corps soldiers have. So, let's call it 'Beitun' – 'the Northern Camp'."

The officers and soldiers of the newly-established production and construction corps were all eager to find a wife. This was an order from the authorities. They must go back to their respective hometowns and then return to the army with a girl post-haste.

The Battalion Commander didn't want to speed matters up. When he left the yurt, the aged Mongolian woman told him: "Wherever you pass by, the forage grass will give out green flames, the flowers will produce a gem-like light and the girls' hearts will leap with joy."

"One girl would be enough," the Battalion Commander replied.

"That is the custom of you Han Chinese, but you are no longer a pure Han Chinese. Half of your life is that of a tree. Where the tree should put down his roots only the earth knows."

"I am already possessed by Altay. A girl will never sway my heart unless she can hold a candle to Altay."

The aged woman admonished him: "Never rule out women on the basis of them being beautiful or not. You can discard them using any excuse in the world except for that. The more you try to turn them down, the more persistent they will be – they will swarm in like bees. "Your blood is sweet – the sort of sweetness that is spiked with salt. Women will love you madly. How can you refuse them in favour of golden Altay? *Ha-ha*, you are pouring oil over a fire!"

When he left Altay, the Battalion Commander stood on the wilderness of Beitun and gazed quietly at the forests, lakes and pasturelands over there and at the clouds, flocks of livestock and eagles that were drifting in between; the aged woman's admonition was clean forgotten.

His subordinates were still in Urümqi. The command he issued was ridiculous: all the officers and soldiers must bring back a beautiful wife. Otherwise, a disciplinary punishment would be awaiting them. The guys all laughed. "We all want a pretty wife, but you can't just take up a brush and paint one."

"Then find a woman who is as pretty as those in the works of art; go and search out the bonniest girl in your village."

The Battalion Commander went back to Urümqi, looking like a birch that had walked out of the great forest in Altay. He recounted repeatedly how he had been shot and how an elderly Mongol woman had used tree bark to staunch the flow of his blood. Apparently, he wanted to use the bullet holes to impress the women soldiers in the headquarters. The women soldiers felt vexed. "We've heard gunfire. We're not little girls at school anymore." The brave ones whipped out their pistols and butted them against their fair-skinned arms. They had grown accustomed to staying in Xinjiang and were now suffused with the strong smell of lamb kebabs. His subordinates clamoured: "It's not surprising that our boss isn't nervous. You are a prince from the grassland through and through. How can we measure up to you!" They then told him their standards for choosing a spouse: "I'll lift its tail to take a look and bring it back as long as it's female."

The Battalion Commander was fuming with anger. He couldn't help feeling outraged. The pasty Mount Bogda in suburban Urümqi reminded him inevitably of the beautiful Altay. His anger didn't have one sole source. If they brought a group of ugly women to Altay to set up camp, Genghis Khan would jeer him to death from the Underworld. Therefore, gritting his teeth, he came back to his home village in Shaanxi in person and brought back a ruddy-faced beauty.

His subordinates returned to the army on time – mostly empty-handed. The Battalion Commander inspected the girls who followed in tow one by one. He was on the point of losing his temper. The Political Instructor drew him to one side and persuaded: "You can never find a bosom friend again after you have gone westwards out of the Yang Pass. We should be grateful that they have come."

"Like our weapons, they come in all shapes and types," the Battalion Commander complained.

"But they are all strong labourers – in the pink of health," the Political Instructor rejoindered.

"Leave it at that, leave it at that. Old-style rifles made in Hanyang County can still be used to overthrow counter-revolutionaries."

"True as this may be, we still couldn't have laid our hands on them until we had sweet-talked and hoodwinked," the Political Instructor confided.

The Battalion Commander heard the young women chirruping comments about the beautiful Altay. He recalled the words of the aged Mongolian woman: "Never rule out women on the basis of them being beautiful or not." His blood then became hot with a *whoosh*. The other fellows seemed to have heard his hot blood was boiling. They ran out to enquire: "Shall we leave now?"

"What will you guys say?" he asked in reply.

"Altay is our home," they remonstrated. "Where's the fun in staying in Urümqi?"

鹿

That winter, they came to Altay together with a heavy snow. Altay stored away her beauty and the earth was blanketed with ice and snow; even the skies were shrouded. Amid the boundless white snow, they reached Altay. They came by truck. Along the way, the

Gobi Desert was also blocked by snow. The world had been made over, clear and clean and simple.

Suddenly the vehicle ground to a halt. The driver said: "Here we are. Get down."

The wilderness dusted over with white snow seemed to extend into space. The great wasteland was empty, spacious and serene; not the least little shred of sound that might denote the presence of life was to be heard. The Battalion Commander was scared. This was another face of Altay. Thousands of people and the great wasteland confronted each other in silence. The veterans came with their families. They had their wives and children in tow. Their children bawled. Their crying appeared weak on the wasteland that extended for 10,000 miles.

"This must be the first kid to ever cry on the wasteland," the Battalion Commander concluded, picking out one boy in particular.

"When his parent was giving birth to him, Papa was fighting Hu Zongnan[j] and didn't hear how he squawked when he dropped to the floor," the child's father said.

The kid, who must have been at least ten years old, nonetheless cried like a newborn babe. His mother clasped him to her chest and neither mother nor son dared to look out of the vehicle.

The Battalion Commander jumped down from the cab. "The sky is our quilt and the earth is our bed. This is our home."

All the men now hopped off. The snow buried them up to their waists or, if they were short, it practically reached their shoulders. The snowy land was dotted all over with dwarfs. The dwarfs were struggling desperately, but the more they struggled, the tinier they looked.

"It looks like your mother is giving birth to you," the Battalion Commander jested.

The others brayed with laughter. The Battalion Commander didn't show even a hint of a smile. He was all seriousness. "Just remember how a baby moves, how a baby comes out of the womb?" He must have been the first one to recollect that. The others took a page out of his book by kicking out their legs and scratching with their hands. Finally, they struggled free. Not until they had patted the snow from their bodies did it dawn on them that they were standing on terra firma.

"*Ha-ha*, I was born on my pins," someone shouted.

In ancient legends, those who were born legs-first were predestined to fulfil some great cause on a par with separating the heavens from the earth.

That day became the most sacred one throughout their lives.

At that sacred moment, the women were originally on the point of crying out. They felt so smothered, they had butterflies in their stomachs. They were mostly daughters from middling-poor peasant families. They had grown used to hardship and no matter how bitter life became, they would grin and bear it. But Shaanxi had no endless Altay wasteland of its own and nor did Henan. Throughout the whole of China, only Xinjiang could boast such a place. The first thought that leaped into the minds of the few young women who had a basic schooling was that they had returned to primitive society. When their men were struggling in the deep snow, they opened their mouths wide but didn't utter a single sound. Later when they were giving birth to their children, they cried out in the same way. They hadn't sensed what a woman crying meant, yet the men's movements were apparently insinuating. The sensation of being profoundly moved surged through their bodies. Presently, in the mysterious Lake Kanas in the abdomen of the Altay Mountains, the red fish surfaced like the sun. The sun didn't rise from the horizon but sprang out of the depths of the skies in one go. Tears welled up in the eyes of the women, but then were held in suspension and never let loose. In much the same way, no matter how high the red fish leapt, he could never go ashore and no matter how splendid the sun was, it would never drop to the earth. A jet of gentle but forceful strength kept their tears inlaid in their pupils, which were shining with the finesse of gems.

Nobody, Genghis Khan himself included, had ever expected that he would possess such a pair of eyes – feminine, feline eyes.

His heart and intestines had been ground into iron and rocks long before. His father Yesugei was poisoned by an enemy and his fellow tribesmen betrayed the orphaned lad and his widowed mother. Time and again, he had narrow escapes and became mean. On realising that one horse couldn't carry two riders, he shot to death his paternal step-brother. The wars that waged to unify Mongolia were grievously cruel. The Khan never showed mercy to his adversaries. Instead, he killed every last one of them, not even sparing their cats and dogs.

He was a symbol of might, though people paid no attention to his catlike eyes.

Still someone did sense the poetic quality radiating from him, namely the Chieftain of the Hongirad Tribe, Daisetsen. When Genghis Khan was five, his father Yesugei brought him to pay a visit to Daisetsen. Daisetsen liked Genghis Khan very much and the two households got spliced. His father-in-law once declared with pride: "I don't care for a territory that extends for 10,000 miles. We only want to have a beautiful daughter." That captivating Mongolian girl, Börte, became Genghis Khan's wife whom he loved deeply his whole life long. Her deep affection towards her husband originated in her adoration for a hero. Among the people of the steppe, bravery and heroic brilliance are the proudest boast any man can have and are esteemed by women as the highest qualities. That pair of elegant cat's eyes was still a mystery to the others, like glittering pearls cast into darkness.

In the autumn of 1204, the Khan and his iron-clad mounted Mongolian warriors marched to the Altay Steppe. The Khan was so startled he couldn't say a word. This was the second mountain the Khan and his Mongolian army had seen besides the Burkhan Mountain. By the time they conquered the world, the Mongols had seen many, many more but none stood out as memorably as Altay. The cobalt hue showing through the mountains aroused something in the Khan's body. From horseback, he issued a decree to his great army: "Never go up the mountains. Our eyes are in there." The *noyans* and *nokeers* shifted their gaze to their Khan. Sure enough, they had spotted his cat's eyes. "Inspect our cavalry," they beseeched their Khan eagerly. "They are the best steeds and the best riders from the grassland."

The Khan urged his mount to trot slowly. It was a most resplendent autumn day in the abdomen of Middle Asia. On the Altay Steppe, all the Mongolian horses and riders appreciated their Khan's delectable pair of cat's eyes. Illuminated precisely by his eyes, the steeds and riders flooded out of Altay and swept across the continents of Asia and Europe. They shed their blood willingly. Though they might end up being pierced by 10,000 arrows, they still could not forget the radiance flashing in those feline eyes.

Altay, moreover, altered the Khan's temperament. When he spurred his colt through his great army, he sensed a fresh vigour from the mien of the riders and their noble horses – a kind of reverence that surpassed almighty power. Hitherto, the Mongols had yet to hail him as their Khan from the depths of their souls. This sacred vigour left the Khan enraptured.

He had already reached the end of the ranks, but he showed no sign of halting in his tracks. He seemed to be inspecting the downy buff-coloured forage grass, the shining bright flowers and the graceful tall birches. He issued laws and decrees which banned the riders from crying – they were not permitted to weep even when bereaved; they were only allowed to be buried in a sea of enemy blood. But the very thing that had been prohibited by his laws and decrees was now surging in the Khan's own eyes. It ought never to have been noticed by his army and the warhorses; he himself didn't want to see it either. He contained his tears. The teardrops that were inlaid in his pupils instantly gave off a peerless charisma that reached the summit of the Altay Mountains. Climbing mountains was also banned by his laws and decrees.

His moist stare landed on the summit of the Altay Mountains. It was a kind of gentle violation, but the tender feelings born in him as he broke his own rule proved a catalyst for martial virtuosity. Many years later, the Battalion Commander and his comrades-at-arms succeeded in developing oases on the wasteland. By the time the delicate crops had grown, factories had been completed too. The workers exploited and ground out the world-famous cat's eye gems[k] from the marl-blue rocks, which sparkled brightly as stars in the darkness. The Mongols on the grassland cheered in feverish excitement: "Genghis Khan, Genghis Khan." Every Mongol after the age of Genghis Khan knew that their Khan had a fetching pair of eyes – eyes that had been ground into the most attractive gems throughout the world.

Genghis Khan's tears hardened. Once a heroic, brave, ambitious heart had emitted majestic light, a world-shaking power would be generated. The Khan seemed to have reached the end of the earth. The warm green River Irtysh under his feet bore the beauty of Altay all the way to the Arctic. The Khan didn't know this. He didn't need to know so much.

An eagle took flight from the summit of the mountains with its wings spreading out evenly. The Khan once shot down two hawks with a single arrow and his fame echoed above the desert. Buzzards, vultures and cranes – without exception – dropped down at the twang of his bowstring. When the eagle of Altay swooped down towards him, he didn't flinch. The bird then flew over along his eyeline and landed on his shoulder.

The Khan ended his inspection in this manner. With the eagle on his shoulder, he settled down on his horse.

He asked himself: "What is it that makes even the eagles kowtow in worship?"

"It's your eyes," his heart replied.

"What are our eyes?"

"The all-embracing world."

This pair of cat's eyes was fated to illuminate and bring beauty to the world.

鹿

On that sacred day on the inexhaustible snow-buried wasteland, the women's eyes were predestined to give out a beam of wondrous light that surpassed tears and the men were fated to take the road that led to their rebirth. With great effort, they scratched away the accumulated snow until they could touch the ice-cold earth. Slapping with their hands and stamping their feet to make sure they were standing on the ground, they felt so excited that their faces became crimson. In this manner, they had completed a baby's heroic birthing process.

The women tossed their luggage down from the vehicles and then brought down their woks and bowls. The men trudged into the depths of the wasteland and fingered apart the piled snow. Hares – reddish-brown like flames – hopped out of the snow one after another.

"Don't hurt them," the Battalion Commander said. "They are flames on the wasteland."

Hare in the Kazakh language means "flame".

"The wasteland has caught fire. We should feed the fire," he continued.

He dived into the snow and took hold of a saxaul tree. The wood was bone-dry, hard, solid and cracked.

"Flames will spurt out of these cracks," he explained.

The Battalion Commander asked the others to weigh it with their hands. The wood was passed around the group for one circuit. They had all handled guns and hoes before, but none had ever felt such heavy firewood.

"Like an iron nugget," they commented.

The women were more scrupulous and their simile more accurate. They likened it to copper.

"Both iron and copper are refined by fire and saxaul wood is used to build a fire," the Battalion Commander exclaimed. He told the others to hurry and gather together some firewood.

The others learned from him by diving into the snow. The snow was as deep as half the height of a man. Half of their bodies were submerged but they still failed to lay their hands on anything. They all grimaced at the Battalion Commander. "A tree was my saviour and so it is easy for me to hit upon some firewood," he emphasised. He told them to scratch apart the snow like they were digging out a tree. The others did as they were told and they did indeed find the saxaul.

The more they scratched the snow apart, the more spirited

they became. The firewood was heaped up high like hillocks. Crowding around the hill-like stacks of firewood, they let out hot breaths that were as white as bushy white beards and their eyes were moist. The women murmured to themselves: "Don't cry. Tears will make the firewood wet." They held back the queer hilarity they felt at having made such a discovery against the odds deep within their eyes. The tears were as round as round could be and their eyes were bursting painfully. They still didn't allow their teardrops to roll out but forced them back in.

Many years later, they wrote in their poems:

The gold in Altay
Has sunk into the eyes of our mothers
And can't be excavated.
The beauty of Altay
Is nurtured by our mothers' tears
And is beyond compare.

They composed many poems. The poets were their children. The slightly older ones were already leaping and bounding there. The slightly younger ones were not even a figment in their mothers' wombs. Many women had barely married into their husbands' homes. They followed them to trudge westwards out of the Yang Pass and braved wind and snow to reach Altay. Before they were born, the poems they wrote and the poems they would write as adults were carried in those mothers' wishes. They would grow up in the company of those wishes. Their poems went like this:

We were born on the primeval wasteland.
Life had started to sprout and wriggle
In the unlit campfire
During the excitement before our mothers' pregnancy.

The firewood was as dry and hard as copper. The women rubbed it with their hands and clutched it to their chests and gazed at it. Their stare brightened up the firewood. Before being ignited by the Battalion Commander, it had already started to burn in their hearts like the lives of their babies sprouting and wriggling in their wombs even before conception. The Battalion Commander told them to settle down at the forefront. The women and children sat down next to the campfire and the men dropped themselves around them. The men were shrouded in darkness and the women and children were red. The hips of the red women and children shimmied relentlessly and their feet and hands all rested over the flames from the campfire.

"The fire is hot," the children yelled.

"So it is," the women responded.

The red women and children were like flames being spat out of the cracks in the campfire.

A massive ball of flame crawled out from beneath the campfire on the snowy wilderness as a fish leaps out of the water.

"This is that fish. Like a horse, it has almost brought me to the Arctic Ocean," the Battalion Commander declared.

The red flames pounced upon them. The flames were ice-cold. People tried to embrace them but failed because they were slippery and agile. The women were greatly surprised.

The young women's upper garments were stroked open by the flames. Their companions who had given birth were experienced. They enlightened the young women: "The size of your breasts denotes how big your baby will be." When the red fish swam over from the flames again, the young women welcomed it bravely and were no longer shy. The red fish never left them again.

"How could he leave us?" the Battalion Commander asked. "Genghis Khan only took a look at him, but I caught him. *Ai*, I caught him with my own hands."

He reached out those birch hands of his. The men all believed that such hands could indeed capture the legendary fish. The Battalion Commander remained modest of course. "But I set him free. He is a sacred creature in Altay. Now being in the River Irtysh and Lake Kanas, he pops out like a god and then vanishes into the ether like a ghost."

"The River Irtysh leads to the Arctic Ocean!" The speaker was the Battalion Commander's wife. She had received an education and was brought by him to Altay while she was still studying in high school.

He appreciated his wife's learned brain very much. "The River Irtysh connects to the Arctic Ocean like a railway line. The red fish can leap up to the forehead of the earth," he echoed to her.

"This creature is miraculous. We can't slaughter it for food. We should set it free," he continued.

"We'd better set it free; set it free. That is the way that leads to life and brings us auspiciousness," the company agreed.

The Battalion Commander pointed at the campfire. "Look, it has come back again to see me."

The red fish crouched down at their feet, wriggling in the fire. "You've been hopping about the whole day and it is already dark. Take a rest," the women told it. The red fish then sank into the flames. The firewood was still solid, but the bark cracked and took on the appearance of fish scales, lining up neatly in row after row. The red fish gathered the saxaul within its perfectly round body and the flames were then well-nourished.

The cold depths of night had already come around. People squeezed together. "The tighter we jam together the better. If we squash ourselves into one man, we can tough it out until the day breaks," the Battalion Commander said. The red fish gathered many people around its perfectly round warm body. Nobody could pick out anybody else except for their eyes sparkling like stars in the snowy world. The snowflakes also started to glisten and then splintered into twinkling stars. All above the wilderness there was nothing apart from the stars. Even the people were indistinguishable from the snow. "Why should we be able to tell them apart clearly? They all fell down from the skies," the Battalion Commander lectured.

Among all the stars, the children were the most poetic. Looking at the constellation that belonged to him, one kid pointed out: "The sun is lying down here."

When the stars were all around the campfire, the dancing flames became the sun over the wasteland.

"The sun is actually a fish in the skies," the Battalion Commander concluded. "The sun drifts up there from the River Irtysh."

The star-like child again remarked on his own constellation: "The River Irtysh has flown to the top of the earth's head and the skies are hanging above the top of the earth's head."

"The fish in the river have all swum up to the skies," the child went on.

"Fish don't shut their eyes at night," the Battalion Commander deduced. "They have stars in their eyes."

"My eyes have become stars," the child said.

The children amidst the constellations all made out the stars in their eyes and so did the adults.

Stars were sparkling in the recesses of the wasteland too – those were the eyes of the animals including wolves, bears, Mongolian gazelles and hares. Scared, the children would have crawled into the campfire if they could. The adults picked up their guns and wanted to fire.

"They neither growl nor bite but keep as quiet as quiet can be. Quiet animals are no longer animals. Come on – stars are twinkling in their eyes," the Battalion Commander dissuaded them.

Wolves and Mongolian gazelles swaggered side by side and bears and hares joined each other. All the animals on the wasteland were summoned to the beacon of the fire. It was the first time they had encountered such a nourishing kind of fire. Their eyes moistened, they forgot the bites and fights between them and slunk up to the big pyre.

"Put your guns away," the Battalion Commander ordered.

The chaps stowed their guns away under their buttocks and behind them were the searing eyes of the animals. The entire wasteland was thriving now.

"I think we can tough it out through the winter," the Battalion Commander reasoned.

The animals formed a fire that was fiercer than the campfire. With a thump, the campfire sank down and scorched a hole in the earth.

"There is magma underground," said the Commander's wife – she who had been to high school.

The others didn't know what magma was.

"Magma is fire found inside the stones," she explained.

The men had been feeling a strong heat under their buttocks.

"Commander, you have married such a clever wife – she is here to heat the *kang* for us," they observed.

"I think you'll find the earth was hot to begin with," the Battalion Commander replied.

The beasts all crouched down and their breath was audible. They were so close to the people. No murderous glare emanated from their eyes, which were still very imposing – both imposing and attractive. One glimpse at them made the women's hearts belch out white smoke with a hiss and their flesh twitch. They were not terrified but excited. They had never seen such awe-inspiring and pretty eyes.

Nights on the wasteland were sleepless.

"Like the fish, we don't shut our eyes at night," the company grumbled.

"That fish has crawled into you," the Battalion Commander joked.

"The fish is still alive," the company responded. "It is leaping within my body."

That night on the snowy wilderness was not black but blue – a kind of limitless, extremely clean, slick and very mysterious blue. Many years later after they were born out of it, they could still feel that kind of blue that was infinite like the sea. They referred to it as "The Night in the Fairytale of Altay".

In that fairytale, people of their fathers' generation blended with the fire. A hole was burnt into the ground. They then sat in the hole. The longer they settled down there, the deeper the hole became.

"The skies have become higher," someone said.

"The night is too bright," another one countered.

The Battalion Commander's words always carried authority. "It is because we are now sitting at the bottom of the earth."

They all picked up the scent of sand and earth. It was the desert earth that had been slumbering for thousands of years. Except for grass roots and jerboas, no one had ever touched it. It was the kind of raw, virgin smell made people giddy.

It was tranquil everywhere. They squeezed tighter together until they became one man – a huge man. Such a giant appeared on the wasteland for the first time. The wasteland was astonished. For thousands of years, nobody had ever got stuck so fast to the earth apart from flocks of livestock and herdsmen scurrying by. The more the giant crawled into the earth, the bigger he became. The earth was so surprised it rustled – the loose earth was sliding down.

"We have crawled so deep. Can we make our way out?" they questioned sceptically.

"The deeper we crawl, the stronger we will become. A strong man can make his way out," the Battalion Commander assured them.

Mongol legends related that their earliest ancestors consisted of only two men and two women – four survivors from the wars. Their tribe fought the enemy and was routed. Shouldering a tribal blood feud, they fled. The enemy wanted to slay every last one of them and they were haunted perpetually by the horror of war. They fled in desperation, scaling lofty mountains and perpendicular ridges before reaching a hopeless uninhabited place. Even they didn't know how they had managed to negotiate sheer cliffs that not even an eagle could fly over.

Where they settled was called Ergunee Hun. *Hun* means "mountain slope" and *Ergunee* "precipitous". Back then, the name signified "precipitous mountain ridge". Nonetheless, this rarely-trodden site boasted large expanses of mellow pasturelands and lush forests. The two men and women who had narrowly escaped combined into two families. On this rustic spot, they regained their vitality. They were sure that they would thrive like a torrent and therefore gave themselves the name *Kiyan*, which refers to the turbulent rapids gushing down from the mountaintop. Believing that vigour and strength was born out of their opposites, they gave their clan the name, *Mongol*, which means "weak and honest". They soon multiplied into a powerful tribe.

Their offspring emboldened themselves with their ancestor's name so that they might charge out of the mountains like a turbulent rapid torrent. It was hard to scale the steep mountains and perpendicular ridges. They gathered together and got firewood and coal ready in large piles in the forest. They then slaughtered seventy of the strongest cattle and horses and tanned their hides into bellows. The firewood and coal were piled up at the foot of a mountain cliff. Seventy pairs of bellows worked together to fan the flames beneath the firewood and coal like seventy cattle and horses were lowing and neighing and stampeding. The men and women and children followed the bellows to roar and scream and jump about. During their carnival, the men created a wrestling game that called for infinite strength and the women invented the most heroic and moving song on the grassland, characterised by its long, searing tone. The tigers, leopards and eagles in and above the rolling mountains pranced about, their roars drowning the skies and the earth. With their lungs bulging, the heavens and the earth blew their tempest-like breath into the flames until the cliff face melted.

The Mongols were fated to become the toughest warriors on the grassland. The mountain they melted down was composed of iron ore. When the rocks melted away, a red river with flying sparks appeared. Nobody expected that such a river would find its way out from beneath the mountain.

"We have burned through the earth and hit the most enormous spring. This spring belongs to us Mongols," their Chieftain exclaimed.

The Mongols then used their national language to shout: "Kanas, Kanas."

The Chieftain harangued: "Like our ancestor Kiyan, we Mongols' have a turbulent and rapid Kanas that won't cease until it has roared its way to the sea."

In the Mongols' imagination, the "sea" referred to the spring water that rushed on forever and ever. The Chieftain naturally became the source of the sea. He was Hoid – the earliest Khan of the Mongols. That delectable, auspicious red fish was predestined to turn up in the sea of the Khan. People saw their Khan stick one of his hands into the boiling magma and retrieve the fabled red fish as if he was fishing in a crystalline cool river. It was a beautiful fish. "Red" in the Mongolian language means "beautiful". Hoid Khan's hands were harder than the rocks. Only such a pair of hands could catch the red fish. The Khan raised the fat, red fish high and announced: "It will bring auspiciousness to us Mongols." "Auspiciousness" in the Mongolian tongue implies "bravery and toughness". The red fish soon became black, but the Khan found a way to brighten it up. When the flames spurting out from the coal took on the shape of a dragon, that column of dull dark iron was again aglow. The Khan cut it into many bars, which were again forged into weapons that were as sharp as sharp could be, together with auspicious stirrups for the horses. The stirrups linked the horses and the Mongols together. The Khan again ordered the women to embroider the likeness of the fire dragon that spurted out of the coal onto their battle garbs. In this way, the Mongols marched out of the dense forests in the depths of the mountains on their horses with fire dragon flags raised high and iron weapons gripped in their hands.

The Battalion Commander didn't call daybreak "daybreak". Rather he called it "coming out". The people were unsure what he was asking to come out. All in one go, the sun, the rolling mountains and the people emerged as if they had crawled out of a cave. Whether the sun was hiding in the cave or not, nobody knew. Whether the mountains were hiding in the cave or not, still nobody knew. The men knew nothing beyond themselves.

What was palpable to them was that they had been hiding in that hollow – a warm refuge – for the whole night. Several dozen folk had squeezed into one heap and made the form of a giant. No matter how cold it was, such a giant could tough it out. When day broke, the heap no longer existed; as the people scattered, they appeared miniscule beyond words and found the daytime chillier than the night. The chills in the daytime were directional and reared up from four sides and eight angles. The sunlight was as flying daggers and the chills became razor-sharp. The children clamoured that they still wanted to wriggle into the dark hole and attach themselves to the adults.

The Battalion Commander and the Political Instructor compared notes and concluded that they should think of a way to dig some dark holes in which the people could hide. They had all fought fierce battles and even been stationed in Korea. The American airplanes had blotted out the skies completely like ravens, but didn't those who were in the PLA dig tunnels that went under the 38th Parallel? Looking about, the Battalion Commander reasoned: "Altay is almost the same size as Korea. If we could dig in Korea, we can dig here."

About thirty campfires scorched thirty black holes into the snow-carpeted ground. After digging downwards one foot, they reached the rock-solid permafrost. The Battalion Commander said: "The Mongols managed to open up a mountain. Can't we melt open the earth?" He ordered that the fires be fed and that while the fires were being fed, they should continue digging. He took off his trousers and propped the legs open with two switches of saxaul to form a pair of makeshift bellows. He told his wife to operate the bellows. The bellows opened and then closed, squirting wind into the fire. The fire started to roar like a wild boar – *ao – lai – ao*. After burning for some time, the glowing ashes were turned to one side and the spot that had burned lay steaming. Iron shovels and pickaxes were then swished spitefully. Obsessed as they were with that sultry black hollow, they still threw themselves into their labour. Never once did they begrudge how dark it was in there, no matter how deep they had dug.

On the seventh day, they finally met the requirements of the Battalion Commander. Every cavernous hole had a ramp. That was the exit. Moreover, there were earthen beds and tables inside and even kitchens were made ready.

The seventh day thereby proved auspicious. The Battalion Commander led the men of the company to the depths of the wasteland and found a patch of forest on low-lying land. As a "tree-man", he could pick out the musk of trees from a great distance so they didn't have to make any detours on the way. The others followed him directly to the copse. All the lofty poplars and elms seemed to have been prepared especially for them. The team brandished their axes and – *clink, clink, clink, clink* – felled the largest specimens.

The cylindrical trunks were laid horizontally on the earthen caves, then topped with tree branches, dry grass and reeds, and finally weighed down with sand and earth. A pitch-dark cave came into being.

The children scuttled in as if they were rats, squeaking wildly. After they had squeaked to their hearts' content, they darted out to leap and bound on top of the caves like rabbits.

The women padded the *kang* with dry grass and reeds and used their buttocks to press it down. The dry grass and reeds were all ground flat by their round posteriors but a sound was still to be heard from beneath. It was not a wild squeaking noise; rather something redolent of an autumnal insect's hoarse chirps. They then spread out the coverlets and under-sheets and folded the quilts up squarely. The quilts and coverlets gave off a radiance. They sat down quietly awhile in the middle of the *kang*. They too were generating a similar kind of warm light.

The children stopped larking about and withdrew to the entrances of the caves to peep at their earthen beds, at their warm quilts and coverlets and at their warm mothers. The muddy walls their backs got stuck to also exuded a warm kind of light. The loose sand and earth dropped down with a rustling sound and landed on their bodies and their feet like jets of hot current. Many among them later went to Urümqi, to Altai,[1] to Karamay, Shihezi and Kuitun. Those who stayed behind were lucky enough to live in houses equipped with central heating. And yet, the warm odour of the earth in the caves would frequently swell up in their hearts. At that sacred moment, they would stop what they were doing and remain silent for a second. The ardour had seeped into their bloodstream. As long as their blood still flowed, this preternatural feeling could hardly varnish. Not a few poets and writers were born of their number. In their literary parlance, "Mother Altay" always resonated with two meanings: one referred to the image of Mother Earth from the ancient times and the other meant their biological mother back home. The two images overlapped and could stand in each other's stead, in effect making their psychological room infinite.

> *The cave carpeted with a heavy snow*
> *The cave topped with round logs and dry grass*
> *Nurtured us*
> *In deep serenity and warmth*
> *Those were weak yet strong lives,*
> *Mother Altay.*

The women were fated to feel the maternal powers of the wasteland. It was virgin land that had been slumbering for thousands of years. Those who had given birth before, babbled as if they were in a dream: "I have become a virgin girl again!"

Another voice came from the heart of the earth: "I want to give birth and bring up children; I want to give birth and bring up children! Give me the seed, give me the seed! Cultivate me, cultivate me!"

Silence ensued – a profound and enduring silence.

Someone whispered: "The earth has been opened up and what is more, opened up so deep."

Another one noted: "Those pickaxes and shovels are all iron implements. Iron can surely open up the depths of the earth."

"The iron is spitting out fire," a third person said.

Like a booming dragon with bared fangs, wielding its claws and curling its mouth, the fire crept into the earth.

Someone said: "It's said that if a woman dreams about a snake, she will give birth to a baby. But we have dreamed about a dragon."

Those women who had given birth in the past were experienced and proud of their bellies. They raised the bottom hem of their upper garments. "His old lady's shanks. Altay is so beautiful!"

The women all lifted the hems of their blouses to study their stomachs. Whether they had given birth or not, they had never observed their bellies carefully before – they were taken aback by their own fertile wilderness.

"Altay is so beautiful. Altay belongs to us women. Our bellies are Altay," they cooed.

Then, they stopped shouting as if they had dined on something moreish and were savouring the aftertaste. The more they did it, the more delectable it felt and then they spluttered into laughter.

The Battalion Commander's wife whispered in a low voice: "There is no wonder. When my old man – the dead devil – mentioned Altay, I was churned inside out and even quit school. My father and mother threatened to commit suicide but I followed him to hit the road without batting my eyes."

"What did the Commander say to you?"

"He tempted me by saying that Altay is very beautiful. If a woman comes here, she will have beauty beyond limits."

"Women can never fend off flattery. Flattering words can make you fling aside your life."

The Battalion Commander's wife was well-read. "Altay originally meant 'gold'. When a woman comes here, she is gold," she said.

"You are gold but we're not," said a woman sniffily to the Battalion Commander's wife. "You haven't consummated your union yet. A woman is gold before the consummation of her marriage, silver after the consummation and is not worth even a scrap of iron after she has given birth to a baby."

"Whether you have given birth or not, you are a woman of Altay all the same and worth your weight in gold after you have come here."

"We are worth our weight in gold," the others cheered.

According to the legends of the Mongols, Genghis Khan issued a special decree in Altay – the most sacred decree ever issued by the Khan from horseback: "Never go up the mountains. Our eyes are in there." This was without doubt the most masculine, most heroic and most dignified imperial edict to come from his lips.

"A woman should never be mounted carelessly. She is cheap if that's the case," the women concluded.

"A woman has lived her life in vain unless she lives in the eyes of her man," they continued.

"Genghis Khan's woman was taken away forcibly by his enemy, but he never harboured any resentment towards her and still took her as a treasure," the Battalion Commander's wife pointed out.

"Tough guys usually have a soft heart," the others surmised.

"Genghis Khan's heart softened after he reached Altay," the Battalion Commander's wife said.

She was a learned woman and all the others were willing to lend her a ready ear.

"Genghis Khan acquired a pair of cat's eyes," she went on.

All of her companions let out an "Oh!" in chorus. Every woman knows what cats' eyes look like. What a sight it would be if such eyes sparkled in the face of a big, tall, valiant stalwart.

"Genghis Khan didn't discover that he had a pair of cat's eyes until he came to Altay. He forbade people from going up there and then the mountain turned to gold," the Commander's wife expounded.

"Our men brought us to Altay and dug such deep holes for us," the other women said.

The more they talked, the more excited they became.

"The ground was so hard. Iron shovels and pickaxes were thrown into work and fire was used to burn."

They were enthusiastic as enthusiastic could be.

"It was such a humongous fire. No one had ever seen one that size – like a snake, a python and a dragon all in one!"

They couldn't be giddier now.

"A cave like this was then dug! A cave like this!"

They crowded around the Battalion Commander's wife. In their eyes, she was a canny lady – a canny lady who had received a schooling. They enjoined her: "Is there any cave as good as this one anywhere in the world?"

"There is an Upper Cave in Beijing,[m] but that was for the apemen to take shelter in."

The other women then commented that it must be a good cave because it lay close to Chairman Mao and anything near Chairman Mao was good. One cave lay beside Chairman Mao and one also lay in Altay. The women all felt their hearts warm as if they were now standing around Chairman Mao. No longer did they fire off questions towards the Commander's wife because they could also say a word or two now. One chirping a comment and another chirping another, they all looked like canny ladies in their own right. Their chatter continued to focus on caves: on the Jinggang Mountains,[n] where Chairman Mao lived in a rocky cave; in Yan'an,[o] where he took shelter in an earthen cave; and in Beijing where there was the Upper Cave. He could take charge of the rivers and mountains.

Still the Battalion Commander's wife was the canniest of them all! "The New China was born in the caves," she concluded.

The other women all let out an "*Ayah*!" and recalled what they should do now.

Kitchen smoke was soaring. The smoke columns were bolt-upright, as if they were rising from the white snow. Several dozen black scars were scratched into the relentless snowy wilds. From these arose a few dozen plumb-straight plumes, which melted directly into the sun. Like a golden yellow, oily naan bread tied atop a pillar of smoke, the sun gave off the fragrance of food.

People breathed in the aroma. The children stopped fooling about and raised their heads to gaze at the huge floating pancake in the sky. The men also stopped their work to look skywards.

"Our women have been digging a hole in the sky. We dug a hole in the earth and they then did likewise in the heavens," the Battalion Commander commented.

If the Battalion Commander said the sun was a hole, then it was. Many glistening yellow crusty naan breads inched out of that bright hole. The pancakes were baked in a pit. When they baked a pancake, Xinjiang people didn't use a pan but dug a deep hole and then pasted it to the side with clay. The hole was then heated red hot and had patties of dough stuck all around its interior. Scores of naan could be baked at any one time.

"They're so bloody nifty. They dug the bake-hole in the sky. They are roasting the sun," the Battalion Commander continued.

"It smells so good, it's killing us to wait," the others grumbled.

Little by little, the kitchen smoke grew weedier and stumpier.

"The sun is a fish. Our women hooked it in," the Commander observed.

The sun had indeed been hooked, and floated over together with the black kitchen smoke. The sun that had bitten the hook was crimson.

"Our women are really bloody capable. They can even catch that red fish. Back in the day, even Genghis Khan could only look on as it swam free. I thrashed about in the river for half a day but still failed to get it. Worse still, it nearly hauled me into the Arctic Ocean. Our women are bloody good. With one stack of smoke they can hook the fish."

The sun was setting bit by bit and the snowy wilderness was left a brilliant expanse.

"The fish has been hooked ashore. There is snow on the banks. No matter how the fish whips its tail, its flesh is still fresh."

The sun set. Only a little residual light was left in the sky.

"The fish has swum into the hole," the Battalion Commander deduced.

The fellows followed the fish in. The cave was preternaturally bright. The fish had crawled into the belly of the kitchen stove; such a whopper. The hole couldn't accommodate it. The fish's tail was left outside undulating ceaselessly to the left and to the right, but finally succeeded in entering. The stove chamber was drilled deeper by the fish and the lid of the wok butted aside. The fish then crawled out of the pan. The adults and children were all whooping, gorging and gulping.

This was their first meal on the great wasteland. For fully one week, no hot food had passed their lips, only dry steamed buns accompanied by snow. Both the adults and the kids were ravenous. Neither their hands nor their mouths could feel the bowls and chopsticks they held. In their brains, there was only that huge, fragrant, oily, crusty naan in the sky and that fat, red fish that had been hooked ashore by the column of kitchen smoke. The guys kept slurping down the food like the mountains were crying out and the seas were reverberating. Their stomachs were round, yet they still threw themselves into it, very greedily. The ravenous feeling was in their blood and in their brains but not in their stomachs. No matter how round their stomachs were stuffed, they continued devouring until they were short of breath, until their cheeks were aglow and their heads perspiring and until their beady eyes rolled relentlessly. The naan and cracked corn soup fed them into big fat fishes – big fat red fishes. Their heads shaking and their tails whipping, they collapsed on the *kang* with their bodies brimming over with comfort and their faces inscribed with auspiciousness.

A blizzard descended on the eighth day. Many years later when they thought of the first blizzard they encountered on the wasteland, their hearts were still gripped by the residual fear. Luckily, their underground shelters had been completed the day before. Otherwise, all of them would have been swept away into infinity.

The men dismissed it as if nothing had happened. They had barely come back from Korea, where the American bombers were similar to Force 12 windstorms, roaring madly above their heads. With a Mohe cigarette clutched between their teeth, they played cards and Chinese chess, struck up a tune on the *erhu* and blew mouth organs.

Women and children huddled together at the corners of the *kang* not murmuring a sound as their beady eyes rolled upwards. Sand and loose earth pattered down from the roof and walls. Inadvertently, the men were their source of consolation: "Take it easy, take it easy. Our underground homes are more solid than air-raid shelters. An N-bomb could be dropped and it would be no big deal."

"Can you tell the wind to stop howling?" a woman asked.

"Who can control a howling wind?" her man retorted.

The woman jumped down from the *kang* with a thud. "Will you do something or not? If you won't, I shall."

The man charged out with a gun. The exit was already plugged shut by the snow. The man fired two shots. The other chaps could only see that smoke was rising from the mouth of the barrel but couldn't hear the bark of the two shots. The bullets were already frozen stiff like birds.

"Don't open the door. Be careful the wind might rush in," the

Battalion Commander reminded.

The other blokes hurriedly reinforced the bolted door.

"The children are terrified," the women wailed.

"Everyone is the first time," the Battalion Commander consoled.

The Commander summoned all the boys together, stopping them huddling together at the corners of the *kang* or nestling against their mothers.

"If a baby son wants to grow up, he must have a taste of fear. Once he's tasted it, he will become strong," he lectured them.

The women clamped their daughters to their chests. The Battalion Commander still didn't promise anything. His reason was very simple: "Even a horse turns his head away from weak grass, why shouldn't we look down on weak people?" The women then loosened their grip. Girls and boys trembled together in the howling blizzard. They trembled and trembled but then no longer trembled at all. Their hands and feet quietened down and so did their shoulders and waists. When they regained themselves, their gaze was steady – steady and straight – and everything was clear in their eyes.

The children sat through the night without a peep.

The men were fixated on what they were doing. Nobody slept during the night of blizzard. The women didn't startle their children but offered up prayers from nearby, not with their mouths or eyes but with their hearts – they were mumbling silently in their hearts. Judging from the postures they struck, they were transmitting a kind of ESP and utilising their unfathomable prayers to help their offspring weather the blustery night in Altay.

The children's bodies found a kind of peace, but their souls were still in terror. Like little worms, their tender, weak hearts were slithering slowly and solitary through the 1,000-mile-wide wasteland. Many years later, they went to school. The titles of their compositions were almost all concerned with "golden Altay". They wrote about the blizzard and about their fragile hearts and souls – like maggots in a cave. When a man felt that he was a very small and weak insect, he would be even-tempered and good-humoured. He could sense the existence of more lives. The children's especially acute ears and eyes pierced through the thick sandy soil. The inner world of the great wasteland became pellucid. They could see the insects and small animals and grass roots in the transparent sandy soil. They all had their respective tiny caves. They were soft and weak, but they were jumping – jumping underground. The dim light of life illuminated the heart of the wasteland. The howling wind grew immediately distant. Their uncle – the Battalion Commander – told them: "You will no longer be afraid. Fear has left you." All the children – regardless of their ages – were predestined to reach maturity on that hallowed night.

The Commander then gave their dwellings a very poetic name – "the underground warren". Lengthy stretches of underground warrens appeared in the abdomen of Middle Asia and near the lakes of the Mongols. The seas could trace their sources back to the lakes and the oases trace their origins back to the underground warrens. Everything was created according to its own design.

Years later, the children grew into teenagers and the wasteland was reclaimed by oases. The atmosphere near the border crackled with tension and the dark cloud of war hovered in the skies above Middle Asia and Asia Minor. The children could hear the boom of the tanks from the other side of the national border. Huge arrays of armoured regiments were drilling over there without ceasing and artillery pieces were growling. Strange lights frequently flashed in the sky. The children thought it was the Southern Lights. From overhearing the adults' conversations, they knew that these were rockets – long-range rockets capable of carrying nuclear warheads. There were also short-range ones. When the adults rambled on about the short-range rockets and nuclear bombs, they seemed to be talking about some sort of grenade. They had been to the battlefields in the past and could never shake off the mentality of aeroplanes, artillery pieces, machine guns and grenades. After they were through with these dangerous topics, they tramped grim-faced to the croplands. The tractors chugged into life. Dozens of them stood in a row and formed a powerful corps to march towards the vast wilderness in an awesome manner. The land changed into a sea. The overturned soil seethed. Next, wheat waves and dense corn sprang forth. Finally, the solemn, pure and plain cotton put in an appearance. Cotton dissolved everything, including the shadow of a possible nuclear attack together with the roars of the tanks from the gigantic neighbouring country on the other side of the border.

During the trial of strength between good and evil,
The multiplication and reproduction of love
Is one hundred times more ancient and valiant than
The devastation caused by death.[p]

When the children grew up, a number of them enrolled at university. Some went on to engage in the study of international strategies and handled confidential documents. Their academic papers were tinged with literary colour. A particularly striking paragraph from one said: "Despite the shadow of nuclear attack hanging over the land, oases continued to burgeon and the crops grew vigorously across Middle Asia and Asia Minor. The local children were unbelievably gallant, handsome and beautiful!" Why should the shadow of nuclear attack lead to nuclear fission in the world of the living? This is a key problem that awaits further study. Only the descendants of the corps soldiers can sense this paradox and only they can conduct research into this topic. When my pen reaches this point, even I can't help doubting if my words are making up a novel, a poem, a length of history or a mythical story. But one thing is clear and that is the fission of life. Now I've picked out something that is pithy, let me resume my narrative.

鹿

In the legends of the Mongols, Genghis Khan was originally a timid child, petrified of the din of thunder, the clash of swords and lances and of the whinnying of warhorses.

A series of terrible experiences befell him, the most dreadful of which was his father's death – his father was murdered by the enemy with wine laced with poison when he was only five or six.

His widowed mother lived a hard life with her brood of young children and every day dragged past like a year. His father's throne was usurped by another. All his father bequeathed to him was his name, Temüjin. This was Genghis Khan's name before he ascended the throne of the Khan as well as the name of their tribal feud. His father had slain the formidable enemy with his own hands at the precise juncture his son was born. He then gave his enemy's name to his son. Temüjin carries a welter of meanings, including both "life" and "death" and "success" and "failure".

"You are the iron of the Mongols," his mother declared.

Temüjin then started a fire, seared an iron red hot and put it on an anvil to be hammered into bars and then into blades.

His mother explained: "We Mongols started from failure. We lost very badly. Only four people were left behind and they fled into the depths of the mountains. When we marched out, we melted a tall mountain with fire and iron flowed out of the rocks. We Mongols thrived from the iron. We are iron, we are *Ergunee hun* – the precipitous mountain ridge, we are the turbulent rapid torrent *Kiyan*."

Temüjin looked at his mother in astonishment. Never before had he encountered the myth of his nation. This story was known by everyone, but his mother refrained intentionally from telling him until now. She felt that the action of him forging iron would weld together with the myth so both would find potency beneath his hammer. In this manner, the Mongols charged out of the mountain passes, marched towards the plains and took to the road that led to freedom and liberation. His mother had descended into grinding poverty and didn't have anything to her name except for this story. Nonetheless, Temüjin shook off the shackles of terror with the help of this tale.

The military campaigns undertaken with the intention of unifying Mongolia were bitter and protracted. Temüjin was regularly trapped in desperate circumstances, but clawed himself out of the jaws of danger every time. He was lonely but fearless. He never forgot his mother's story. New connotations were folded into the mix when this household tale was related by his mother. He had never forgotten how to strike the iron either. After the unification of Mongolia, one of his decrees ordered that all Mongols fire up a furnace and hammer out a piece of iron symbolically on New Year's Eve so that they would fix in their minds how the Mongolian nation had won their new life and liberation.

Altay was very important to him. Barely had he unified Mongolia, when he realised that he and his great Mongolian army ought never to be confined to just the Burkhan Mountain and the Mongolian grassland. *Mongol* means "endless multiplication and reproduction" and *Kiyan* refers to the "tumultuous torrent". He and his great army marched to Altay. Taken aback by the dignified and elegant rolling mountains, he first discovered that he had a pair of beautiful cat's eyes. He was moved by his own virility. The Burkhan Mountain and the River Onon didn't possess this. It dawned on him that there was something still dormant in his life. He strode into the waist-high wormwood. The rustling forage grass failed to distract him. After a bend, the mountain valley opened up into a broad expanse. The River Kelan flowed through and the banks were even and moist with plentiful sunshine. Spying a large patch of tender green sward, the Khan made his way to an open area to the south of the mountains and the north of the water; even the earth couldn't blot out this greenery. It was already late autumn. The forests and the grassland were both withered yellow. What plant was still budding and bursting into leaf at this time? Pleasantly surprised, the Khan brought to mind his mother's story and how his body grew flesh bit by bit when he was in distress. That expanse of grassland belonged to an old Han Chinese lady. She was so old that she couldn't recall her own age. Many moons ago, her ancestor had been dispatched here by a dynasty from the Central Plains to claim more acres of the Western Regions for the soldier-cum-tiller folk. That dynasty had ceased to exist ages before. The soldier-cum-tillers scattered sporadically across the boundless deserts of Middle Asia.

"We are so hard to find," the old lady confessed. "You are my first guest besides the sun and the eagles."

She poured some water for the Khan. It had the leaves of an apple tree steeped in it. The old lady explained that this was "tea".

The Khan didn't know what *soldier-cum-tiller* meant and was keen to know if the people on the Central Plains were all soldier-cum-tillers.

"A soldier-cum-tiller is basically a farmer."

"Can the land be farmed?"

"You just need to dig it first and then you can grow whatever you want."

"*Ayah*, the land must be too vast."

"You are smart. The more a lazybones horses about, the smaller the land will shrink; the more a diligent man toils, the larger the land will become."

"This patch of grass is the result of your graft and grind?"

"This isn't grass. It's wheat."

"*Aoyao*, wheat!" The Khan bent over to observe carefully. The ears of wheat were tiny and tender. Deep was his astonishment. He already had the grassland in his sway. Even the eagles in the skies were his possessions, but he wasn't familiar with this kind of plant, which alone remained green in the season when grasses and woods had wilted and become sparse. Even the stones on the grassland are bound to be cracked frozen in the winter, the Khan thought.

"It should be eaten before the arrival of winter," he said.

"You can't get a taste until next summer," the old lady replied.

"How can it survive through the winter?"

"Because it is tender and weak."

The Khan was even more surprised. "Old ma, can you give me a wheat seedling?"

"This is our grain."

The old lady was in a real quandary.

The Khan beseeched: "This is precisely the myth my mother related to me when she was still alive: the tender and weak will surely beget the strong."

The old lady plucked out a wheat seedling and gave it to the Khan with the soil still clinging to it. The Khan's capacity for self-control was remarkable. No matter how violently his heart was buffeting, his face remained impassive. This kind of superhuman composure always brought him the richest harvest.

"Where did the wheat come from?"

"Our ancestors grew it."

"How did they get it?"

"Our earliest ancestor gained it in exchange for his own life."

In the old lady's story, a hero called Kuafu[q] swore an oath that he would catch up with the sun. He chased the sun from his resting place in the Yang Valley until the end of the skies (in other words to this very place in the vicinity of Altay). When he was on the cusp of capturing his quarry, the sun let rip its fiercest heat to roast Kuafu alive. Kuafu had been across many deserts but still felt unbearably parched. The mighty rivers he supped from were drained dry, yet he still felt so thirsty. Back then, Altay was a desolate land used by the sun to entrap Kuafu. The sun had baked this place into the massive Gobi where not a blade of grass could grow and the mountains were all bare. The sun then squatted on the summit of a bald mountain waiting for Kuafu. With a yell and not caring for his life, Kuafu charged and collided with the sun. His body caught fire. The sun hooted with laughter, believing that Kuafu must have been burned to death. Conversely, Kuafu collapsed to the ground and prospered. His head was metamorphosed into dignified mountains, his sinews and flesh into fertile expansive plains, his blood into great rivers, his hair into lush grasses and woods, and his eyes into clear, clean lakes. No longer could the sun flee from him. The grasses and woods ensnared the sun like fishing nets. Kuafu's offspring now sow wheat on the most fertile lands. When the sun is at its most insolent in the summer, those dense prickles of wheat sting it savagely, so it feels them as thorns in its back.

The feuding enemy Genghis Khan had barely defeated was known as the Sun Khan (died 1204 AD). Genghis Khan felt that he was listening to his own legendary story. What startled the Khan more was that wheat could put out thorns.

"It is called *wheat awn*," the old lady continued. "Like arrows – they are the gold arrows shot into the sun by Kuafu."

The Khan was apparently shocked by this legendary hero. He

also sensed his own mission: he and his great army must scale Altay to give chase to the sun. He issued his third decree to his great army with a flick of his mighty hand: "Pursue and attack the Sun Khan. Wherever the Sun Khan flees, that is the direction in which our army should march."

How many times was the Khan to shout out those heroic words on Mount Burkhan: "Hunt down our enemy and deprive them of their wives and daughters; make them shed tears of sadness." Everything was altered by the autumn of Altay. The Khan truly did become the favourite son of Heaven in Altay. He chased the sun. No longer did he use powerful bows and blades. He adored the fresh plant sent to him by the old Han Chinese lady. He announced with pride: "We will use this puny blade of tender seedling to conquer the world."

The blacksmiths copied the shape of the wheat seedling when forging a new weapon from the iron produced in Altay. The weapon was pointy and delicate. The generals and soldiers were gleefully surprised. Forged from the superlative iron, this was the thinnest and most minute weapon in that material throughout the world – like a piece of tiny cutlery. The Khan said: "The Han Chinese from the Central Plains make meals out of wheat. They feast on the most beautiful grass on the earth." Not until the spring of 1959 did the Battalion Commander and his comrades-at-arms cultivate the first plot of oasis where green vegetables grew. The herdsmen hooted with laughter. "The Han Chinese from the corps are eating grass." But that was another story. In the late autumn of 1204, Genghis Khan announced to his great army: "Our courage comes from Tengri and our weaponry from the earth. The weak will surely become strong and this weapon is named 'Seedling'."

That seedling thrived more than any other. Like the lakes and underground dwellings, Genghis Khan had created the sharpest and most imposing as well as the most poetic weapon between the heavens and the earth.

What is more, his legions – each consisting of 10,000 warriors – followed the shape of the seedling in their battle formation. The

Khan rode at the forefront with a long wheat-seedling-shaped blade in his hand and two generals behind him. One begot two, two begot three until the 10,000 were assembled. The generals donned gold armour and the soldiers iron. The Khan's outfit was plain. He sported a bronze helmet and had a Mongolian gown wrapped around him. The armour beneath the gown had changed into tree bark – the Khan had stripped the bark from a comely birch with his bare hands.

"We will capture the Sun and tether him to a tree to watch over our yurts," the Khan bellowed.

His great army took to the road. Whenever the generals and soldiers thought of their Khan's beautiful eyes, that seedling-shaped weapon and the pure white birch bark armour, their hot blood coursed so as to make them invincible. The 10,000-warrior legions marched westwards, westwards and further westwards like a whirlwind, driving the Sun Khan to the sea. The Mongols named that expanse of sea the Atlantic Ocean, which means "the westernmost sea on the earth".

The sun in the east was bright red but became a sallow-faced hag when it dropped down into the western sea. That was an unwelcome sight for the Khan. His great army reached the River Volga and he lost interest in the sun.

"The sun was really fine while he was still strong," he judged.

He had seen how decadent the sun was.

"Kuafu fell down in disappointment. At the very beginning, he thought the sun was very alluring and very tough. He charged to his front to take a look and then felt disappointed. He himself was the most alluring and imposing.

"We are quite satisfied with ourselves. Kuafu caught up with the sun at Altay and we defeated our Sun near the River Volga. As Kuafu's descendants, we weighed our hearts and concluded that we hadn't brought shame upon him."

Unwilling to follow in Kuafu's tracks, which had finally led to disaster, the Khan returned to the East. An ugly sun was aghast. The Khan told his princes to inform the Europeans: "The sun is good for stirring up people's desires, but human beings should never be too greedy." The Khan went back to Altay. What he admired more than anything else was the manner of Kuafu's demise. That was a hero's death.

He stayed at Altay for one year. His children returned after their conquest of the West. The Khan accompanied them to the Central Plains. At the foot of the Helan Mountains, he fell mortally ill. He knew that death was close at hand. The princes had conquered the better part of the whole world and the wealth of all the kings had become their war trophies, yet the Khan wanted none of them – not even the gold.

"People take gold as the sun," the princes persuaded. "Even the kings make no exception."

"There are no kings in this world except for one and that king is me," the Khan blustered. "This king doesn't need mortal gold. The gold you see is only an illusion. My gold is invisible."

The Khan wanted nothing – not even the imposing seedling – as his funereal objects. The seedling was bald when they went on the western expedition. Whenever an enemy king or generalissimo was slain, one hair would be plucked from his head. By the time they returned from their conquest of the West, a thick wad of hair was draped around the seedling.

"This is a warning given to the people of the world. They should mark what it represents and leave the wheat alone on the earth," the Khan said.

By the time he rose from the grassland, the Khan had already focused on a vaunted green tree at the foot of Mount Burkhan.

"Put us in that tree and bury us on the spot," he ordered.

The princes cried. "Then how can we offer sacrifices to you!"

"A king needs no memorial monuments. A king is simple and plain."

The Khan was brought back to the grassland and slotted inside a round log. An extremely deep pit was dug in the ground with a ramp serving as the exit. The log was slid painstakingly into place. When the hollow of the underground mausoleum had been refilled almost up to ground level, the princes, afraid that they might not be able to find the grave again, buried a baby camel near the surface. The next spring, the mother camel led them to their father. Green grass had already covered the spot, blending with the great grassland. The mother camel rushed to a grassy spot to mourn and the princes cried their eyes out too. They didn't call it a tomb but an "underground warren" instead. Like a pond, it signals the beginning of a new life.

鹿

The Battalion Commander awoke from his dream with a start. He had been dreaming about sleeping in the underground warren and how a tender wheat seedling was growing out. When the seedling was on the point of butting out of the earth, his head ached as though ready to explode. The seedling had pierced his head. His wife touched his hair, which was standing on end.

"What made you have a dream like that?" she asked.

"Isn't it good to dream of a wheat seedling?"

"The wheat seedling is growing out now, but you have almost thrown your life away because of it." His wife held him tight. "Why are you like a tree?" She touched him up and down and her hand told her that his skin was like birch.

"I got shot and an old Mongolian biddy staunched my bleeding with tree bark."

"Does it still feel painful?" His wife caressed the scars again and again.

"Those aren't bullet holes anymore. They grew solid long ago."

"Have the bullets been taken out?"

"Bullets? My body chomped them into a pulp like kidney beans."

"Don't try and pull the wool over my eyes me. Bullets are lethal."

"You haven't been to the battlefield and don't know what blood is capable of doing – it can melt away a bayonet."

"You have chomped bullets to a pulp and melted away bayonets. Why then was your head pierced by a wheat seedling?"

"That is a legend from the Mongols. The strong traces its source back to the weak."

Spring arrived in Altay. The ice and snow thawed out. A dozen-or-so-metre-wide stone-paved road appeared in the midst of the wilds – all pointy stones. That was the renowned Genghis Khan Thoroughfare. Back then, the Khan's curtained carriage galloped to the West from here. Boundless drought-stricken wastelands lay on both sides of the thoroughfare. The surface soil was very thin. Sand and rubble were dislodged with the chop of an iron shovel.

The Battalion Commander said: "The strong originate from the weak. As long as there are seedlings – no matter how weak the seedlings are – the sand and pebbles will be kicked down."

"The earth crawls out of the sand and pebbles," he continued.

The guys were all peasants before they joined the army.

"The peasants in Altay can sever the heavens from the earth," the Battalion Commander encouraged them.

A swish of his iron shovel produced a shower of sparks.

"You see," he pointed out. "To sever the heavens from the earth we should first bring out the earth."

"After generations on the land we are back to being novices," the other chaps said.

Sparks started to fly under their iron shovels.

Ditches and furrows were shovelled out and water coursed in from the river. Tilth was retched up from beneath the pathetic topsoil.

Crouching down on the field ridges, the company was overjoyed. "*Ayayah*, it has been brought up, up!"

The water was gurgling and bubbling. Clear water then became muddy and the earth was dissolved into the muddy water. After the water was swallowed by the earth – *glug-glug* – a layer of mud was deposited on the ditches and furrows. One day of baking out in the open was enough for it to crack. Again, clear river water was released into the cavity until it was brimming over. After half a morning, the water again seeped underground to the very last drop. In the process of being released and baked dry like this, the water became muddy every time and crawled underground to bring up the earth like a rat.

"It is not being brought up but sucked out of the earth grain by grain," the Battalion Commander corrected.

"Holy mother," the others cried out. "Like a baby suckling from its ma."

Someone then sat on his haunches and took a handful of sand to examine it left and right. It didn't look like a woman's nipple. He dropped it into the water. The sand turned soft and creamy like a woman's nipple again.

"The earth is our mother," the Battalion Commander said.

The guys had heard this from their cultural instructor before.[1] A Battalion Commander is a Battalion Commander. He knew what a cultural instructor knew; he also knew what a cultural instructor didn't know.

"Stones are the mother of our mother," the Battalion Commander went on.

The cultural instructor made a wisecrack: "Today, I've learned that rivers flow with milk and not water."

The cultural instructor had barely consummated his union with his wife.

The others then pulled his leg by saying: "You got that last night?" They then nicknamed the cultural instructor's wife "River". Feeling the name poetic, the cultural instructor asked to go to the river to help release the water. The Battalion Commander promised. The cultural instructor's wife was labouring merrily in the field. With her sleeves and trouser legs hiked up high, the ruddy-faced young woman rose and then bent low on the wasteland, looking, in fact, like a river.

"There was only one river in the land to begin with. Now another river has come along. We have two rivers," the Battalion Commander mused.

Glug-glug – the river water was swallowed into the viscera of the earth. The clear water turned muddy and the muddy water then congealed into mud.

"I have never seen such a parched land," the others grumbled.

"Kuafu died of thirst here," the Battalion Commander recalled.

The others then asked him who this Kuafu was.

The Battalion Commander proffered that Kuafu was the father of many, many people – a father who was as old as antiquity itself. "This ancient father of ours died a heroic death. His head changed into mountains, his flesh into earth, his hair, beard and eyebrows into forests and pasturelands, his blood into rivers and his eyes into lakes."

It dawned on the other guys. "The wastelands are our ancient father's bones."

"Then let's put some flesh on the bones," the Battalion Commander suggested.

A layer of fine yellow earth had by then accumulated on the sand and stones. The others were unexpectedly jubilant.

"A beauty is plump.[5] Now the bones have put on some flesh," the Battalion Commander declared.

The others stroked it with their hands. The creamy, soft, delicate feeling moved them as well as choking back their words. "Beautiful, beautiful, too beautiful," they still managed to cry out.

"A hero is hairy," the Battalion Commander resumed. "Bushy hair all over his body makes a man handsome beyond belief."

The corps then gazed at the mountain to their north. The Altay Mountains had barely walked out of winter and banked-up snow was still layered on their northern slopes. The forests, pasturelands and greyish-blue rocks appeared tender and clear. An eagle was wheeling overhead with its wings spread out very evenly. Someone mumbled: "It seems to be ploughing the land. I have seen those furrows."

A brilliant light was flashing in the mountains and above the grassland. Wherever the eagle flew, a whirlpool arose from among the brilliant light.

"It looks like a man spread-eagling himself," somebody said.

The others whooped in agreement.

"A sprouting leaf is a man spread-eagling himself," the Battalion Commander said.

"A stalk still takes on human shape – one man is piled on another. That means you have children already," he continued.

"One seed is sprinkled into the earth. When it is fully grown, we can harvest a hefty handful," he finished.

Startled, though in a good way, the others' eyes were sparkling incandescently.

In the spring, they sprinkled wheat seeds. They sowed the seeds in the daytime. A windstorm darkened their door at night. The seeds and the topsoil were blown clean away and even the ditches and furrows were flattened. Only the desolate Genghis Khan Thoroughfare was left on the wasteland. Not until now did the fellows know why Genghis Khan had built such a solid road using only jagged stones. All the stones were triangular with their sharp corners directed skywards. Their bulky ends were buried in the earth as if they were growing out of it. Only those growing out of the earth were eternal. Genghis Khan grew the stones so that they would sprout and spread into a road to pass through the deserts, mountains and pasturelands from the East to the West as far as the seas.

Crops originated from grasses. The Divine Peasant tasted numerous kinds of grass and finally identified each crop.

The Battalion Commander crawled out from beneath his warm quilt as if a god had entered his body.

"What are you doing? What are you doing?" his wife asked.

Like one possessed by the devil, the Battalion Commander rushed out of their underground dwelling. His wife was hot on his heels. Crouching down, he crammed wheat seeds into the cracks between the stones.

"Can't you wait for daybreak?"

"If daybreak arrives, the miracle won't happen."

His wife held a torch in her hand. With the help of the torchlight, he picked out the earth from the cracks between the stones.

"Those that grow in the cracks between the bones are all good flesh. Seeds which sprout here will be like fired-off arrows – Genghis Khan's arrows."

When the day broke, all the men came and the women helped the Battalion Commander's wife back home. The men tugged at the Battalion Commander, but he wouldn't budge. He persisted in watching the seeds being crammed in grain by grain.

It was another stormy night, yet the seeds in the cracks between the stones were safe and sound.

Two banks were built on either side of the road. When water

flooded in, the stones started to tinkle and their sharp corners were gone – buried by the yellow earth that had been brought up by the water.

"Genghis Khan took to this road in birch bark," the Battalion Commander pointed out.

Birches were planted 50 metres away from the road and elms were planted 100 metres away from the birches. Both belts of trees extended several dozen metres wide. The elms were blown askew by the wind. Those in the outer circuits were all short and bent low. The posture of the wind was apparent. The wind roared its way over. Encountering a barrier, it started to swirl like an armour-piercing projectile and twisted the trees into fried dough twists, but still failed to charge through. Some trees were slain to the ground with their crowns raising a little, like warriors who had taken a shot and fallen; still breathing, but with their blood draining away. The further inwards one went, the taller the trees. The branches of the few innermost rows of elms spread out very wide and let go of themselves completely to surge skywards. The birches on both sides of the road could well be regarded as a picturesque landscape in their own right.

The wheat seedlings prospered between the stunning belts of impressive trees.

They grew out of the cracks between the stones at the very beginning. With only the tiniest of shoots, the young seedlings sparkled brilliantly to illuminate the whole wasteland. Those needle-tip-like shoots soon sprouted two leaves like an eagle with its wings outspread. No longer did the eagles need the protection of the stones. Like an old man's teeth, the stones loosened. The cracks between them were too narrow to accommodate the vigour of the wheat seedlings.

"The seedlings are growing well. Let them charge out like rapid torrents," the Battalion Commander said.

The life that originated from the weak charged out by melting away a great mountain.

"The stones have loosened already. Pluck them out," the Battalion Commander said.

The stones were plucked out one by one. The holes left behind were drenched with water and then refilled with earth. Like an old man whose teeth had been extracted, the wasteland, whose teeth had been pulled out, looked young immediately.

Windstorms loomed large again, but no longer could they wreak havoc on their homeland. The wheat seedlings flew more and more energetically in the windstorms and sprouted another two leaves to pair up with the former two. The tip of the seedling remained in one piece. Akin to Genghis Khan's cavalrymen in the legends, they marched westwards from the east until the seas.

The chaps stared skywards. The sky in Altay in the spring was an endless blue. It was a kind of delicate blue; it was an ocean of wheat seedlings. When the wheat seedlings captured the sun, they were immediately ripe.

New oblong fields that stretched out both to the north and to the south were reclaimed on both sides of the Genghis Khan Thoroughfare. The wasteland was truncated and surrounded by belts of trees, and ploughed and irrigated. The earth was sucked out by water from down below. When seeds were to be sown, stones were paved above; when the wheat seedlings grew out, the stones were removed. All the seedlings struck the posture of an eagle as they shot out from the cracks between the stones. They pierced the earth and the air, spreading out their wings in the windstorms and flew with a mighty sound.

In this way, the oblong fields were reclaimed all the way to the River Irtysh. Mountains and pasturelands stood on the other side of the river. The great wasteland between the southern foothills of the Altay Mountains and Ulaandaban disappeared and so did the Genghis Khan Thoroughfare. Wheat and maize were prospering.

The Battalion Commander was struck by a thirst that could not be quenched. Everyone else felt thirsty, but no one was as dehydrated as him. He was originally a legendary figure. When he shouted out "I feel parched to death", they were reminded of the legendary Kuafu. Kuafu chased the sun from the Yang Valley where the sun was supposed to rise in the ancient times until the western heavens – in other words, the abdomen of the great wasteland in Middle Asia. Kuafu fell here, but the Battalion Commander didn't. He was still standing. "I am quite satisfied with myself. As a descendant of Kuafu, I've searched my heart and concluded that I haven't brought shame upon him."

The other chaps handed him water, sugared water, black tea and milk tea.

"Drink the river water," his wife advised. "River water can put flesh on you."

The Battalion Commander was so bony that he was out of shape. He jumped into the River Irtysh and the water level plummeted.

"His mouth is dry as dust. So are his hands, feet and bones," his wife lamented.

"Let our Battalion Commander drink like a fish, drink to his heart's content," the others echoed.

The Battalion Commander didn't clamber ashore until he had been floating in the river for days on end. The others all heard tell of his legendary stories and none felt startled. The jaws of the Russians dropped. Back then, the Soviet Union was China's Elder Brother and Altay saw many Soviet experts and expatriates. Witnessing how the Battalion Commander was floating in this great green river, they exclaimed: "He is tougher than our Yermak. Yermak was drowned in the River Irtysh."

Yermak began as a bandit who slaughtered people along the River Volga with the ease of mowing down hempen stalks. The House of Strogonov, which was entrusted with conquering Siberia, hired a gang of bandits and drove them over the Urals to invade Asia.

Yermak defeated Kuchum Khan from the Khanate of Siberia and presented the whole of Siberia to the Tsar. Ivan the Terrible not only pardoned his past crimes but also rewarded him handsomely. "A victor won't be made to stand trial." He emphasised the national interest. Yermak, who received the awards, attacked Siberia with even greater frenzy. One stormy night, Genghis Khan's descendent Kuchum Khan heard the wisdom of an oracle:

"The enemy of the steppe will perish in a river – whether it be the River Tura, the River Amu, the River Syr or the River Irtysh, each of them is able to drown Yermak."

Yermak was subjected to unremitting ambushes. His powerful blunderbuss couldn't help him. Kuchum Khan hid underground and always caught him on the wrong foot. He would suddenly crawl out of the earth, launch a volley of shots to hack down a batch of Cossacks, and then retreat like a windstorm to a very distant place. There he would dig trenches in wait for Yermak. Every time, Yermak would lose a large number of mounted Cossacks. He whipped his colt spitefully, but a horse raised along the River Don could never outrun one raised on the Mongolian steppe. The Mongolian horses were short and small. The short and small Mongolian horses had only to fling themselves forward with little effort to dart ahead. A wind would tail them and they would disappear from the wilds.

Yermak was the lone survivor of his company, and he fled here and there across the grassland with an arrow wound. An old Tartar woman saved his hide with milk tea and told him that he must disrobe when he swam across the river – he should never violate the decree issued by Genghis Khan. According to Genghis Khan's laws and decrees, rivers should never be polluted. Yermak wore the armour bestowed upon him by Ivan the Terrible. The old Tartar woman implored: "This is a dead weight that will drag you down."

"Old mother, I am a good swimmer. No river can stop me."

"But in front of you is the River Irtysh – a river that even Genghis Khan felt in awe of!"

"The Tsar has given me fame and honour. What has Genghis Khan given me?"

"What Genghis Khan has given to the earth is his oracles. His oracles surpass the honour given by all the kings."

"You want to persuade me to take off my armour? But I am a warrior of the Tsar, old mother!"

"A warrior has more awe-inspiring armour."

"Then show me, old mother."

The old woman pointed at the birches on the wilds. "Our Khan walked throughout the earth in a suit of birch bark."

"Birches are poetic, but they can't ward off a bullet, old mother. Ivan the Terrible's powder shotgun can shoot down goshawks. Eagles leave the skies to crouch down on his crown. He used powerful mines to blast open the city walls of the Khanate of Kazan. The grassland belongs to the Tsar."

"Kings will perish, but trees never will."

"But trees are so lonesome and bitter. All the way from the River Volga to Siberia are just grief-stricken little birches. I have been loitering about the wasteland for too long. It is time for me to get a taste of the good life. The Tsar's palace is like the Heavens. I should go to see my Tsar."

When Yermak swam across the River Irtysh, his armour became a millstone and dragged him down to the bottom of the river. It was the height of summer. His swollen body burst through his armour and the gold plates on it reeked unbearably – it was a kind of egregious auric stench. Yermak was not fished out until he had been left to rot for more than forty days. The middle and lower reaches of the River Irtysh and expansive Siberia remained desolate until the age of Khrushchev, who spared no financial resources in reclaiming that expanse of ancient wasteland and sprinkling tons and tons of corn seeds. Nonetheless, the golden seeds went rank faster than Yermak. Siberia became desolate as ever before and crops could never be sowed there. The only harvest was large stretches of N-bomb bases and large groups of tanks, which lined up along the border and formed a dense dark mass that made people short of breath.

鹿

The air above the border was charged with tension, which kept the settlers company until they reached adulthood. The tense atmosphere constituted a part of their formative years.

The Battalion Commander was a rare figure from the very beginning. People still remembered how he swam like a fish in the River Irtysh for several days and made the Russians slack-jawed. Naturally, he charged to the front line. His masterstroke was growing crops. A man who could grow wheat in the cracks between stones was a miracle in his own right. The dense dark masses of crops he had planted spread out along the border from Altay to Tarbaghatai to the Ili River Valley to the southern and northern sides of the Tianshan Mountains. The green sea knew no borders.

The Battalion Commander was very happy. He had opened up oases at the gate of his motherland and planted crops.

This story has now almost come to an end. The crops planted by the corps soldiers flourished to the accompaniment of the booming tanks and the shadow of a possible nuclear attack. There is nothing strange in the story ending like this.

In Tarbaghatai there lay an area which was disputed by China and the Soviet Union. The horses and iron wire meshes from the other party frequently crossed the boundary illegally and encroached deeper and deeper onto home territory. Sheep were undeterred from grazing on the forage grass however.

By then the Battalion Commander had gone back to Altay.

He got wind of the information at a cadres' meeting. He studied the map. Surely, there was a blank space there. It was said that the land was very fertile. He loved crops. If he didn't farm, he would feel uncomfortable. It was such an expanse of fertile land and what is more, it belonged to his people. But their animals couldn't graze there. He then thought of cultivating crops there.

His wife wanted to follow suit. For so many years, she was always with him just as the body and its shadow are inseparable. He didn't know if she was carrying a baby in her womb or not. He had farmed so much land. It was time for him to bring back home a harvest from his wife's plot of land. Apparently, his missus wanted to give him a surprise. She had braced herself to inform him. The meeting was barely over. He was talking about the patch of fallow land in Tarbaghatai over his meal; he was on a high. His wife was only too familiar with his passions. The most sacred things to him were the crops and the land. Crops were his Allah.

The Battalion Commander worshipped the crops like a pilgrim. When he strode out on the field, he would unconsciously pray to Heaven with his palms put together and murmur quietly in his heart: "The Grey-blue Heaven in the Highest, let the crop prosper. Prosper unflaggingly like the turbulent rapids." Every time, at this same moment, his wife would fix her eyes on him in silence. Back on the street in the small city to the north of the River Wei when he had described the beautiful Altay to her, he wore a fanatical look like this. This fanatical expression was always fresh, familiar and yet novel.

"I shall follow you there," she promised.

The Battalion Commander hesitated. He didn't know why but his wife persisted and he no longer sought to dissuade her.

Their company was within the range of one arrow from the national boundary. The incident occurred while the men were in the middle of their meal; some were wiping the tractors and some were putting away the corn seeds.

The radio announced: "The corn seeds sowed by Khrushchev have all become rotten in Siberia. Chairman Mao has written a poem, which reflects that Khrushchev has released a fart. A fart won't bear seeds." The corps soldiers were in a festive mood, cheering that their Xinjiang was a fine place. The wastelands on the southern and northern sides of the Tianshan Mountains had all been turned into granaries.

"The shepherd has been taken away," someone shouted.

The folks charged out with a *whoosh*. They didn't go to the armoury to fetch their guns. They had got accustomed to wielding agricultural tools. With the tools in their hands, they charged over and tussled with the soldiers of the Elder Brother. Their opponents were all Cossacks on horses raised along the River Don. They had in their hands long sabres and horsewhips. Later, they threw their guns into use.

The Battalion Commander was shot. He was not afraid of this stuff. His body had been riddled with bullets from Hu Zongnan, the Americans and the bandits, though not the Cossacks. With a swish of his iron shovel, he chopped at the gunner's arm. The arm then flew out together with the gun.

The Cossacks retreated to their side. They had all been injured, not by weapons but by agricultural tools. Who could stand this kind of humiliation?

The one who received the bullet was a woman. The Cossacks all witnessed it. A woman was shedding blood on the ground. She was the Battalion Commander's wife. An armour-piercing bullet had sliced through the Battalion Commander's body and then hit his wife, who was standing behind him. Not until the men tried to rescue her did they find out that she had a swollen belly. The Battalion Commander knelt down in front of her, but words failed him. His wife shared with him the joyful secret: "We have a baby now." Tears then plopped down her face. The tears of the women in Altay had always been kept captive within their eyes. Now they flew out. "I don't want to die," she bleated. The Battalion Commander crammed a corn seed into her wound. "Our baby," she murmured. He put another grain into her mouth. No longer did she mumble and nor did she shed tears. He whispered into her ear: "A dignified life will never perish. We will regain our lives from the plants."

鹿

A new voyage of life started like this.

The Battalion Commander whispered into his wife's ear: "Life returns to its budding stage."

The corn seed cast out shoots from his wife's wound.

He again whispered into her ear: "Life goes back to the earth."

A very big, deep pit was dug in the earth and her body was lowered slowly down. People could still see the golden yellow seedling, which was like a palomino horse.

The Battalion Commander was still confiding in a voice that uncannily resembled the rustling of the tree leaves. It was a birch from Altay. Everyone unconsciously raised their heads to look up at the dignified tree. The tree murmured: "You have heard plenty. When you have anything to say, you can go and summon Hong Ke." In the belly of Middle Asia, *hong* means "beautiful" and *ke* refers to "a small tree switch". The tree switch swayed gently and captured large patches of wind:

> *I have spoken my mind and written a book.*
> *I have grasped two worlds.*

The Tears of the Trees

He has woken up; he knows not how. He does not turn on the light. Instead, he crawls up and pushes the window open. It is pitch dark outside. So distant are the stars that it seems as though they are germinating in a long tunnel. The stars are so tiny, like pinheads, but are still clearly discernible. He has risen early in order that he might watch them.

He half-squats like a dog on the bed. Canines gaze at the stars in this posture. They are capable of gleaning almost any message from the stars, but the less they are able to glean the more they are likely to continue watching them. The longer one looks at the stars the smaller and more remote they become. The stars moisten as if juice is seeping out from the sky, and this is cast down onto the man's face. His cheeks are now damp. He realises he is weeping. He closes the window and draws the curtain to.

Sitting on the bed, he cannot fathom what on earth has just happened. A huge shadow migrates over from afar and sidles up towards the window.

"Who is that?" he asks

The shadow moves slowly and steadily.

He raises his voice: "Who is that?"

The shadow pays no attention whatsoever to him and prepares to leap onto the windowsill.

Having had no time to put on any clothes he pushes the window open with a *pang*. It turns out to be the blue sky, which is sprawling inch-by-inch through the darkness just as an estuary gradually broadens and empties into the sea. The blue sky bumps against the window. The sky deepens and starts to drown the faraway stars. The stars appear very much like tadpoles, wriggling about in the water. The blue waves pitch higher and higher. The stars sink in their entirety to the bottom of the water.

Daybreak comes in this manner.

He dresses and sticks his head out through the window. The corner of the wall remains shrouded in darkness. He is the earliest bird in the company. The brick house and the clay-built house are still asleep. The scattered chimneypieces on the roofs are visible. The chimneys have awoken; they are smoking. Most of the stacks have been fashioned from rough, thick porcelain jars, some out of brick. They all open their large mouths. The blue smoke licks the blue sky like a tongue. It licks and licks until sparks start to appear in its midst. These sparks float a great distance as though they possess wings.

He goes out of the room to stare at the big chimneys. Blue is the sky and the smoke is black. The blue sky gulps down the black smoke together with the sparks. No matter how bright the sparks glow, they cannot withstand the icy coldness of the blue sky. The sky seems somewhat wet. Actually, the sky is dry and so smooth and so vaulted that a hard blade of light shaves across the spectator's eyes.

He stands at the entrance to the village, smoking a cigarette. The cigarette glows ruby red. The village is encircled by forests; the exclusive domain of poplars and birches. Their bark is white and the leaves golden. Within the forest, there is a lustrous sheen. Behind the forest stand the grey and blue Altay Mountains. He knows they are there without even needing to look at them. His back possesses eyes of its own. He smokes a cigarette, radiant and red as a ruby.

The day becomes lucent in every quarter before the sun has even come out, making things clear from a great distance off. A generous road hastens out from the village, unfurling towards the roomy, plump expanse of the wild plain. The wild plain swallows the generous road. The man walks along the road for a while and then stops. Even if he walked along it for a month, he would be unable to ascertain anything.

Later on, he sees a dog. The dog is squatting on a hulking rock as if it has sprouted out from it. The dog lolls out its long tongue. It is watching the sky conscientiously. When a dog is in a conscientious mood, its tongue will protrude as though it is preparing to lick at the blue shade of the sky. There is nothing in the sky, nothing save for that blueness. He touches the dog, but it neither moves nor acknowledges him. He gives it a kick, but still it refuses to acknowledge him, instead remaining fixated on the sky. There is nothing in the sky. What on earth is the dog watching?

He touches the dog again. Its fur is snug, while its body is icy; it must have been squatting there the entire night. This much he can read in its eyes. The stars are reflected blue in the dog's eyes. The blue stars flash in them. They flash until an edged figure appears. First, there is the form of a cross, then a pentagon. The pentagon-shaped star glistens before disappearing, and then glistens back once more. Within the hound's eyes, the stars are soaring.

He shouts at the dog: "There are no stars in the daytime. Are you looking for an escaped fart?" It jumps up and runs away, scurrying about in the tall grass and the woody shrubs before vamoosing into the forest. The dog now scans a tree, scrutinising its top as though there are stars up there.

What would happen if the stars fell into the trees?

The man's heart is aflutter.

He stands on the rock where the dog was previously. He slips a cigarette into his mouth without lighting it. He watches the forest.

The sun is rising up from the intensely iridescent glade. The poplar trees and birches are all red; the same shade a girl's face turns when she is kissed by someone. He once kissed a girl in this manner – on the face and then on the neck, which felt like the back of a fish. The taste of the girl still lingered on the tip of his tongue. It is a pity he had not bitten the tip of her tongue. A girl's tongue-tip is her treasure, like gold. Gold is a soft metal. The tip of the girl's tongue must be soft too. Gold is red. The tip of the girl's tongue must be red as well. Gold is sweet. The tip of the girl's tongue must be sweet also. He had failed to bite the tip, so bit his own. It was like sawdust. One nibble was enough.

The sun has been floating in the forest the whole day long. It now lounges among the trees. How big this forest is nobody knows. It spans from the north of the village to the foot of the mountain without seeming to have any other boundaries. The

Altay Mountains are, in fact, huge beyond belief, forested all over. The sun walks from the mountain little-by-little and after that starts to glide. That is the temperament of the sun. It likes to hike through the mountains, but on reaching the plain it wants to fly. The sun never ventures to a bleak place; it loves to lodge inside the woods. The white birches are spoiled by the sun, which decides to hover the entire day along the treetops.

The dog raises its head assiduously and looks on with a serious mien. He has mistaken the sun for an oversized star. Skimming above the trees, it has become a star in the dog's eyes. The hound watches from morning until night and then until the stars disappear one by one. The dog's eyes become blurred and it believes that the stars have tumbled down into the trees. The canine has confused the stars with birds. Birds fly in the sky. When they can fly no more, they perch among the branches. Very small birds bulk up their build by roosting in the trees. The birds are black as polka dots when they are in flight and gain colour when they perch. They become chromatic and alluring. The sun is red to begin with and then turns gold like the dog's coat. Its fur is pure yellow, being both smooth and glossy.

The dog lets out two barks. It is greeting the sun.

The dog charges towards the forest.

The man can only see the tail of the dog. The tail is yellow as well, being both smooth and glossy.

He jumps down from the rock and follows the creature into the forest. He does not run. His pace is slow. There are poplar trees and birches on the fringe of the wood. As he peers further in, there are no more poplars. Successive birches appear whiter and whiter. With fewer leaves on the trees, the space in the forest becomes fluorescent. The golden tree leaves hang among the branches after the fashion of gold earrings. The trees bow noticeably. When they emerged from the ground they were perpendicular, but developed a kink from a height of five or six metres. The trees also taper from this benchmark. Shooting further upwards, their curves are more acute. These angles cause the white birches to form a multi-varied spectacle. Each specimen is different from the next. This is why birch trees are more eye-catching than poplars.

The dog is not too far from him, though he is unable to see it. The ground is completely strewn with leaves. The falling leaves cast the yellow dog into the shade. The man can hear the sound of it panting and running just as if it is the golden leaves which are panting and running. The forest looks spacious and empty. The ground seems to be growing thicker and softer in texture. The sandy dust is soft too. The tree leaves are yellow and delicate, fracturing into small pieces like gravel when they are stepped on.

At this moment, a huge shadow stalks over. The dog halts and so does the man. The shadow approaches nearer with a martial bearing, seemingly dressed in a radiant overcoat. That grandeur envelops the unbounded forest. The forest is now quiet. The area the general has patrolled is quiet. One after another, the trees brighten. They are simultaneously white and radiant. They are radiant from the root to the canopy.

The sky is so blue. There is nothing in the sky save for its blueness. The limitless blue sky is perpetually blue.

Both he and the dog can see clearly. The sun is careering through the forest. The sun is golden. When the golden sun treads along the land, the falling leaves cannot eclipse it. There is the sound of the sun moving within the forest together with its gargantuan shadow.

The dog bounces up and then disappears. The man hears the dog leap up several times. The dog cannot see the shadow even if it jumps up. It becomes agitated. An agitated dog can scale a high wall, but it cannot escape from torrents of falling leaves. Big rocks become evident within the forest in the manner of archipelagos in the sea. The dog mounts one. The rock is more than three metres in diameter and most of the leaves that were upon it have been brushed away by the wind. A few remain. The rock takes the dog as a tree leaf and so twitches a little out of contentment. There are splendid white birches on every side. A snatch of tree leaves are shed. One rests on the dog's body almost like a contour incised into copper. The animal's body bears this contour and appears itself to be a contour on the surface of the huge rock. The hound raises its head and watches the white birch. It then lowers its mouth to the rock and whines for a while. The dog lifts its head once more and its eyes are damp. The canine is now directly facing the white birch. The leaves drop one at a time. The golden leaves swirl down one at a time as if somebody is perspiring. The happy sweat sprinkles onto the ground like raindrops, generating a whistling sound.

The man recalls those sweat-filled days, when they were in the grassland. They rode a motor-mower and chased about wildly. They drove the machines to the heart of the grassland. The young fellows in their company rode the best mowers.

The grass became taller and taller. Enticing designs miraculously appeared in the unlikeliest portions of the grassland. Many blocks of colour were configured by the flowers. The motor-mowers splayed out from their column. Some bumped into the scarlet patch, some into the aquamarine and some into the violet. When the motor-mowers glided into the sea of flowers in the manner of a butterfly, the sound of the engines could be heard no more. The cries of the young men echoed throughout the grassland. They screamed with the last of their strength, their faces turning red and their necks dilating. They screamed until their throats were sore. After that, there was silence.

The grassland fell silent. The green motor-mower mimicked the calls of insects in the autumn. It jerked about the tall grass with the movements of a grasshopper. The stalks were flattened everywhere in the zone where the green grasshopper bounded. The vegetation must have been tired. The grassland was so massive that even a horse would become fatigued upon roaming there once. How many times had the grass traversed this place? The grass was as fast as the wind. The grass galloped in tandem with the wind and the horse ran alongside it. The wind could rest in the mountains. The horses could rest in their stable. The grass, however, must stay in the grassland.

Now that the grass was reclining, he shouted: "Hello! Hello! The grass is all laid out."

Nobody answered. His words were too sincere. Obviously, he had discovered something among the fallen stalks. He jumped down from the machine and patted it. The machine stopped moving.

He took out a scythe from behind the driver's seat. That was why he was different from other people.

When leaving home, he removed the scythe from the wall. Others laughed at him. It was really comical to place a tool on the back of a great big motor-mower. Now the machine had been metamorphosed into a small grasshopper. Still, his scythe was there to be used.

He took off his overcoat. The autumnal sun was warm, marvellous and Herculean, appearing somewhat swollen. He was clad in riding breeches with elongated boots reaching above the knee. He had on a collarless white T-shirt and a brownish-red cowhide belt gripped his waist like a steel ring. The copper buckle covered his navel as a mirror would protect the heart of an ancient warrior. It reflected the shadows of the grass.

He simply stood there for a while, though his large scythe could not wait any longer.

With a *whoop* his scythe dived across the ground. Another *whoop* followed. His shoulders and waist moved extravagantly. First, he through his head backwards and then moved forward, lunging to and fro. The grass mimicked the sound of whistling. His feet sank down as he advanced along the ground. The low stubble he had trodden on rose again in his wake. The moisture from the grass left behind many wet prints as if the ground was sweating. From the gaps in between the stubble, he could glimpse the dark face of the ground. The fragrance of the grass pervaded the air.

He couldn't move any further.

The large scythe stood tree-like in the midst of the grass – a curved stripling, the sharp blade of which flashed like a rainbow against the sky over the grassland. The grass was twitching and whistling. The blades of grass wriggled like fish in the blade of the scythe. He was standing together with his tool and panting. His face and neck were covered in sweat. The perspiration fell onto the grassland in imitation of the soothing pit-a-pat of the rain.

The grass-collectors came over and called him to drink some water. He answered them but did not go. He stood amid the tall grass, still sweating. Someone carried libation over to him. He received the flask and the contents gushed out. The water tinkled onto the grass as if it were rain. He exclaimed: "A sudden white downpour."

"You are sweating all over?"

"I'm also in the middle of a sudden white downpour."

The person offering the water turned out to be a girl. She handed over her half-drunk water and said: "Sorry, deal with it."

He drank the girl's remaining water. There was a kind of aroma around the mouth of the bottle similar to the flavour of the grassland vegetables.

He shot the girl a glance.

The girl offered: "Let me go and exchange it for another."

"No need."

The bottle gurgled and was empty.

The girl advised: "Drink slowly, nobody is pressing you."

He spluttered continuously.

The girl lifted the scythe. She gave it a try. The leftover stubble was too leggy and slanted in a criss-cross fashion. With the scythe in her hand, the girl found herself at a loss, yet did not want to surrender it.

He said: "Let me do it." He cut for dozens of metres and eked out a clearing amid the tall grass.

The girl screamed: "Ha! Such a big pit." The girl plopped down on the ground: "You can sit down too."

He then took a seat. The two disappeared from the view of the others. He was still sweating and came over a little embarrassed. He mopped his face a number of times, but it was no use.

"Don't try wiping yourself anymore," the girl pleaded. "It is a good look, having sweat all over your head." The girl tilted her head and looked at him. The sweat ran to his chin and then dropped down. The droplets of sweat gleamed in the sunshine before dripping onto the leftover stubble and percolating into the moisture from the hay.

"The grass is sweating all over, like you."

The girl could hear the whistling sound of the sweat.

Rain sprinkled down like this. The sun was lucid and intense.

The blue sky dispensed a sudden white downpour before the sun's very eyes. A blurry white haze accumulated over the grassland. The pair stood up like grass. Just as the grass used to be, they had become – flora caught in the rain.

The girl screamed: "I now know why they call it a 'sudden white downpour'."

The wild land and the sky were all white. Since it was sheltering from the rain, the sun appeared as only a golden-red shadow. The grass rustled and blanched too.

The girl shouted: "This rain is so white. I can see its shadows."

He could also see the white rain. Its shadows were slender and vigorous. They were jiving along the wild land.

"How wonderful it would be for a woman to have such a fine physique," the girl whispered.

She herself had a slender figure. Owing to the rain, her clothes had become tacky against her body, like a second skin. "Why are you looking at me?"

"Your clothes are all wet."

"I know."

"Like mosses growing out from the land."

"Don't look at me."

He stared at the white rain. It was both slender and strong, like a horse. Its long white shanks flashed about the grassland.

"The rain is the same as the light."

"What did you say?"

"The rain is the same as the light."

"You can look at me now."

The rain abated at this very moment. Downpours come and go easily on the grassland, like a pack of wild horses. The sun abruptly recovered its glow and sunny rain flickered over the grassland. The pair was still intoxicated by the atmosphere of the sudden white downpour. The drenched girl stood slender and strong.

He said: "You are the rain."

"Thank you." The girl was tearful.

He grew upset. His hands fumbled around, though he could not speak a word.

The girl smiled: "I'm alright. Don't be nervous."

"You are crying."

"Who says that I'm crying?"

Tears were all over the girl's face. She wiped at them and tears soaked her hand.

"I am sweating," the girl corrected him, and then went away.

The girl traipsed into the tall grass. A pale leg flashed out from beneath her skirt. The grass rustled. The rain galloped along the grassland in this manner.

The whole of the Altay district rustled. The season of autumn was always loud with rustling noises.

It was strange how when he got back to the village he could no longer recall anything distinctive about the girl. When he encountered her in the midst of a crowd, he could only recognise her when she called out to him. He was an impetuous soul. He burst out: "Rain! Rain!" Her face reddened. She was smiling. Her smile made no sound. It was just an attitude cast back from her dark red face. The smile was in her posture. He had found the shadow of the rain in the way she held herself.

"How could she resemble the rain? She is dark and strong."

She genuinely was a strong girl. Her chest and waist and her arms were all extremely dynamic. The same was true of her legs. How could such strong legs have seemed so slender on the grassland? The noise of the grass being trampled sounded wonderful. He had felt almost flattered there among the stalks of the empty grassland. In the throng of the noisy crowd, he became serious.

He felt guilty. Stammering, he asked the girl what she was there for.

"Window shopping," the girl replied. "We've been busy for dozens of days. Come out for a spot of relaxation."

The two parted.

He watched the girl walk into a shop.

He and his friends played billiards for a while. His luck was poor and his rage lousy. Even though everybody yielded to him, he became even more troublesome. Everyone was angry. They bounced up together, carried him out and deposited him on the embankment. His body and face were covered with dust. Someone cursed him: "He must have been dumped by a girl. He has taken these brothers as his punch-bag." All the others cursed him for being a good-for-nothing.

He stumbled towards the deepest part of the embankment. Altay is the kind of place where no matter whether you are on a manmade embankment or in a wild forest, the leaves of the trees are all yellow as if coated with wax. The trees are universally golden and aglow.

Later, he ran into the girl again. They were in the same company. It was impossible for them not to meet. They merely nodded when they encountered each other. The girl was walking with many other girls. They were talking and laughing. She nodded casually at him. The trees along the roadside fluttered as if caught in a heavy shower. The fluttering of the leaves always made one think of rain. For so many years, the tree leaves had fluttered like this. He expected to hear the sound of rain falling from them.

One day, he was driving a tractor across the land. The girl, who was working in a cotton field, stood up to wipe away her sweat. She wiped her chin and flicked away a series of glittering pearls. The leaves of the cotton plants crackled.

The tractor was roaring loudly, but he could still hear the sound of the girl casting down sweat like rain onto the cotton field.

The girl's hands and feet moved swiftly. She had not noticed that someone was observing her. The cotton boughs were little chicks in her hands. With a number of tugs up and down, the fibre was all removed. The white flowers appeared milky. Women love cotton. When they stand in cotton fields, they turn even whiter.

He reversed his tractor and covered the same distance again. He spied the pale arms of the girl. To his surprise, even her face was wan. He knew that was the effect of the cotton. He dared not imagine what it would be like if a man's hefty hand came into contact with the cotton. Those who had served in the army claimed: "A bullet can pass through solid steel, but not cotton."

A captain was roaring at him from the end of the field. The captain cursed him for getting distracted. He was raking over the already-sown land. The captain stamped with fury. When this guy lost his temper, he beat people. The man was a little scared. Nevertheless, he became bolder. The tractor rumbled directly over towards the captain. The captain grasped the tree and scaled it like a monkey. Then, the captain fell down. He rolled along the ground a few times. The captain's temper had subsided. He beat his waist and asked: "Young man, have you never seen cotton before?"

"I just wanted to take a look."

"You should have stopped the engine and then taken a look."

"I see, Captain."

"That's fine, as long you know that." The captain patted him. "Such a fine young man should get to look at the cotton. If your uncle had kept an eye on the cotton a few years earlier, your auntie would never have given me the push."

Several years ago, the captain's wife went off with another man, leaving him an old bachelor. His disposition was fearful. The captain commented: "Your temper is even worse than mine. I am old, so it's OK. You are still young. You must find a way to solve this problem."

The season drew to an end in this way. The land became empty. It had been picked clean of cotton. Melons and fruits had been transferred into storage cells. The grass had been mown and dried and piled on wooden frames within the courtyards. Only the forest was still enjoying the fall. These were the limitless forests connecting with those of Altay. There one could perceive the shadows of the white birches.

During the night, lots and lots of birches streamed into the man's dream in the style of wild horses, causing him to wake. He pushed open the window and watched the stars. The stars were zooming through the night sky and casting off colourful light, exposing white arms and legs from beneath the skirt of the night. The stars trod on the grassland with the rustling sound of rain. A white shadow was pulsating from within the midst of the grass.

The rain sprouted leaves. This was the denouement of autumn.

The dog jumps off the rock. With a whine, it huddles into the roots of a tree. The dog – a pile of gold – seems to find itself decked with all the ornaments cast down from the tree. Suddenly the dog becomes glistering and phosphorescent. It has turned into a golden hound. The golden dog whimpers. The sound is tender and soft, being absolutely not the sound of a dog. Instead, it is a strain that leeches out from within the depths of the earth. The earth and the falling leaves chant.

Like insects, dogs are at their strongest and most passionate in the final days of the autumn. The dog's neck grips the tree root tightly. Its head is buried in the crevice between the tree root and the land. It too appears to form part of the roots. The tree is still growing. The tree, it seems, is on heat in the springtime. Suddenly, it becomes swollen and lets off a whistling sound. The bark is smooth and white. In the smoothest, whitest and most tender place, the sap of the tree oozes out.

The flow of the tree-sap makes people twitch and shudder.

The man knows that he is weeping. He squats on the square rock, which is surrounded by white birches. Every one of the birches is exuding sap.

He has already walked out of the forest, but the sound of flowing tree sap is still audible alongside him. He stumbles across the wild land like a drunkard.

The village is far, far away. The sun is astoundingly bright. Some people continue to labour in the fields. In the stark fields, people, no matter who they are, all take on distinctive features. He, however, remains something of a blur. He knows he is a hazy spectre, and walks towards the distinct figures.

He asks: "Can you see me?"

"Yes, I can."

"Who am I?"

"You came out from the forest."

"I came out from the forest."

"There is a small birch tree in your eyes."

"A small birch tree in my eyes."

The birch sapling is indeed growing out from his eyes.

The birch sapling stands on the wild land.

He grasps the arms of the birch. The arms are supple – supple and white. Arms full of sap all seem like this. A kiss falls on his face, bigger and fiercer than raindrops. He cries in his heart: "White rain." He cannot say anything out loud.

    The man and the dog saunter across the fields towards the village. The dog crouches on the bare layby watching the sky dumbstruck. Its pupils ascend into the blue sky and splinter into white stars.

Snowbird

Old Nana is having a sleepless night. She can hear the sound of snowfall and is bracing herself for it bursting into the room. She doesn't know why this strange fear has popped into her head, though as the night deepens, the idea takes a firmer and firmer hold.

The break of day comes.

The tin gate rattles and someone enters the yard. Old Nana now sits up. The person knocks on the door.

"You are a girl," Old Nana deduces.

"How did you know that?" The visitor is startled.

"You are having to strain yourself to open the door."

The door creaks more than once, and the person comes in with a bang and nearly falls over.

It is indeed a girl, tall, white-coated and wearing a white hat like a snowman.

"You are from Xinjiang, aren't you? Shut the door quickly, please."

The girl tries twice before it shuts tight.

"Not from these parts?"

"I'm from Urümqi."

"Oh-yoo, Urümqi girl, step over to the fire wall. You are frozen."

The girl peers curiously at the fire wall. She stares at the substantial stove that blazes and burns. The old woman nudges the fuel inside the furnace to one side and the flames bank up to waist-height, quavering. They are toweringly well-built.

"Such a fine figure." the girl comments.

"Your figure is finer." Old Nana's eyes are eagle-like and nab at the girl's body a few times.

She blushes in response, whereupon she is told she is "not nearly red enough".

Those eagle eyes scrunch themselves into a tighter squint, provoking the visitor to snap: "Don't look at me like that. I can't stand it."

"Such a tender girl can't handle the fire.ᵗ Let it blaze up higher, from your feet up to your head." The flames in the stove grow taller, surpassing even the height of a man, and they continue their balmy dance. "How is it, sweetheart?" asks Old Nana.

"Oh, so tall and slender! Look, its legs move so fast!"

"It's jigging."

"I've always wanted to dance as well as that, but I can't."

"It's a joke that girls from Xinjiang can't dance like this."

Her face blushes. It was crimson before and, presently, the flame dances on her complexion. Old Nana's eagle eyes catch the redness of her face with great alacrity: "Don't be embarrassed. A lot of girls are taken in this way. You aren't the first."

"You are always so flattering."

"You want to excel. You have what it takes, but you don't play it out to the end."

Old Nana balances the pot on the stove and the flame vanishes. So does the dancing. The girl reaches out to catch the shadow of the flame, though the old woman stops her: "It's time for it to be put to work." The flame reaches out from beneath the vessel and the water in the pot lets out a creaking sound. The girl scans her own hand and the hand of the flame: "It dances so well. Its hands are like this and this." She imitates the action of the flame. Old Nana steeps a brick of tea in the pot.

"You haven't seen a fire before?"

"Not such good-looking one."

"You don't have a stove back home?"

"We burn gas."

"Gas. Gas is great. Does gas burn without a fire?"

"There's only a little pilot light."

"Like a cigarette lighter. You mean that's enough to cook on? How does rice taste when it's prepared on a fire that doesn't dance?"

Old Nana stares at the ceiling, mystified as to how such a dish might taste without fire.

"I have had sons but I've never had a girl. If I had a girl, she would be a fairy. You've come to be my daughter."

The girl nods with a grin.

"You came to see my son, not me."

She rouges over again.

"Shy girls are good girls. Shy girls are few and far between."

"He is not home," the girl whispers.

"He is home. How could he not be?"

Surveying the house, the visitor detects nobody else.

"You aren't looking in the right spot." Old Nana fixes her eyes on the iron nail on the wall, which is as ample as the branch of a tree. "It's for hanging up a rope. Such a large coil of rope is now suspended from it. When the girls in the fighting-farming regiment visit, they check to see if it is there. If it and the pickaxe on the back of the door are gone, they know the householder is away and so leave."

"What do you use that for?"

"Didn't my son tell you?"

"He said he belongs to the hydraulic regiment."

"How honest that lad is. He lets a girl in on everything. He told you all about it, so why don't you understand?"

"What a good job that must be, in the hydraulic regiment."

"It certainly isn't bad."

"A lifetime of dealing with water. The water in the river."

"Snow on the hills, water in the stones."

"There is water in the stones?"

"The spring. It spurts out from the stones."

"That's what he does."

"No one does it if he doesn't. When the snow and spring water gather together, they are a gang of bandits, fiercer than beasts."

"He tethers them with a rope."

"Tethers himself."

"I see. The rope goes around his waist. Abseiling down the cliff, he uses the pickaxe to catch the untamed river."

"How clever you are, my girl."

"He rushes to the river, and the river rushes to him. Not with a sword, but with a pickaxe – two swords crossed. He doesn't face a charging bull, but a roaring river. Awesome! Better than a Spanish matador."

"My son doesn't have big front teeth like a handsome fella.[u] His teeth are neat – strong and neat. Don't you know my son's teeth? You should know about his teeth."

"He has good teeth."

The girl is frightened by this, and her face reddens again.

Old Nana brews milk tea, which they drink together with naan bread. The girl's blush lasts for an eternity. "You have it," Old Nana insists. The girl thinks about the young man's teeth as she chews on the naan bread. Her heart beats so fast that she worries it will jump out of her chest. But, being famished, she cannot make do with milk tea alone. Nervous and excited, her pace of eating accelerates. She devours three naans in a breath: "I've eaten so much. This is enough to feed my whole family."

"Feel for your ribs."

The girl can feel nothing at all.

"Are they bulging out or not?"

"No."

"If your ribs don't poke out it doesn't count at all. Have more, have more. Take your fill."

"I can't eat any more."

"They aren't bulging."

"My ribs have never stuck out before."

"Is that how your mother raised you?"

"All the mothers in the city bring up their children in this way."

Old Nana has never been to the city, and she cannot imagine how kids can grow to adulthood if their ribs don't bulge. There must be something wrong with them. This young lady is in fine fettle, and she cannot diagnose what the matter is.

"My son is taken by a city girl like you."

"He is charming."

"His is so strong, but we are poor, and that strength doesn't count for anything however great it might be."

"He has great strength and charm."

"Maybe he has got what you call *charm*. He's got many good things about him."

"When will he be back?"

"Who knows? He will come back after work. You're not in a hurry, are you?"

"No."

"Wait then. Some men are not worth waiting for; some men are worth your life."

"Such people don't exist nowadays."

"Didn't you come all the way from Urümqi?"

"You flatter me."

The girl is now sweltering and brushes the buttons of her coat with her hands.

"I know why you don't unbutton them. If you do, your heart would jump out."

The girl looks at the old woman in astonishment, as if she is some sort of a sorceress.

"My ticker beat worse than yours when I was a girl. Clothes couldn't hold it in."

"What should I do then?"

"Use a hemp rope. Fasten it around and around your chest, and then go and see your sweetheart. The tighter it is, the harder your heart will beat, like a horse that has the comfort of the wild and can jump and dance to its heart's content."

Old Nana pats her own wizened chest, where there is a concavity. Maybe there was once a big heart there.

"I guess some old guy rode it away like a horse."

The girl opens her eyes wide, stares at the old woman, and looks at her chest again: "Can a horse dash out of here?"

"Every woman is meant to have a horse in there. Only a few girls get the chance to let it jump free. Many of them are trapped inside and die."

"I want it to run out."

"Give it to your lover and let him take over the reins."

The old woman is so spindly, like a tree consumed by fire.

"I'm long in the tooth and ugly. I must be a ghastly sight."

"You are really quite different from other old ladies. They carry their years lightly, pay attention to their appearance and have their own particular charm," says the girl, removing her overcoat.

The walls are grey without so much as a hanger or hook, which is what she is searching for.

"I'll hold it for you."

The old woman lays out the white coat across her knees and strokes it like a plump sheep.

"Such good leather. Cost a pretty penny, did it?"

"My brother bought it back from Australia."

"Foreign goods – very pricey, but good with it. Just like the snowbird."

"You know about the snowbird?"

"Sure I do. Everyone here knows. It must have been my son who told you that."

She nods.

"My son is an honest man. People seldom speak frankly to beauties like you."

"I am lucky to have heard it."

"This is where I feel uneasy. He must have told you an altered version of the snowbird story."

"Why do you say so?"

"Girls who have heard the proper story daren't come here."

This is, in fact, a spine-chilling tale in which all the snow in the sky was borne aloft on wings and fell down to earth. Old Father Heaven's most beloved daughter wanted to come down to earth too. She was a little princess with dainty flesh. Old Father Heaven tried to strike fear into her by saying: "Go down there and you will lose your life." He was telling the truth; so much snow fell down and was never seen again.

The little princess pored over the snow that was drifting down outside, all the while dying of envy. Heap after heap of snow descended from the sky. Along the way, it was transformed into gorgeous birds which, upon landing, became clusters of flowers.

The little princess did not want to stay in the sky any longer.

She could hardly bear to listen to another word from Old Father Heaven. What, after all, was the purpose of being up there alone? She jumped out of the sky.

White-mouthed with fury, Old Father Heaven unleashed the wind to crumble the snow into powder. The stronger the wind, the prettier the flake. Far from the earth, the little princess changed into a flower.

Snow had lain on the ground for the whole winter. In the snow's dreams, it yet had the chance to blossom. Here in Xinjiang, it is not too difficult to realise this dream. In winter pastures, the plants lie just beneath the snow. As long as everything goes according to plan, on the first day of spring the buds will pop out directly from the snow.

But when spring came around, an ice-cold river surged up from the Tianshan Mountains. The herdsmen's flocks were frozen to death, and horses coughed loudly and struggled for breath. No one had ever seen such a violent river, churning with chunks of ice as hard as iron. These glaciers, crowding fore and aft with a thundering sound, redounded with a terrifying name: Kuitun, Kuitun. The name was chanted by people petrified out of their wits. They were too afraid to shift from their nests and word of the terror spread abroad across the earth.

In the spring, the snow princess sprouted haggard flower buds, but she still had to exert all the strength she could muster to grow a pair of wings that would burnish her beauty. Once they had developed, she had to overwinter into another season. A living creature that could survive two seasons was able to fly. Herdsmen and their flocks moved from winter pastures to spring pastures and then to summer pastures, passing all the seasons of the year. Snowstorms couldn't hinder them. They had faith that they could weather every disaster, and so did the snow. When the fierce and freezing River Kuitun yelled over, the snow lay quiet and motionless on the ground. In those places swept over by the river, the snow was degraded into mud and the ice was still in disarray. The snow had been put to death.

The little princess was the last in line. When the River Kuitun roared in her direction, brandishing its large chunks of ice, mud pelted against her face. Gone was her white complexion and there was no scarlet to pick out her cheeks. She started to sing:

Gone are my chicks,
Gone are my flowers,
My foal has left the stable.

Engulfed in the icy torrent, the little princess was turned into a pile of black mud.

Deep in the desert, the river was finally tired and, as it lay down, it could hear the song of the little princess:

Gone are my chicks,
Gone are my flowers,
My foal has left the stable.

The river raised its head to look around. Green grass overran the wasteland it had trampled over and flowers burst out of the sward. The river had no alternative but to stare blankly: it would have to wait until next year to splash the little princess with more mud.

"Mud is spattered on your little face."

"It's not mud. It's his child. I'm pregnant with his child."

"Let me see. Let me see. Wow, my son, how great you are."

The girl is powerless against Old Nana's hands. The eagle's talons jump up onto her and fumble around as if searching for something in a pocket.

"You liar. There's nothing in it."

"Can such a thing be bogus?"

"Was mud really dropped on your little face?"

"Why do you rattle on about mud? It's a little life."

"So you would like to have this little life. I thought he cheated you, little girl."

"He didn't cheat me. He is an honest man."

"I only have one son left. I can't instruct him to fool others. He'll get his comeuppance if he cheats."

Old Nana's eagle-like talons reach for her head again. The girl hid once but stopped hiding after that. The claws comb her hair so that it sparkles.

"Such a tender child! How did your mother raise you – sealed you in a bottle?"

"We live in a house."

"We live in a house too but the girls here are black and coarse like the men."

"That's how you choose to describe them."

The girl's mouth is waxing bigger and bigger, as if someone is clutching at her neck.

"Handle me tenderly. Yawns should be let free."

The girl yawns with a long sigh.

The old woman leads her to the bed chamber. The bed is next to the window. She has never seen such a large window, massive as a plate glass frontage and capacious enough to contain the Gobi Desert and the glacier too. Old Nana slides the inner pane open to wipe the frost from the outer pane, and all of a sudden the glass is radiantly bright. The girl stretches out her hand but she soon recoils and blows warm air on her finger. "Don't touch it; it bites." Old Nana slips the girl's fingers into her mouth, and she feels a tingle like they have been daubed with thick chilli paste. The girl is worrying about how exactly to retrieve them, when they are expelled, feeling a little warmer. She kneels in front of the window and surveys the whole snowfield and valley through the large and glistering eyes of the glass.

The sky is blue and black; the snow-white breast of the earth balloons outward; the valley is precarious and deep, and the snow is shining. The girl clings to Old Nana's hand, and the old woman, like a real eagle, bends over with all her strength.

"Whatever it is that's alive in that river, they have seen you."

"They're moving."

"They will climb up on you."

"Will they eat me? I want them to eat me."

"They have eaten me more than once."

"How many lives do you have in all?"

"They ate my two sons and a husband, and I am so thin because their lives have been taken from me."

"How about him?"

"He's all right. He's the third son. He can make it to fifty like his father."

"You're his mother. Why don't you let him live for decades?"

"It's quite good for ice-breakers to live to fifty.

"Every winter he becomes a young man and so can act as a youngster dozens of times in his lifetime. Could there be such a wonderful man in the world?"

"It's so scary."

"Don't you think my son is great?"

"He is great."

The girl sounds like a mosquito; a flame jumps in her face.

The frost seals the glass and the glacier disappears.

"Close your eyes. You won't be able to bear to watch it for much longer."

The girl lies somewhat crumpled on her pillow.

"Every year I watch this through the window and each time I turn limp. Summer too becomes limp on that stone beach. That deadly river makes people drunk and restless."

"Let the glass shine a little longer."

Old Nana's eagle claws creak on the glass, and the glass lights up, shining on the girl's face, as if the light is streaming out of her eyes. The light is still flashing when she falls asleep.

Old Nana slips out quietly and heads to the stove outside. The flames in the stove jump violently. Old Nana is out of breath: "I prayed for peace for you. You must come back. Your woman came from Urümqi. You have to find a way to let her follow you all her life."

There is a whimper of wind outside. There has been no wind for days. Her body seems stiff and taller, since she has been listening for a long time. That is indeed the wind. The wind blows in from the Dzungar Basin, down from the mighty sky, into the mountains, and into the valley.

"The wind is able to carry my words away. Just one phrase is enough – 'keep safe'. I only ask you to take this."

The wind does transport her words to the mountains. It caterwauls and gusts hundreds of kilometres. In the heart of the Tianshan Mountains and at the source of the river, her son and five others are treading lightly along the channel with thick ropes around their waists and pickaxes in their hands. The river resembles a huge pane of glass and the layer of ice is transparent. Underneath the ice, the water flows in torrents, and the steep cliffs on both sides appear like strong men peppered in white snow. The ice-breakers brandish thick ropes in their hands as they stalk the river like a flock of hounds. Under the guidance of the hills, the hounds patrol the river.

When Old Nana sees the gleaming ice glass, she murmurs in a low voice: "Ice, ice, you are my son's longevity lamp. You must keep on shining. You must."

The ice glass shines constantly. She cannot perceive her son's face though.

The six men are clad in fur coats and leather hats, with a snow visor shielding each of their faces. They look like blue aliens, with pickaxes flashing as mysterious new weapons. The beasts are too frightened to move and so hide under the snow and breathe lightly.

Old Nana knows there are bears and wolves amid the snow.

The river channel is quiet. The wind does not gust into the mountains, but is able to funnel along the river. The valley, like the throat of the mountain, clears the waterway by inhaling and exhaling. Snow engulfs the valley, yet does not touch the river, piling up instead on the shore.

Those half dozen strong men tread onto the ice. Despite being thick and hard, the surface is, nevertheless, glass. The light on the pane freezes and the ice-breakers hasten to the shore, groping to find their way against the cliff. Where the light is absent, the ice begins to rattle. The ice-breakers cover their ears. The river bursts and roars out from underneath the ice as if a heavy breath is being exhaled. The broken ice, carried by the force of the flowing river, is crammed together in stacks, which soon become mountains.

The ice-breakers turn into real hounds, with a ferocious wheeze in their mouths, and dart towards the iceberg together. They strike frantically with their picks to tamp the bergs open before they can freeze shut again.

Old Nana extends her hands over her chest, her mouth shrivelled and her eyes sparkling with a mystical light.

"Damned ice, you can't stop my son. My son has magic powers; my son is an iron rod. They will crush you. Old man, old man, open your eyes and see. Our son has crushed the ice! Old man, keep your eyes open. You lie in the grave and your eyes keep on squinting from the sand, damned sand! Blow it clean, old man. Look carefully. Our son has raised the mountain."

The mighty man lifts a large block of ice and throws it as hard as he can. The ice lands in the hole and spews up a high column of water. The whole berg-like lump lands in the torrent. Some chinks of broken ice bump against the shore before falling back into the river. The cold soon seals up the river, so that the surface is patinated with frozen scars.

The ice-breakers clamber out between the rocks on the shore and resume their work.

One ice-breaker, who employs a pickaxe, sets to work on the scars and cleaves the ice glass flat and smooth like he is grinding jade.

Old Nana knows that this ice-breaker is her son. There is a woman in her son's heart. A man with a woman in his heart always does his job with panache.

Her son folds up his pickaxe and chases after those ahead with bounding feet. The blue light from the ice glass rises behind her son. When he manages to catch up with his companions, the blue light shifts forward again. The huge glass of the river is shining.

The Gobi Desert beyond the mountains also flashes with blue light, all the way to the old woman's house. The light wakes the girl up. She sits up in bed and rubs her eyes.

"What's the matter? Is it daybreak?"

"It is not daybreak yet – it is my son who is doing his work beautifully."

"How does he do that? It's not like the light from the stars. It's not like moonlight either. Does that light come from gems?"

"It's my son's light. You've come to see him. He's too away far from you. He's looking this way towards you."

"How wide his eyes must be!"

"He's standing on the river and looking at you, and his eyes are as big as the river."

"No one has ever looked at me like this except for the sun and the moon."

"It's a big river looking at you."

"I am so happy about it."

"You should be so happy all your life. Living with a man like that all your life, you will be happy every day. The sun will not shine on you every day, but he will shine on you every day."

"I want him to shine on me."

"But he will only shine on you for a moment."

"Yes, just for a moment." The girl stares at Old Nana in a state of infatuation. "I envy you."

"I've been married to this river for life. What woman can compare with me? It waters an oasis. It is so violent that it can run out of the mountains, over the great Gobi and pour out such an oasis – a one-thousand-*li* oasis that a quick horse can hardly escape from even after days of running. An oasis filled with crops and orchards. Have you ever seen such a rich woman? A marauding river waters a woman."

This is beyond the girl's imagination. It is a true story. Years ago, near the mouth of Yellow River, pretty girls were recruited from secondary school into the army and came to the foot of the Tianshan Mountains full flush with dreams. A large group of women soldiers spied the river at the edge of the reclamation area. With the roaring sound of the torrents, some strong men emerged one after another from under the stream, glistening in the sun. They were trying to bridle the River Kuitun. The men from the reclamation unit told the newly-arrived girls: "This is our death squad. Dozens of us have been killed already."

The bonniest female soldier asked: "How come there are no lady troops in the death squad?"

The people were astounded: "What use would the death squad have for women?"

The bonny soldier said: "Am I or am I not a soldier?"

Everyone laughed. This attractive soldier was destined to marry the army chief. She did not know that yet though.

Everybody made fun of her and said: "Anyone who wants to get on with the River Kuitun must marry it."

"Is the River Kuitun larger than the Yellow River?" She asked the arrogant men: "I come from the Yellow River. I don't believe that I cannot join the death squad."

The girl was serious and wouldn't leave. The army chief had to satisfy her curiosity. The chief took it as a woman's curiosity. That's what they all thought. The chief warned the head of the hydraulic regiment, and the head of the hydraulic regiment warned the captain of the death squad. The death squad captain was anxious to keep a close eye on that woman soldier, taking care of her at every turn.

She dared to enter the water. No matter how hot the weather was, the water in the River Kuitun was always ice cold. Women who entered the water risked becoming infertile.[v] The health officer reminded the captain and the captain's head hummed. He jumped into the river, grabbed the girl's hair and carried her to the shore. She slapped his face. No one would risk stopping her from getting into the river again.

The chief had to let the commissar make it clear: "You came here to become the chief's wife and you cannot let the chief be childless." The female soldier was shocked and angry, biting her lips so blood redder than her lips seeped out.

It was winter, so the soldier wrapped herself in a fur coat, tied a thick rope about her waist and scaled the valley into the mountains. The captain was close behind her. He was on a mission to protect her. They climbed all the way to the source of the river, and in the midst of the snow and ice, the death squad captain took the greatest risk of his life. The fierce girl welcomed his bold advance. All the time they were entangled, everything was lit up by flames of snow and ice. In that flame, the female soldier told the captain of the death squad that she knew what a young man was when he rose from the waves of the great river. He was a god of heaven, full of bright copper-like flesh.

She said: "You will always be a young man."

The captain had fought in the river for 30 years. At the age of 50, he was still a virgin. The 50-year-old boy was swallowed up by the glacier when he entered the mountain. He had been a boy for the river for thirty years, and kept his boyishly innocent body for thirty years in expectation of this beloved female soldier.

The chief called the death squad captain to headquarters and gave him a punch: "Damn you. How wonderful to be young. Keep young all your life." The death squad captain stood to attention and was wed in high spirits.

The veterans said this was all the will of heaven. The troops had been fighting all the way from northern Shaanxi to Xinjiang. In every hard battle, the chief always called on him to be the death squad captain. The dead squad members died one by one but the captain did not yield a hair. When the army faced the River Kuitun, the chief handed the violent river over to the death squad captain. The captain conquered the river and the woman too.

The captain remained in the hydraulic regiment, and the death squad became an ice-breaking unit. A couple of valued warriors died every year. The dead valley was lifeless, and then crops and orchards were irrigated by the river. What had been desert for thousands of years was turned into an oasis in the blink of an eye.

The locals were shocked by what they called the 'good fortune' brought by the bonny woman soldier. They regarded her as not just the wife of the captain, but the woman of the River Kuitun.

Their great ancestors had endeavoured to conquer the river and each attempt had ended in fiasco.

Centuries ago, a group of refugees from the Central Plains joined them. The most delightful refugee was selected as the daughter-in-law of the river. She was to perch on a sedan chair and be hauled up by several strong men to the source of the river deep in the Tianshan Mountains. The bride and the sedan chair flew hundreds of metres downstream and were swallowed to the bottom of the river. Those on the shore cried disconsolately and, when they had cried enough, they started a debate. They discussed and discussed. They reached a conclusion: the River Kuitun disliked their women. That's also what the herdsmen said. The herdsmen had sent a Kazakh girl and a Mongolian girl to the river. They were both elegant girls like swans. But the river refused them all. What a waste. People were expecting more beautiful girls. It was not until hundreds of years later that the bonny female soldier from the Yellow River leapt into the water, and the river opened its eyes. The ice on the river turned into bright glass, reflecting clearly the death squad captain and the ardent female soldier. The captain exclaimed: "The river eats people."

"Let it eat if it wants."

"There are Kazakh girls, Mongolian girls and Han girls."

"They were the prettiest of girls, and I'm better than them."

The captain was speechless.

"These legends are too old. There should be a new legend in which the man escorts the girl to the river source. The man is no longer a bodyguard and a labourer. He becomes the river himself."

With the lightest of touches, the female soldier broke the secret of the river.

Despite supposedly being rendered infertile, she gave birth to one strong boy after another, three in a row.

"I brought a good harvest to the earth." Old Nana pats her withered belly. "I had three sons and the river had even more."

"Our show is about this river."

"A movie?"

"Opera."

"An opera must be better than a movie. Look at your figure and your little face. My son must have taken a fancy to you while he was watching it."

"Yes, it happened when we were rehearsing. He came to visit his classmate, sat in a corner and then suddenly yelled out, which scared us. He said that our play was not good and began to make modifications, even though he had no professional training."

"He is the son of the death squad captain. He has guts."

"The original screenplay complained about how women were mutilated by the old customs. As he yelled out his instructions, the play became a great river teeming with life. Instead of belittling women, it brought out the pride in women's lives. Even the director and the scriptwriter recognised this."

"He grew up in this river. He knows it."

"He even changed my dance movements."

The ice-breakers taught her the authentic dance. The big river danced with the mountains and the world changed in that instant. They strode out of the theatre to the south gate, to the big crossroads, where snow was floating down like birds. Old Nana's son said: "This is the snowbird." Once again she was amazed. A snowbird had fallen into her small red hand.

She declared, her voice catching: "I have lived in Urümqi for twenty years and I never realised that the snow is a bird."

"Why should the snow not be a bird?

"Is there any bird that can fly for such a long distance?" From the tone of his voice, not even the eagle was a match for the snowbird.

Snow was indeed a kind of bird, an ethereal kind of bird. She must have one of these birds. He made a promise to her. She looked forward to it with great elation. Now, she has become a snowbird and, on that day, found a little life in her belly, a little life smaller than a bird.

Old Nana insists: "A woman should have a good harvest. A woman who has not had a good harvest is not a woman."

The girl holds her belly and maintains: "I'm not scared."

"At first you must be afraid, but it just lasts for a moment."

"I'm not afraid now."

At daybreak, the girl falls asleep. Old Nana tucks the quilt around her. The elderly woman wants to sleep but cannot. She mutters: "What's the matter with me?" She goes to sit alongside the stove. She spots apples on the table. The fruit is wilting. She eats them, reasoning that the girl should have only fresh ones.

The yard is packed with snow. She shovels snow from the vegetable cellar. Someone knocks at the door, which comes as a shock to her. Daybreak is just here and the sky is full of snowy light.

Suddenly, Old Nana is struck with a slightly laborious feeling as she goes to gently open the door. Outside the door, there stands an ice-breaker, and Old Nana pleads: "Please try to keep your voice down."

"Brave grandma," he says. "We all know that you are brave."

"Don't say any more, I know."

"Six of us. Only two came back."

And he begins to weep.

Old Nana kicks him: "You are still a man. Don't cry!"

"We're going to look for the body."

The man departs in tears.

Old Nana peers at the mountains on the other side of the wasteland and at the silent glacier. The eagle in her eyes has suddenly flown away and the bright light in her pupils is no longer to be seen. The eyes are now grey like those of a sparrow.

She heaves a long breath. She closes the door. Old Nana treads down to the cellar to pick out the best apples and misses one of the steps while climbing the ladder. Resting her elbows at the mouth of the cellar, she pants for some time before climbing back out.

The girl is still asleep when she comes in. She washes the fruit and sits beside the girl. She has no eagles in her eyes, only grey sparrows. The grey sparrow chirps up. She quickly closes her eyes, but cannot bring the chirping under control. At last, two tears with a fishy smell coat her face. She squeezes them in her hand, whispering: "Ugly. What ugly tears. How can you show yourselves without feeling ashamed?" There are no more tears in her eyes, which become empty and broad. She can look at the pretty girl with ease. No matter how wide she opens her eyes, no matter how desolate her eyes are, the girl is still a redoubtable beauty. She touches the girl, causing her to wake. She looks at the girl as she dresses and asks: "Does your mother know?"

"Mum knows."

"Does she know about the baby?"

"She doesn't. She just let me come here for a few days."

"Your mother is right."

"She never forces me."

"Don't force a woman if she loves someone. Everything is OK when the passion is over."

"I don't understand what you mean."

"Good girl, listen to me; you've seen this river. You are still young. I will take you to have the abortion and then you can rest for two days and go back to Urümqi."

"I want the child."

"How can you have an ice-breaker's baby?"

"Aren't you the wife of an ice-breaker?"

"That's a story from the past."

"Is the story not good enough?" The girl jumps up and says: "I'll finish the snowbird story for you as he told it to me. In his version, the snow princess did not become mud. She waited until she met her prince. They loved each other. Winter passed and the snow princess swore to stay. She gave herself to her prince. The pregnant princess turned into green grass, which was the feathers of the snowbird. The prince became a white horse, which galloped on the grass. This is the story of us. I'll have his baby. When I have his baby, the snow will have become the real snowbird."

"Being pregnant is very painful. When my two elder sons died, their wives had terminations, then went away and got married to someone else. So my third son banished the thought of finding a wife. His brain was not muddled by being in Kuitun. He lost his mind in Urümqi though."

"He didn't lose his mind. It is the snowbird he brought. There was always snow in Urümqi, but there was no snowbird in Urümqi. He brought the snowbird."

"The child will bring you misfortune."

"When an oyster gets just one grain of sand in its shell it is very uncomfortable. Still, it can transform it into a delightful pearl."

"How come you have such a strange idea?"

"My mother is from Suzhou. I heard the story from her when I was a kid."

"These damned stories."

"A woman without a story is not a real woman."

"He knows you're pregnant. He won't talk to you again."

"This is not possible."

"He likes the way you dance, and so do I. How can you dance with a big belly?"

The girl is befuddled. While the girl is befuddled, the old woman accompanies her to the snow-plough, which ferries her to the regimental hospital. It is minor surgery. The girl is an in-patient for two days.

On the third day, she waits at the intersection. The bus is more than an hour late. For more than an hour, the girl glimpses what will prove to be an unforgettable scene. The doors open and people head for the bank. No one is talking, only breathing, with a pious gaze, and looking at the mouth of the remote mountain. An earth-shaking rumble emanates from the mountain pass. Icebergs roar down through the river. The desert is immeasurable; the onslaught of snow and ice grows fiercer and fiercer, sparkling under the sun.

The men's faces gush with blood. Women like to murmur in their dreams:

Ice-breakers' horses
Ice-breakers' horses.

Little girls also twitter:

Ice-breakers' horses
Ice-breakers' horses
Snowflakes fall on the horse's mane
Snowflakes fall on the horse's mane.

The girl's mouth keeps on gaping as if she is dreaming. When she climbs onto the bus, her mouth is still misbehaving. The passengers think she is about to say something and so watch her for ages without seeing anything.

Hometown

'When the chicks must sleep, it's for their mam they'll peep'
West Guanzhong proverb

THE ROAD BACK to one's hometown is the road to visiting and seeking out one's mother. In the local dialect of Shaanxi, it is put like this: *When the chicks must sleep. It's for their mam they'll peep*. Hereabouts, people pronounce "ma" as "mam." That's the proper form of address. Irrespective of how senior an official you have become or how great your achievements in the outside world are, it designates you as being a kid, and a very small kid at that. You may even have risen to the rank of emperor, yet when you return to your hometown you are a kid, as the saying goes: *No loftier than a dick and no bigger than a bollock*. From afar, you can hear your mam calling through the deep valleys and roomy gullies of the loess plateau: "Sweet puppy come back! My sweet puppy, come back! Come back to eat bean porridge." Your tears roll down in great drops like the big beans in the porridge your mam is cooking in the pot.

The ancient Zhou Plateau encompasses the counties of Qishan, Fengxiang and Fufeng. Qishan is the cabbage heart and the walnut kernel of the region; Fengxiang and Fufeng just skirt its edge. Zhou Jian's home is located on the boundary between Qishan and Fufeng counties. Several times it has been transferred from the jurisdiction of Qishan to being administered by Fufeng and back and forth. No matter how the village is shunted about in official terms, locals maintain: "Squirm as the creature might, it's always rooted in your thighs." Rendered into more civilised parlance, it has never been cut asunder from the Zhou Plateau. There are two routes back to this particular hometown on the Zhou Plateau. Regardless of whether one is approaching from

Xi'an City or from the farthest west of the region to the north of Weinan City, a train must be taken to the Cai Family Slope and then a bus to mount the plateau to the county town. After that, the various villages and towns become accessible.

For a long time, Zhou Jian has felt that returning home is like passing through a tunnel, a phenomenon by which he echoes the exploits of the mythical hero Tuxing Sun.[w] He burrows into the earth at Xi'an and then resurfaces in the village. In so doing, he manages to bypass the village itself and appears immediately inside his family home before his mother. He even bypasses his father, his brother, his sister-in-law and other family members, as he is going back to his hometown simply to see his mam. His mother will shout: "My sweet puppy, my kid, my sweet puppy!" The mother and son then exchange greetings in long and short phrases, tears covering their faces. This is followed by a generous bowl of savoury noodles with seasoned pork.[x]

This feeling of passing through tunnels began after he graduated from university and found himself unable to find a job. Each time he came back, the villagers and his kin would repeatedly ask him where he was working. He would fabricate a company that did not actually exist, though his lies were soon seen through by others. The folks in his hometown were not strangers. They did not poke his deception into the open. Even so, they not only possessed x-ray vision, but ultrasound and could pierce like a CT scanner too. Ultrasound is capable of telling whether the embryo in a woman's body is a boy or a girl. How could these people not ascertain what Zhou Jian's true situation in the outside world was like? They had the ability to know something with their eyes but would not say it out loud. That really was a great affliction for those anxious for counsel. At moments such as this, his hometown could seem as remote as the mountains and rivers. Commencing from the courtyard of his home, the houses, the trees, the pigsties and the chicken coops, the fields and the gullies, the rivers and the sky, all disappeared. Passing to and fro between his hometown and a strange place guided entirely by feeling, his situation was precisely that of a cataract-sufferer who ambles along the textured track paved to assist the visually-impaired.

A man who does not lead a decent life in a foreign land has no hometown. Even if he comes back to his hometown he can only see his own mam.

Zhou Jian can still remember how in years past he always caught the last bus and entered the village when it was dark, like a swordsman in days of yore who shrouded his face with his hat or a mafia member in modern times who wears dark glasses. Anyhow, no one could recognise him. It was fortunate that his home was situated on the western end of the village. His method of turning off all his senses was akin to conducting an underground nuclear test. With the passing of time it became a force of habit. As soon as he stepped onto the road back home, all his sensory functions shut down automatically. They only resumed their operation when he saw his mother. He could not let his mother find her son wooden, a living corpse or an embalmed mummy. That would grieve her to death.

For some time, Zhou Jian went so far as to imagine himself as being a big parcel in the post, which could be delivered directly into the hands of his mam, never to be intercepted by others, not even his father or his elder brother. Only a mother understands the mind of her son. In the tranquil night beneath an oil lamp or a candle, his mother would open the package and her son Zhou Jian would awaken inside. As soon as he opened his eyes, his mam would be there in front of him. How a loser in a foreign land loves the dark night. How fortunate it is to be a man who travels in the evening, quietly entering and leaving the village like a secret agent.

For a long time, no matter how dire his life in the foreign land was, Zhou Jian never came back empty-handed. His mother told him countless times not to bring anything home, only himself. How could he return empty-handed? His mam shared out the worthless sweets and biscuits he brought back among the villagers. He could imagine her going from one household to another. Zhou Jian could also envisage that when his mother distributed them among his kinsmen she would constantly mention her son Zhou Jian. Of course, the villagers would praise his mother for having raised such a good son. The villagers knew the ancient etiquette. Zhou Jian had been to the South, to Guangzhou and Shenzhen as well, but these places were too remote. Even though he didn't have the feeling of being Tuxing Sun then, he was still unable to tolerate the Spring Festival transportation. He had to try his hardest to return to his hometown, to join the reunion banquet on New Year's Eve. Missing that meal would spell ill fortune for the whole of the coming year. It was a sacred rite. The only achievement of his short period as a migrant worker in the South had been that his hometown became a holy shrine within his heart. From then on, he never left Shaanxi Province, travelling to and fro between his hometown and Xi'an. He might do any kind of work in any part of Xi'an, but his hometown on the Zhou Plateau remained a fixed point.

On the way back to Xi'an from the South, his hometown itself turned into a holy shrine. After resting for a short while in Xi'an, he went to the bulk sales market at Kangfulu with a little money. He bought cheap sweets, biscuits, clothes, shoes and socks, and hurried back to the Zhou Plateau with a large package. The moment he got out of Xi'an, the whole world vanished. This time it was not like Tuxing Sun passing under the ground. The whole world vanished. There was not even the sound of the wheels of the vehicles. The houses in the village were all transformed into temples or shrines. Every one of the villagers metamorphosed into holy attendants. He didn't even use the old terms of "monk" and "Taoist". Of course, he didn't employ the foreign term "priest" either. He had witnessed the brilliance of the outside world, so such absurd and paradoxical images of holy attendants sprung up readily in his mind.

The guardians of one's hometown always pass comment on the sincerity of a wanderer from afar. His gifts, offered up to his parents, would be distributed all over the village. Each of the villagers' comments was deemed to be extremely important. There was no need to make mention of a loser like Zhou Jian. Even his uncle and those still more brilliant than his uncle were mocked and jeered at ad nauseum by the villagers. The gossip would gather pace, snowballing or generating a butterfly effect. Such is the price that must be paid by those who leave their hometown.

The road to one's hometown is a road of pilgrimage. Whenever somebody is mocked by the folks in their hometown, they come to think that their Tibetan counterparts must be more fortunate than themselves. The Buddha never mocked his disciples. The temple has never cared how much a pilgrim gives by way of donation. The hardship and piety of a single kowtowing step is considered worthy enough. Auntie Golden Flower laughed in an unprecedented fashion at the irrational injunctions of the guardians of the hometown. She called these "fearless demands with entrenched support". It is said that the Hebrew prophet Jeremiah warned the guardians of the Holy Temple in Jerusalem in this way. Uncle Zhou Zhijie and Auntie Golden Flower were sadly cheated by their kinsmen. No one took any notice of the warnings. Everybody knew that Golden Flower would compromise for the sake of her husband. From the day when Golden Flower married his uncle, the people of his hometown took her as a good woman. Still, the warnings of a good woman are impotent.

Countless times Zhou Jian has imagined the most wretched days of his Uncle Zhou Zhijie's life. When the uncle and nephew chat, the uncle makes repeated mention of his mam. This signifies the future life of his nephew. Zhou Jian was supported by his uncle through the four years of his university education. He vowed solemnly that he would repay him. His uncle just spoke casually: "Go home often and visit your mam." Years later, Zhou Jian realised that his hometown was in fact his mam.

Apart from the underground tunnel and the parcel in the post, Zhou Jian experienced the sensation of his soul returning to his hometown. Customarily speaking, this is the way that a dead man returns home. And yet, Zhou Jian had this feeling while still alive. Needless to say, this was in the most wretched period of his life. He didn't have decent clothes, even his fig leaf was gone. The more miserable one becomes, the more one misses one's hometown. At this point, his soul would migrate from his body and be transmitted to his mother like microwave radiation. His mother called him "sweet puppy" repeatedly and fed him bean porridge. Her spoon would rise and fall and rise and fall as she continued to ladle up the porridge. She believed this was not a dream. Her sweet puppy Zhou Jian was in front of her. Her son in the foreign land was eating the bean porridge in his dream. She asked him when he would come back. He answered honestly: "Your son will return home after he has acquired wealth and honour." His mother also intoned some honest words in the dream: "Whatever you may be wearing, you must come back. Even if you are naked, you must come back." Another interlocutor told the mother and the son: "This is wishful thinking." The mother and the son awoke from the dream. They both saw each other's surprised look. The dream disappeared like melting snow transformed into tears.

The most wretched time in the life of Uncle Zhou Zhijie was when he sang and sang *The Song of the Kushan Empire* and *My Mother*. Zhou Jian, then a high school student, secretly monitored his uncle in case he took matters too much to heart. For an entire month, his uncle roared out or hummed these two simple folksongs from the Western Regions as if he were chanting incantations. *The Song of the Kushan Empire* was easy to understand, but *My Mother* left people baffled. His uncle's mother was alongside him. It was hard to comprehend why a man should rant about his mother in their own hometown. Singing *My Mother* in a foreign land carried significance. Just like *Sawu'erdeng*, this was a folksong of the Oirat Mongols.[y] The song had accompanied the Mongols as they returned to the bosom of the Tianshan Mountain from the River Volga. *My Mother* goes:

> *Take the clean spring water,*
> *Wash my clothes;*
> *Washing my clothes,*
> *I bring to mind mama.*
> *Take the bitter spring water,*
> *Wash my hands;*
> *Washing my hands,*
> *I bring to mind mama.*

The very day when he went to sign up at the Fengqing Construction Materials Company Ltd in Weibei City, Zhou Jian dropped by at the Blue Sky Kindergarten to look for his beloved, Zhang Haiyan. Auntie Golden Flower would later claim that this action represented his evolution from a sparrow to a hawk. Golden Flower thinks that men from the interior of the country are about 3,000 years from becoming true men. This is the same distance that separates a sparrow from becoming a hawk. Zhou Jian had witnessed firsthand how Golden Flower had come to his uncle in the Zhou Plateau from distant Beijing and how she had weathered her despair. As a high school student, Zhou Jian then fully understood the position of Zhang Haiyan in his life. Further down the line, no matter how hard or how unfortunate his life turned out to be, in the depths of his heart he would never forsake Zhang Haiyan.

Many years later, when Zhou Jian appeared in the Blue Sky Kindergarten in Weibei City, it's easy to see why Zhang Haiyan acted extremely calmly and confidently as she was teaching the children how to sing and dance. Her eyes told Zhou Jian she had always known that one day it would happen. Next, they went out for a sightseeing stroll. They sauntered to the free market in Horse Road Lane and then to Huatong Shopping Mall. They ate steamed dumplings and porridge in the Sunshine Pavilion. By the time they parted, Zhou Jian had already become a man brimming over with confidence.

Zhou Jian goes to visit his parents over the weekend. The moment the bus starts up, he glimpses the sun amid the blue skies and white clouds, as well as the large streets and small lanes, high mansions and colourful crowds in the city districts along the banks of the River Wei. Next, he sees the dark green Qinling Mountains and the golden plateau. The hues flash in the pupils of his eyes. Just like a newborn baby, the first colour he can recognise is red. He remembers clearly how Zhang Haiyan's smile gradually blossomed and his eyes grew even brighter. The children around Zhang Haiyan lifted up various balloons, though he only noticed the red one. He stayed with the children for half an hour. He noticed red, blue, purple and flowery balloons. That day Zhang Haiyan was wearing a red dress resembling a ball of fire. It was the first spectacle to lighten Zhou Jian's eyes.

Zhou Jian raises his head and sees the sun. The sunshine starts to pervade his body. It seems as though as he is holding a flame in his hand. The world begins to awaken.

The bus mounts the northern plateau. His hometown is no longer a tunnel or a subterranean cave of darkness. His hometown, much like an oil painting, possesses crops, forests, villages, rivers, plains, deep valleys and roomy gullies. Each of these delectable features encircles his mother. His father, his elder brother, sister-in-law, nieces and all the villagers encircle his mother as well. The sky, the earth, the sun, the moon and the stars orbit his mother. This is a vigorous and flawless mother. The son in the mother's eyes also constitutes a world of overwhelming vigour. His mother has no time to appreciate the gifts her son has brought back. She takes her son by the hands and visits her neighbours one by one. She wants to show off her high-spirited and energetic son to the whole village. Today, Zhou Jian fully experiences what is called "being reborn in the fire" and takes on a new self. Zhou Jian witnesses his mother's heartfelt sense of joy and calm. A mother always worries about her son when he ventures outside. All these years his mother's heart has been suspended in the air. To come back to one's hometown and to one's mother's side with the love of a girlfriend is to return truly with wealth and honour. Thinking about this, Zhou Jian's heart is flooded with tremendous gratitude towards Zhang Haiyan.

Yesterday, Zhang Haiyan had taken him to Huatong Shopping Mall. They were busy there for the whole morning. Since he has been with Zhang Haiyan, the gifts he brings home are different. Intuitive as she is, his mother knows in her heart what has happened. No matter whether it is at a country fair or a palatial city mall, women are born shoppers par excellence. Men know nothing about it. Unmarried men know less still.

This time Zhang Haiyan has prepared two great gifts. It goes without saying that his mother knows the other present is destined for another family. Her son tells her the family lives a dozen miles away beyond the two adjacent villages. He says his colleague's elder brother is getting married. His mother then realises that this colleague must be important to her son. So many people from that particular village have achieved considerable things in the outside world. There are county heads, bureau directors, departmental deans and vice-mayors. Within the county, it is the village most famed for spawning officials. Her son could have gone directly to the village to attend the wedding banquet, but he chooses to visit his mother first. This is the arrangement made by a diligent girl.

A fortnight earlier, when her son brought the girl named Zhang Haiyan back to the village, her presence caused all the villagers to treat them with heightened respect. In Uncle Zhou Zhijie's life, two women had appeared, Tian Xiaolei and Golden Flower. One was more vivacious and capable than the other. This time, Zhou Jian brought back with him the doll-like Zhang Haiyan. People said that the uncle and nephew of the Zhou family enjoyed good fortune when it came to women. The girl named Zhang Haiyan was not at all like ladies from the big cities. She voluntarily did household chores and was keen to learn how to cook savoury noodles with seasoned pork. She acquired the skill swiftly and mastered it easily. The aunties and sisters-in-law all thought that this unwed girl had appeared with the purpose of flattering her would-be mother-in-law. The mother was clear in her heart that this city girl was not as straightforward as she seemed. Regardless of whether the business in hand was complicated or simple, she busied herself for the sake of her son Zhou Jian. The mother was clear about this. Hence, her fondness for the city girl grew.

Zhou Jian borrows a neighbour's motorcycle and arrives at the village where the wedding is being held within half an hour. Before he left, his mother urged him: "Watch your tongue when staying with new acquaintances. In the countryside, people divide kinsmen into those who are long-established and those who are newly-made. When a guy goes to his maternal uncle's home, he can behave freely. In other households, you should mind your manners. A slight slip-up can be laughed at by others. 'Colleague' is a new term in the countryside. This is a novel type of relationship. One more friend, one more road. One more friendship, one more new word." The mother from the countryside and the girlfriend from the city cooperate perfectly in tacit agreement. Nobody dares tell the mother about the ticking time-bomb that is Zhou Jian's cement mixer.

Zhou Jian is greeted at the entrance to the village by his colleague Liu Jun. Zhou Jian has brought with him not only a red envelope containing money, but a gift as well. The two become entangled for a while as if they want to wrestle. Zhou Jian says repeatedly that his mother has prepared all of these items for him. They are for Liu Jun's mother and grandma, given to show respect towards his elders. Liu Jun stops and pushes the gifts back. In the city, men take their wives as their mothers; only in the countryside do men take their mothers as their mam. Liu Jun leads Zhou Jian to see his mother and grandmother first of all. Liu Jun's grandmother is in her nineties, yet still has good mobility. Liu Jun's mother is in her seventies, yet half-paralysed. She has suffered much. Zhang Haiyan's large pack of gifts is divided into three smaller bundles. There are nutritious foodstuffs for the elderly and various confectionaries, biscuits and toys for the children. The small kids share the food and toys with their great-grandma. People become child-like again when they are old. The nonagenarian granny is as over the moon as the kids. She chews and swallows in high spirits, genuinely feeling rejuvenated.

Liu Jun's half-paralysed mother is the backbone of the family. While driving away the small children, she asks the old granny to eat slowly and tells her that nobody is fighting with her for the food. Liu Jun's mother is elated: "Your grandma is happy today. She is more chuffed than her grandson who is getting married." Liu Jun's mother asks Zhou Jian from which village he hails. After a brief chat they establish that she and Zhou Jian's mother attended the same cotton-planting course organised dozens of years ago by the commune. "We learned how to use pesticide and spray 1059 and DDT over the buds. I wore a pink Terylene blouse and your mother wore a bean-green one. Your mother's pale complexion suited the bean-green colour, but I was as black as a pig." All the people in the room laugh. This is the bred-in-the-bone humour of Zhou Plateau folk. They often make fun of themselves, while actually being very contented.

Liu Jun has seldom seen his mother so happy. He pounds Zhou Jian repeatedly on the back with his fist. This is the way fraternity works in the countryside. Liu Jun's mother accepts Zhou Jian as a member of her own family. Assuming the tone of one of his elders, she declares: "You two should be blood brothers. On the plateau, you are brothers. When you go down from the plateau into a strange place you stay as brothers." Liu Jun and Zhou Jian hug like foreigners in a movie and pat each other on the back. Liu Jun's mother again urges them: "You two should help and support each other." The duo bow like small children to the old woman, letting out a rash "yes", and then leave smiling.

The proceedings go off exactly as Zhang Haiyan had expected. The banquet is boisterous. Everybody exchanges greetings. Several countrymen and colleagues present their gifts and sit down at the table. Before the ceremony begins, everybody drinks tea, munches sunflower seeds and watermelon seeds and chats freely. Zhou Jian finds time to send text messages to Zhang Haiyan to the tune of: "Liu Jun's ma knows my ma. His ma treats me as her own. Keeps on urging 2 b blood brothers. Help and support." Predictably, this surprise makes Zhang Haiyan happy. The first sentence of her answer goes: "Wah, U R wonderful … U R 2 talented … the mixer'll turn in2 a hot stove." The day when they received the invitation card, Zhang Haiyan told Zhou Yan: "The dangers of operating the cement mixer will soon be behind you. The mixer will turn into a hot stove." Liu Jun is in charge of operating the No. 5 cement mixer. By "becoming a brother" of Liu Jun he means becoming cement-mixing brothers. In the second message, Zhang Haiyan warns him: "Drink less, eat more veg, less meat, more noodles." Zhou Jian's mother's outlook is old hat. Zhang Haiyan is far more flexible.

In the countryside of the Zhou Plateau, the host treats the wedding guests twice a day. In the morning, noodles are served and, in the afternoon, comes the liquor banquet. Zhou Jian allows his belly to loosen and devours twenty bowls of savoury noodles. The savoury noodles have the capacity to transform newly-made friends into old chums and old chums into blood brothers. When Zhou Jian eats the noodles one bowl after another, the people around them realise that his work relationship with Liu Jun is exceptional. Liu Jun is delighted too. He persuades Zhou Jian to consume two extra bowls. Zhou Jian does not decline the invitation. He stands up and loosens his belt. This is the greatest sign of praise one can communicate to the chef. Everyone laughs and believes that Zhou Jian is a pragmatic fellow. Zhou Jian becomes more civilised when it is time for the liquor banquet in the afternoon. He prevails upon the others to drink more and to eat more sophisticated dishes. He sticks only to the cheaper vegetables laid out before him. The people around see this and feel that Zhou Jian is not greedy, but rather understands etiquette.

Before returning to work, Zhou Jian sojourns for a while at home. He wants his mother to share in his success. With the air of a leading actor, he relates how Liu Jun's mother recalled the situation when they were together on the cotton-planting course. His mother listens gleefully whilst patting Zhou Jian on the back of the head. She says: "My boy is a fine boy. My boy is handsome. My boy is smart. The day after tomorrow I shall visit the Liu family village and seek her out. I remember that there was a woman like her who was black and scrawny like a pig. It should be easy to find her. Her boy is named Liu Jun. if I shout 'Jun Jun's mam!' she is sure to bounce out like a flea." While they are talking, a text message from Zhang Haiyan arrives: "Don't be in hurry to meet Liu Jun's ma. Go before end of year." Zhou Jian adapts Zhang Haiyan's words into his own. Nevertheless, his mother can read his mind. Her face grows sullen: "My boy has good fortune, a good life, and he has now become a city-dweller. People in the city take their wives as their mam. Zhang Haiyan hasn't married him yet; she hasn't even become engaged to my boy. Already she has turned herself into my boy's young mother. My boy is flashy with his humility; he flashes even faster than lightning and makes the eyes of heaven blurry." Mothers in the countryside always employ this method to prick at the hearts of their sons who have married a city wife. Each sentence jabs at her son causing him to be breathless and to suck his teeth bloody.

Zhou Jian escapes in a hurry. On his way, he pants and unbuttons his shirt. Half of his chest is exposed. Passengers on the bus take him for a hooligan and shy away from him. When he meets Zhang Haiyan, the anger is still hovering in his face. Zhang Haiyan knows what is wrong with him as if she is a roundworm in his stomach. She offers him a cup of water.

After he has finished the water, she puts Zhou Jian at his ease with a single sentence: "Liu Jun is a migrant worker. You graduated from university and are a technician. When the two mothers meet each other and chat about their sons, Liu Jun's mother is sure to be no match for your mother."

Zhou Jian tries his best to retaliate: "My mother is not so shallow as that."

"That is not being shallow. A mother who has a son like you is sure to be proud. Whatever praise your mother may heap upon you is insufficient. Even if she doesn't speak, her expression will convey to all in the world how excellent her son is."

Zhou Jian can speak no more.

Zhang Haiyan smiles and paws his nose: "I cannot supplant your mother's goodness towards you. I know this myself. Don't be nervous. Be at ease. Keep your heart in your belly."

Liu Jun starts to speak about his mother with Zhou Jian. Only people with an exceptionally close relationship indulge in this kind of heart-to-heart exchange. It is both solemn and holy just like foreigners sharing each others' perspectives on religion. Chinese men talk about beliefs and women casually, even when they are discussing their wife or their mistress. However, when they talk about their mother, even a blackguard becomes serious. Liu Jun does not want to settle down in Weibei City. His ideal solution is to buy a two-bedroom apartment in the county town on the Zhou Plateau. He can take his mother to the county seat and thereby have a place to stay in the village and in the town.

His older brothers work as government employees in Xi'an and Weibei City. They are not ordinary members of staff, but each of them has accrued some renown. Liu Jun does not speak in detail about how renowned his two older brothers are. As a lowly migrant worker who only matriculated from junior high school, his decent job at the city company was secured for him by his brothers. Mothers in the countryside like to live in the old village home. No matter what their children have achieved and how big a house they have obtained, they simply come over to visit as though it were a rare occasion such as a country fair. Staying for ten days or a fortnight, they become uneasy and want to go back to the old village home. The situation of Liu Jun's newly-married third brother was better than his own. Following graduation, his eldest brother and second brother had grown into lofty trees in Xi'an and Weibei cities. After matriculating from high school, his third brother had sat the college entrance examination in five successive years, faring worse each time than on the previous occasion. He only attended a self-funded college programme with a great deal of assistance from his eldest brother. His third brother was not stupid by nature. To begin with, he worked for a few years in Weibei City and then marched to Xi'an. Receiving help from the eldest and second eldest brothers, he was even able to buy an apartment in Xi'an.

Some kind-hearted people gave Liu Jun the following advice on how to cultivate himself: "Pursue a totally different track to your three brothers. You should try to find your feet in your hometown. Your hometown is your great camp." Their guidance straightened out Liu Jun's horizons for him. He even said goodbye to his then girlfriend. He turned the page on her with the phrase: "People whose courses are not the same can't make plans for one another." His present girlfriend shares the same course with him. "My girlfriend's situation may be considered nothing in the cities of Xi'an and Weibei, but is really something to be admired in my hometown. The key problem is that a woman should have brains. If she has the brains of a pig that will antagonise you to death." Liu Jun is more than satisfied with his current girlfriend. The important thing is that the two of them can communicate with one another. She fully understands Liu Jun's strategy and can take it on board herself. Liu Jun is earning money in Weibei City. She manages a shop for a relative in a small county town on the Zhou Plateau. They have found a suitable apartment that can be secured with 30,000 or 40,000 yuan. At that stage, they will take his mother to the county seat.

All of the county towns in China are basically large rustic settlements. From the County Head to the Township Head, they all speak in the local dialect. Local expressions float about their streets. The teachers in the county high schools have a marked preference for speaking Standard Chinese. The farmers either listen to the highly-refined Standard Chinese of national television hosts or to the local tongue. They call the half-learned Standard Chinese "vinegar-fried Mandarin". A more favourable advantage to living in the county town is the local cuisine. Savoury noodles with seasoned pork, chilli-filled flatbreads, cold wheat-flour noodles, fermented rice wine, melons, fruits and vegetables are all locally-produced. No matter how wide or how thick the streets in the county town are, they still supply a sort of humid, soft and easy down-to-earth feel.

His girlfriend is even cleverer than the kind-hearted people in his home village. Liu Jun's eldest brother and second brother both married women who were the only child in their family. His third brother's wife grew up in Xi'an City. She is slim, white and beautiful. Young people regard her as if she is a film star, although older people look upon her adversely. They all say that he has wed a "bean shoot of a girl". That bean shoot is not even of the thickest, whitest variety, being instead a wheat-straw-like green bean – charming to gaze at yet utterly impractical.

Liu Jun's girlfriend has revealed her great assets. Her buttocks and breasts are the proof of the pudding. Since her Household Registration Card[2] rendered her a country resident she is entitled to give birth to two children. Liu Jun's girlfriend has started to assume her role in advance. She has begun to imagine their future life thus: "As long as we can give birth to a baby boy, we will be the Living Buddha of the Liu family and the only hair upon the Liu family scalp."

Liu Jun tells her: "If you want to be my wife you should be obedient to my mother."

She promises without hesitation.

Liu Jun's second condition is that they should settle in the county town.

She butts in and exclaims: "You wouldn't be making your home in the county town if it wasn't for your mother."

The girl then further points out: "If we grasp our mother in our hands it is like tugging at the balls of the three brothers."

The couple is obviously pissing into the same pot. Liu Jun starts to smoke. He wants to listen to Zhou Jian talk about his twelfth "Five-Year Plan".[aa] Zhou Jian's idea is far simpler. Buy a house and settle down in Weibei City then bring his parents to live in the city.

"Will your eldest and second brothers agree?"

"From high school through university I was supported by my third uncle. My third uncle and auntie's words carry more weight than my father's."

"Your key problem is Zhang Haiyan. She is a native of our home county. It would be hard for you to overcome the barrier of her father and mother."

Zhou Jian and Zhang Haiyan have been seeing each other for several months. Zhang Haiyan has been to Zhou Jian's family home, but he has never been to hers. Everybody knows this. Liu Jun sucks in deeply and then lets the smoke billow outwards: "Brother, listen to me. You have it made with Zhang Haiyan and can have the rice cooked. Her mother and father are powerless in that situation."

Zhou Jian's head shakes like the drum-shaped rattle used by a peddler: "No, no, no, I cannot do that."

"You are an honest man, a benevolent soul. You are a university graduate. Reading more books has made you soft and delicate."

The two just smoke in silence for a few of minutes.

Liu Jun then says: "City girls are more complicated. There is no use resorting to force. They are not like the girls in the countryside.

If you have got it on with them they will follow you down the line without a thought."

Liu Jun gives Zhou Jian a pat on the leg and adds: "The learned and the unlearned are different."

Liu Jun really does take Zhou Jian as his brother. He even tells him what is in his heart: "Even though I've only been with my girlfriend for two months, I've already got it on with her. She was so sad that she cried. I told her, 'I was with my first girlfriend for two years, but we never did that. I did this with you so soon because I sincerely want to live with you.' She then stopped crying and asked me if I were genuine. I said nothing and pressed her down on the bed and we did it again. This time she believed me. A man cannot simply make things up with his mouth."

Liu Jun beats around the bush and then comes back to the point: "Listen to your older brother. Find the chance and make out with Zhang Haiyan. Such an attractive woman and you will only know the flavour of life after you have got it on with her."

While they are talking, Zhang Haiyan comes over. Liu Jun draws two deep drags from his cigarette and puffs out the smoke slowly so it masks his face. Zhang Haiyan gazes at the two men with a smile. Her gaze unsettles the pair. They toss away the stubs of their cigarettes and rub their hands like a child who is clueless about what to do. Zhang Haiyan bends down and cranes towards their faces: "It's great to see you two guys putting your heads together like brothers."

Liu Jun insists: "You two enjoy yourselves." He then departs.

Zhang Haiyan continues to rib Zhou Jian: "What were you talking about? You two are so mysterious and tight."

"Nothing secret. Just casual chatter."

"Won't you let me share in this?"

"Just village matters. Honestly, even if I told you, you wouldn't understand."

"I don't understand village matters, but I know that you shouldn't put on airs like a university student in front of a migrant worker. Liu Jun received only a little education, but he has much more life experience than you have. He's sure to talk to you with a true heart. You must take it seriously."

"I have to digest this slowly."

"What type of porridge must Liu Jun have offered for a university graduate to be given an upset stomach?"

Zhou Jian's expression has already become queer. Zhang Haiyan draws a cold breath: "You two rogues are sure to have been up to no good. Your hearts are surely possessed by a demon."

Zhou Jian will not tell her about the demon.

Zhang Haiyan's anger modulates into happiness: "Men's relationships are out of the ordinary when they are conspiring over something. This is the effect we need. I shall forgive you. Don't be nervous. Relax, just relax. You have started to put down roots at work. Now you have a brother and a network. Your uncle and auntie are talking about the warmth under a quilt in a special tone. Everybody knows how warm and cosy it is. I don't want others to allow you to endure the coldness outside the bed."

While Zhang Haiyan is nagging like a clucking hen, Zhou Jian is all ears, placing his arm around her shoulders. After her nagging ends he holds her in his arms as if his chest were a bird's nest. The bird may come to the nest and then fly away. After parting, Zhou Jian stands there until Zhang Haiyan has disappeared. When she has almost disappeared, she turns around, waves her hands and smiles. Zhou Jian's train of sight has tracked closely that bright smile.

For rather a long time, whenever they embrace and kiss Zhou Jian recalls that wonderful fantasy he had imagined before. Now the fantasy has become a reality, he is truly experiencing it for himself.

For rather a long time, Zhou Jian has been a spectator at the dance. As a high school student, he witnessed first-hand how, in the deep valleys of the Weibei Plateau, Auntie Golden Flower had relit his uncle's hope in life. More than once, Zhou Jian enjoyed what he thought of as the dance spectacle being staged in his uncle's family home. Zhou Jian and his friends and the kinsmen of the family construed this as a habit developed in Xinjiang. They even thought that Golden Flower did this consciously in order to foment a harmonious relationship between herself and her stepdaughter Zhou Jingjing. The whole family grew so close in the dance and was held together in tacit agreement. Even the village elders believed that Golden Flower was far more maternal towards her than the girl's biological mother. Zhou Jingjing always hugged and embraced her stepmother and would lean into her arms, placing her own face against hers. She did not even feel self-conscious about doing this when her actual mother Tian Xiaolei was present. Some even felt that the Mongolian woman must have been a witch in her previous life. Had she not been a graduate of Beijing Normal University, people would have taken her to be a witch. Auntie Golden Flower then proudly declared that she was the sultana and the cardinal of the grassland. *Ha ha ha ha!* This beautiful woman of the grassland, she bent herself double with laughter.

Soon after Zhou Jian had begun his relationship with Zhang Haiyan, her roommate Fang Jing told him: "Because of you, Haiyan refuses to dance in an adult way. She dances like a kid all day, so much so that she has nearly been turned into a giant white bunny." Fang Jing brought this out into the open and urged him to dance with Zhang Haiyan.

He told Fang Jing: "I really don't know how to dance."

"Are you going to tell me that you never went to university? What era are we living in? Universities always arrange weekend dance parties."

"There are students who never attend this kind of party." Zhou Jian spoke these words with a grin.

In the staff dormitory of the Blue Sky Kindergarten in Weibei City, his bright smile outshone the summer sunshine of the loess plateau which was peeping in through the window. Fang Jing, Zhang Haiyan's close friend and roommate, had for the first time seen something cold and forlorn behind the vivid sunshine and that smile. Several close-up shots of that time in university flashed through Fang Jing's mind – in the university canteen there was free vegetable soup and some students habitually arrived earlier to buy a bowl of rice or two steamed buns; they would finish one round of soup before everyone else came along. Then they would take a second bowl with ease. The free vegetable soup seemed to be their non-staple food. On weekends, when all the dance parties or gatherings were assembling, there were students who left the school in a hurry and went outside to do odd jobs. On red letter days, those students would be as tired as migrant labourers. They would come back to school with unsteady steps and a feeling of exhaustion. The smiling guy in front of her now would have pulled off countless turns of this kind on the university campus. The situation continued like this for three years after his graduation. That was until he returned to Zhang Haiyan's side at Weibei City a few months ago.

The smiling guy peacefully told Fang Jing: "At that time, my heart was reserved for Zhang Haiyan and I didn't pay any attention to other female students."

Fang Jing told him: "If you could dance it would make Zhang Haiyan very happy. You see those dancing couples and ice-skating partners all go on to marry."

Zhang Haiyan had never forced Zhou Jian to dance. That was until last weekend when they were in his uncle's home. Their former auntie, Tian Xiaolei, had come over to visit her daughter Zhou Jingjing. Their uncle, Auntie Golden Flower and their two children together with Zhang Haiyan danced *Sawu'erdeng*. Zhou Jian was unable to sit there as a wallflower anymore. He clumsily joined in. All of a sudden he was entranced by the dance as though thunder and lightning were coursing through his body.

Auntie Golden Flower coached him, saying: "Silly lad, you should put on a good turn; then Haiyan will have the confidence to dance *Sawu'erdeng*."

She pushed him over in the direction of Zhang Haiyan, who was overcome with tears of excitement, repeatedly sobbing: "I am OK, I am OK, just too high."

On the road, Zhang Haiyan told Zhou Jian: "You are very fortunate. You did pretty well considering that was your first time. The dances I've performed before have been purely for show. *Sawu'erdeng* gave me a fond feeling. Do you know how hard I've tried to advance beyond those shallow and formulaic dances?"

"Is *Sawu'erdeng* really so miraculous?"

"The twelve forms of the *Sawu'erdeng* dance imitate the gestures of the heroic hawk, the steed, the bull, the ram, the camel and the rabbit. They evoke the lives of every species of flying bird, running animal, flower, grass, fish and insect found in this world. The portal of your life has been opened. You become connected with the sky and the earth and everything on the earth. Man and man, man and all the things of the world are fused together as one. This is the most emotional connection. It is delicate, gentle, passionate, unrestrained and majestic. This is the most splendid moment. Auntie Golden Flower has been a part of your family for so many years and yet you have only come to learn about these matters like a wooden ninny."

"I've been waiting for you."

"Correct answer. I shall give you a small red flower as a bonus."

A kiss fell down onto Zhou Jian's forehead as swiftly as a fish leaping onto the bank and then back into the water again. Zhang Haiyan scuttled away like a fish. She didn't forget to exhibit her classic smile before disappearing into the crowd.

家

When Golden Flower got married her parents, her sisters-in-law and her younger brother journeyed to Shaanxi Province to attend the wedding. Her parents mistook Zhou Zhijie's parents for his grandparents. Golden Flower and her folks lived together on the grassland. Later Golden Flower's elder brother, who was working in Hejing County, transferred her to the county high school. Her parents, still living on the grassland, were weather-beaten but, compared with their counterparts in the Shaanxi countryside, they looked like people from two different generations. Upon bidding farewell, Golden Flower's parents told Zhou's parents that they would be sure to make a return visit a few years hence. Her parents-in-law took this as a mark of courtesy. Only Golden Flower understood the weight of those words in her heart.

Their hometown on the Zhou Plateau lay more than 70 kilometres from Weibei City, which was situated in the foothills to the southwest. In the eyes of the people of the Zhou Plateau it was a foreign and distant land, but in the eyes of people from Xinjiang the two seemed close at hand, lying just beneath one's eyelids. No one should mention that they were 70 kilometres apart. Even if there were hundreds of kilometres between them, they would still seem close at hand. On weekends, Auntie Golden Flower asked her students to house-sit. She followed Zhou Zhijie back to his hometown on the Zhou Plateau. They installed a bathroom inside the house. Uncle Zhou Zhijie attended to his aged father. Auntie Golden Flower attended to his aged mother. They returned to Weibei City in the afternoon. Sunday belonged to their children. During the summer and winter vacations, they transferred their elderly parents to live in Weibei City.

The other two sisters-in-law were regarded as kindly wives in the village, though they never showed their filial devotion in this way. Her sisters-in-law matriculated from high school. Nowadays illiterate folk are scarce in the countryside.

Her sisters-in-law asked Golden Flower: "Even your parents in the grassland aren't able to take a bath every week?"

Golden Flower answered: "When you scrub our mother-in-law's back you have the sensation of feeling her skin has texture. You Han people don't dance. People from the grasslands will die if they don't dance. I'd been wracking my brains for a long time before I hit upon this idea. It is sanitary, healthy and you can also get closer to people's hearts there."

The sisters-in-law thought that Golden Flower would try to encourage them to bathe their mother-in-law too. They had already prepared the words with which to refute this request. However, Golden Flower said that she was inclined to mind her own business and did not interfere in other's affairs. The two sisters-in-laws swallowed their spittle. The countryside in the Guanzhong Plain is now, to some extent, open to the outside world. Several years ago karaoke venues and amusement arcades started to appear in the town. All of the big girls and young wives now know how to dance and sing songs. This kind of singing and dancing is virtually a prelude to the advent of decadence. During the temple fair, erotic model shows were put on by amateur troupes. This really took Golden Flower by surprise: "My God, how could such singing and dancing be allowed in this world?"

The two sisters-in-law once triggered a fight through their dancing. Golden Flower did not know about this tender spot of theirs yet she found herself unconsciously poking at it. This didn't arouse any trouble because they had been getting on rather well under normal circumstances.

The spirits and appearance of the aged couple began to improve. The two elder brothers could wait no longer. They started to take turns to bathe their elderly father. Zhou Zhijie then seized the opportunity to go and visit the homes of those brothers. The two sisters-in-law had been holding out on that duty for quite some time. To bathe their mother-in-law should be the business of a daughter, unless the mother-in-law is paralysed or seriously ill. The sister-in-law ought then to wash the clothes and deal with the contents of the bedpan. This behaviour would go on to be recorded in the local annals and greatly praised on the radio station. Their parents-in-law were in outstanding health, so there was no need for this.

Auntie Golden Flower had been looked down upon by the wives of the village for a considerable length of time. Solidarity between women is not long-lived. It has to be shored up through various favours. When some small friction flared up between the two sisters-in-law they were incapable of holding out anymore. They began to alternate the task of bathing their mother-in-law. They did a risible job and with reluctance. The mother-in-law was an honest woman. She was rather satisfied with this, yet found it impossible for her to compare the two sisters-in-law in the countryside with Golden Flower. She still spread positive words about the sisters-in-law in the village. Half a year later, the two daughters obviously felt that they were being isolated from their mother. Their mother no longer needed the small padded cotton coat they offered.

When a married daughter returns to her mother's home she always plays the role of a strategist like Su Qin and Zhang Yi of the State of Qin.[ab] Even her husband will become annoyed at her for having gone back to her maiden home to fan up trouble in the manner of a treacherous Court official. Parents always subconsciously assume the role of a small feudal emperor, even if they are a puppet one. The earth nourishes everything, the sense of being an emperor included. Treacherous officials and petty men are the predictable entourage of the emperor. Auntie Golden Flower unwittingly transformed the dragon throne[ac] under the buttocks of those seniors into a sofa and a carpet.

The two daughters could not come back to their mother's home where they were apt to stir up trouble. All they could do was sit to one side on a small bench. They returned home less and less frequently, and peace descended upon their husbands' households. Upon marrying and having a baby, a woman is just like water that flows across the surface of the earth. From being a young wife to being an old wife and then a respectable old wife after that, it takes at least eight or ten years, sometimes even twenty or thirty. Certain women do not even achieve the status of being a family member until they are decrepit. Throughout their lives, their bodies reside in their husband's home, though their hearts remain in their maiden home. As soon as Auntie Golden Flower entered the household, she started to act with the demeanour of a family member and this was hard for the villagers to understand, harder still for the people of Weibei City.

As folks grow older, they begin to cough and spit. It is as if they are patients being treated for hepatitis B. People prepare special bowls and chopsticks for them. Even their cooking wok is kept separate from that of the other family members. When Auntie Golden Flower quit Xinjiang to go to university, she found that the senior citizens in the countryside and the city were all senile and had runny noses and teary eyes. This formed a striking contrast with older people in the desert of the Western Regions. The seniors of various ethnic groups in those parts remain healthy and clean like the diversiform-leaved poplar. Even at the last moment as death looms, they still keep the dignity and composure of the living after the fashion of a work of art.

Golden Flower commenced by sorting out the sanitary habits of her parents-in-law. Gradually she reformed their eating habits. They ate at the same table and the food was cooked in the same wok. In winter, they ate mutton and in summer beef, cutting down on their intake of pork. All year round, they drank tea brewed with dates and sweetened with sugar just as Hui Muslims do. Auntie Golden Flower also introduced Islamic cuisine into the household. She always frequented the Hui market street where she would purchase sheep's eyes. What was more, she imported the living habits of the Western Regions, adding fruit and a variety of dried fruits and other nutritious products to their daily routine. Two or three years thereafter, her parents-in-law had nearly been converted into Xinjiang natives. They looked healthy and vital with ruddy skin and glistening eyes. Their bearing was uncommon. No matter whether they were in Weibei City or in the village on the Zhou Plateau, people took them to be retired senior cadres. Auntie Golden Flower appeared to have accomplished a great project. She wired a telegram to her own parents in the depths of the Tianshan Mountains: "*Abu* (Dad), *Erji* (Mum) come to Shaanxi to see your daughter." This time when Auntie Golden Flower's parents stood together with her parents-in-law the couples were virtually indistinguishable in age.

Golden Flower's parents told the in-laws: "This is a fine turn up for the books. Had it been any other way we would not have had the face to meet you. We would have had no face to return to the Tianshan Mountains."

When the in-laws praised their sister-in-law, Auntie Golden Flower's parents said glibly: "This is her duty. If she were not able to do it well, would she be qualified to live in this world?"

This was how Golden Flower's parents ventured inland for the second time. Three years earlier when they had first gone there, they were rather surprised. People, whether they were old or young, men or women, all appeared to have pale or sallow visages. Their eyes were blurred and every one of them seemed poorly. Drawing closer to their in-laws this impression deepened into shock. That was why they had left those words of promise to their daughter. The daughter was indeed a good daughter. She did not bring shame to her parents. Upon leaving Shaanxi, the parents told her: "We folk of the grassland have only tents and herds. We don't admire gold, silver and pearls, nor do we like spacious houses. We only admire healthy seniors and dutiful kids. Our hearts are put at ease because we know you have a pleasant family."

The parents left and never again returned to Shaanxi to see their daughter. Their hearts were truly at rest; so simple.

During vacation time, Zhou Jian, who was by then a university student, again heard Auntie Golden Flower singing songs to the accompaniment of his Uncle Zhou Zhijie's Xinjiang Mongolian guitar. After singing *The Song of the Kushan Empire*, Auntie Golden Flower started to intone another number, *My Mother*. Zhou Jian, the undergraduate, sensed that Auntie Golden Flower must miss her beloved relatives. It was natural for her to miss her beloved ones because she had been married out of Xinjiang and into Shaanxi.

Three years ago, when his uncle returned to their hometown, he became a stranger. It was Auntie Golden Flower, by means of *The Song of the Kushan Empire* and *My Mother*, who had helped him to find where his permanent home should be. Now when Auntie Golden Flower sings *My Mother* there is no more bleakness and sadness. This is extirpated by the joy and gratitude.

The mother in the song has relocated from the Tianshan Mountains to Shaanxi. Her mother-in-law has become her own biological mother, this being the authentic habit of the people on the grassland.

Zhou Jian was due to graduate from university the following year. He had no intention of returning to his hometown. He planned to temper himself in the outside world. His future might be harder still. He was more willing to imbibe the blood-boiling *Song of the Kushan Empire*. He found *My Mother* inscrutable. In a foreign land he may miss his mother. Perhaps he would sing *My Mother* in a plaintive key. At that moment he could not understand why Auntie Golden Flower sang the song with joy and gratitude. Anyhow, he was touched by this joy and gratitude.

In the forests of Chinese scholar trees on the opposite side of the valley, he silently memorised the lyrics.

Take the clean spring water,
Wash my clothes;
Washing my clothes,
I bring to mind mama.
Take the bitter spring water,
Wash my hands;
Washing my hands,
I bring to mind mama.

Zhou Jian came back from Shenzhen and Guangzhou after having stayed for barely half a year. He was really unable to regard the foreign land as his hometown. He rushed home from Shenzhen at the end of the same year he had graduated from university. The transportation during the Spring Festival period was fearful. It was akin to a military tournament. By New Year's Eve he had not made it back to his home. He ate steaming and delicious dumplings on the train. While feeling grateful to the conductors, he simultaneously bemoaned his bad luck. He arrived back home early on the morning of New Year's Day. His mother persisted in asking him whether he had eaten and what he had eaten. Although he spoke highly of the boiled pork dumplings offered for free by the government, his mother kept on saying how unfortunate her lad was. In the eyes of the folk in their hometown the dumplings offered by the government were nothing but the scraps doled out to the starving during a period of famine. What could be more unfortunate than to eat this on New Year's Eve? After the New Year he did not return to the South. He settled down in Xi'an. When all was said and done, he had stayed there for four years while studying. This place was both strange and familiar for him. Apart from the train, there were two highways which could be used to get back to his hometown on the Zhou Plateau. As long as he could squeeze onto the bus, two or three hours later he would be back on the Zhou Plateau. From there to his village was about thirty kilometres. He had to walk back home.

In the provincial capital of Xi'an, he undertook various kinds of odd jobs. From the office buildings to construction sites, from working in shopping malls to driving taxis, he ran through all the big streets and small lanes of Xi'an. The city became stranger and stranger to him. The truth was very simple. He was not able to set up a home and secure a career in Xi'an. He was only an itinerant worker, no better than a migrant labourer. The only difference was that he wore spectacles and had a summer suit and a winter outfit. He wore them when he went back to his hometown on the Zhou Plateau. Facing the detective-like interrogations of the villagers, he could reel off so many enterprises and companies without difficulty. What was annoying was that before he left the people had started to comment freely. What was more hurtful still, they lumped him together with his Uncle Zhou Zhijie. Not Zhijie when he was in full plumage, but the Zhou Zhijie who lived a wretched life in his unit and was abandoned by his first wife.

When in a foreign land, one always wants to go to one's hometown, but before one has spent even a whole week there the need to escape becomes unbearable.

Three years on, his uncle's life has become fixed. Auntie Golden Flower has successfully made her parents-in-law assume a new look and pass the evaluation of her own parents. She now has the ability and the heart to sort out her nephew. When Zhou Jian comes back to Weibei City, his Uncle Zhou Zhijie says at their first meeting: "It's grand to be back. It's grand to be back." His parents in his hometown on the Zhou Plateau echo how it is grand to be back. When the honest folks of the Zhou Plateau go to undertake work outside, as soon as they leave the Zhou Plateau they call their surroundings a "foreign land". Those who attend university and leave Weibei City are said to possess a hometown. Everybody chants in the same tone to Zhou Jian: "Back home." Zhou Jian too has the feeling of having returned home.

When Uncle Zhou Zhijie chats with his nephew, he sighs: "You are back now, but your small uncle is still drifting."

"Are you and Auntie going to relocate to Xi'an?"

"My silly nephew."

The uncle touches the back of his nephew's head and pats it gently: "If we struggle to feel rooted in Weibei City and are exhausted here, how could we go over to Xi'an? To be frank, your small uncle is a stranger in his own hometown. It was your Auntie who asked somebody to help with your job."

"My Auntie's achievement is your achievement. How could you draw such a clear line between yourself and my Auntie?"

"This is not your small uncle's meaning. Your small uncle is living like this in his own hometown. How could he not sigh with emotion?"

"That's true. My Auntie comes from Xinjiang. My small uncle is an authentic native of the Zhou Plateau in Shaanxi. You are not as sociable as my Auntie. Don't let this weigh heavily upon your heart. My Auntie is the living Buddha of our Zhou family."

"That's true. She is a living Buddha; also, a Mongolian Buddha at that. From ancient times, nomadic tribes began to select where to set up home according to where grass and water were plentiful. They have the inborn ability to turn a foreign land into their hometown."

This might be the reason why Uncle Zhou Zhijie divorced his ex-wife, Tian Xiaolei. From the day she returned to Shaanxi, Xiaolei became a stranger in her hometown as well. Women are more sensible and delicate. Zhou Zhijie's resentment towards his ex-wife proved transitory.

From that time onwards, Zhou Zhijie changed his field of research from primitive cliff-paintings to the history of the nomadic peoples in the North of China. His focus was upon the migration and living patterns of the ethnic pastoral herdsmen of the grasslands. Maybe he felt grateful to Golden Flower or perhaps Golden Flower's swift assimilation into his hometown was what stimulated him. His first study was into the history of how the Torghut branch of the Oirat Mongols returned from Russia. He went by his own means to investigate from the Kalmyk Republic in Russia to Kazakhstan and to Kyrgyzstan and Ili and the Bayingolin Autonomous Mongol Prefecture in Xinjiang, and the Ejina

Region in the Gansu Corridor, and the Hexi Autonomous Mongol Prefecture in Qinghai. Along the eastern return route of the Oirat Mongols, he accomplished a rare long march of 10,000 *li*.

When abroad, he only had himself to rely on; at home, it was far easier. He could investigate together with his graduate students. The funds, being insufficient, could only cover research undertaken at home.

When he returned alone from the River Volga to Golden Flower's hometown, the Bayinbuluke Grassland, to visit his parents-in-law, the entire grassland was hurrahing all over. They regarded him as a true Mongolian. Even the sound of the Mongolian guitar was different to his ears. Singing *The Song of the Kushan Empire* and the ancient western Mongolian *My Mother* made everyone feel like they had been transported back to the heroic age of Ubashi Khan.[ad]

After the Mongols rose to power, they galloped on horseback across a vast area from the Greater Khingan Mountain Range to Vienna. During the Ming and Qing Dynasties, the Oirat tribe of Western Mongolia became the masters of this vast terrain. Mongolian riders even traversed the Parmir Plateau, the Hindu Kush and the Himalayas. They established the Mughal Kingdom in the ancient Indian subcontinent. That was the Mughal Empire.

In order to memorialise his beloved concubine, the Mughal Emperor Shah Jahan constructed the fairyland-like Taj Mahal. When the European powers began to conquer the world, the Mughal Empire, the Arabic Empire and the Persian Empire all fell into decline. The Great Qing Dynasty was the last remaining piece of bone the European powers conquered.

Before the decline of the Great Qing Dynasty, under the attack of the Russian Tsar, the Turkish Empire and many Mongolian Khitan states also collapsed.

From the seventeenth century, the Torghut people, a branch of the Oirat Mongols, lived to the west of the Tianshan Mountains in the vicinity of the River Volga for more than 150 years. The River Volga was known as the "River Yile" in the magnificent Mongolian language and the grassland steeds also left iridescent and colourful place names for forests, grasslands, mountains, rivers and lakes across the sprawling area between the Greater Khingan Mountains and Vienna. These included the palace of the Russian Tsar, the Kremlin, which means "castle" in the Mongolian tongue.

Confronted with the conquering iron hooves of the Russian Tsar, the Torghut Mongolians fought back.

The Torghut people cherished freedom. They had never been enslaved by anybody. Other than God, they feared no one. They thought that it was natural for the people of the grassland to chase after habitats who had abundant water and grass. They treated the tribes they conquered with magnanimity and shared with these people the twists and fortunes of daily life. The emergence of the empire of the Russian Tsar was like the first manifestation of a demon on the earth.

Ayuka Khan, Tseren Donduk Khan, Donduk Ombo Khan and Donduk Dashi Khan[ae] fought in succession against the tighter and tighter lasso of the Russian Tsar. The Torghut people faced extinction; *to be or not to be?*

During the reign of Ubashi Khan, the Torghut people decided to return from the east to Tianshan, the mother mountain, leaving behind the River Yile, where they had lived for more than 150 years. For thousands and thousands of years, the people of the grassland had built sumptuous homes unremittingly, always forsaking them in their quest for a new dwelling place. They migrated freely back and forth, never again having to suffer such humiliation. The Kushan people ran into this disaster more than 1,000 years ago when they travelled across the Qilian Mountains and planted their feet in the River Ili Valley. From there, they had to breach a tight encirclement and travel along the Tianshan Mountains to cross the Pamir Plateau and find a new home. *The Song of the Kushan Empire*, left in the River Ili Valley by the Kushan people, enshrined the innermost pain of the people of the grassland. It represents the secret history of the nomads. When one of them was lost forever in the abyss and about to enter the gateway of hell, this ancient song welled up in their heart.

Child, if you are thirsty, don't drink the water from the river,
The river has been poisoned by the enemy;
If you want to drink, drink the enemy's blood.
Child, choose death over submission,
When you are dead, don't let me see you sleeping in a coffin;
Your body should be carried back on a shield.

On 5th January 1771, the Torghut people left the River Volga and rushed eastward like they were competing in a race.[af] More than 200,000 people belonging to about 30,909 tent families followed Ubashi Khan. The river started to freeze over. In excess of 70-80,000 individuals from 10,190 tent families were left behind on the grassland of the riverbank because they could not cross the waterway from the plateau. This tribe was later to be known as "Kalmyk", meaning "those who were left behind". The 200,000 Torghut people who followed Ubashi Khan crossed the River Ural and went through the Enba Desert, walking along the Mugodzhar Hills and arrived at Yiergizi, Sarail Batu (the capital of the Golden Horde) and Jiersakan. From Jiersakan, they bypassed the Siberian forest and turned in a hurry to the southeast. Then they came across the Karakoram Desert and journeyed towards Lake Balkhash.

The company passed through the Kekaisi-Yuhansike Grassland and the Halatuoer Wilderness before arriving in the River Ili Valley. Among the 200,000 people, only 70-80,000 survived. Two-thirds of them lost their lives. During the seven-month-long march they covered a distance equivalent to half of the Earth, going through the largest forests, grasslands, deserts, wastelands, rivers and lakes. Pursuing from behind were the soldiers of the Russian Tsar. They were attacked by the grassland tribes on the road. In their hearts, they only had the paradise-like grassland to hold onto. They dashed to the grassland; from the grassland of the vast deserts and the great seas to the grassland in the endless wasteland. Perpetual wars and natural disasters fortified the grassland on the Earth.

At last, the paradise-like grassland was found in the arms of the mother mountain, Tianshan. One hundred and fifty years ago, their ancestors relocated from the grassland in the heavens, which was situated about 3,000 metres above sea level, to the River Volga Valley. The journey of the seven-month-long march again and again recalled the national memory of the Tianshan Grassland. The Tianshan Grassland had become the last refuge of these people. The grassland below the mountains may have disappeared. Their peripatetic lives, which began in ancient times and saw them chase water and grass for survival, were about to come to an end. On the grassland, people had no sense of national boundaries. They did not have the concepts of country and nation, as put forth by Western powers. Nonetheless, they realised that this was a fearful, strangulating lasso. Human beings will fall into the abyss, never to return. The world will be full of demons.

The mission of the Torghut people was to guard the last heavenly grassland on the Earth. They darted thousands and thousands of miles from the River Volga as though competing in a race. The Tsarist soldiers, who were chasing them, witnessed this wonder. The soldiers and officers of the Russian Tsar regarded them as the third Roman Empire. They took the authentic Greek religion as their guardian and must have brought to mind the Olympic Games in Ancient Athens. They must have brought to mind the more than 40-kilometre-long marathon and the Thermocretian Campaign. The angry Torghut people rushed for tens of thousands of kilometres and defeated en route the Russian armies and attacks from the grassland tribes. They conquered deserts and forests one after another. The European mercenaries in the Russian army left a record that went like this: "The spirit of the Mongolians when rushing towards the grassland made people think of the British navy song – *Britannia rule the waves! Britons, never, never, never shall be slaves!* The sentiments of this shanty could be applied to the Mongolians. Rushing towards the grassland represented their spirit of freedom and resistance to ever being slaves. The grassland was the sea and the Russians were the earliest Europeans to make contact with the Chinese. The Russians told the Western Europeans that 2,000 years ago the Chinese people named the grassland of the Gobi Desert "the great sea" and "the endless sea".

At the very beginning, the Torghut people used *The Song of the Kushan Empire* to lift the soldiers' morale. However, more and more troops and generals perished. They could not be carried back on their shields. Most were abandoned in the wilds. Further livestock fell and died too. These were the lifeline people needed for survival. The Kushan people, the creators of this ancient song, found a new home in the Hindu Kush to the south of the Pamir Plateau. Their contentment caused them to forget to travel home, so they refused the request of Zhang Qian,[ag] the envoy from the Han Dynasty, to stage a two-flank assault against the Huns before returning to the Qilian Mountains. Were the grasslands on the high mountains also their home?

After the Kushan people had grown prosperous, they expanded their territories into the Indian subcontinent and established the Kushan Empire. They spread and promoted Buddhism and transformed that place into a nexus for introducing Buddhism into the Western Regions and the Central Plains. The One Thousand Buddha Caves of Dunhuang situated at the foot of the Qilian Mountains, in their home region, and the golden roofs of the temples built by the Kushan Empire in the Hindu Kush and the Indian subcontinent burnished one another's beauty. This presented a propitious impression of the Buddhist paradise. The Torghut people who believed in Buddhism were mercilessly enslaved by the Tsar. Tens of thousands of soldiers and generals offered their lives in battle in support of the Tsar, yet he still transported hundreds of Torghut nobles to Moscow as hostages. What is more, he exhorted them to relinquish Buddhism and embrace Eastern Orthodoxy. Thus, returning to China via the eastern road became the collective wish of the whole nation.

The catastrophe faced by the Torghut people is the catastrophe faced by all Oriental peoples and mankind in its entirety. This catastrophe far surpassed that confronted by just the Kushan peoples. *The Song of the Kushan Empire* could exorcise the horror of that disaster. At the time, a beautiful Torghut maiden started to dance *Sawu'erdeng*. Then all the women danced *Sawu'erdeng* as though they had been awakened from their dreams. In the successive days of battle, women were responsible for tending to the old, the weak, the sick and the disabled. They fed domestic animals because they were the food necessary for their survival.

Originally, *Sawu'erdeng* was danced in praise of the horse, the cow, the sheep, the camel, the flying birds and the running animals. It was a fusion of human and animal. The ancient *Sawu'erdeng* had fifty or sixty varieties. During disasters, the Torghut women selected the most representative dozen. The first maiden who danced *Sawu'erdeng* did so for a lamb that had just died. She only wanted to revive the lamb. Months later, that lamb was capable of producing milk for soldiers on the frontline. Assuredly, in the first few days, women danced only to revive expiring domestic animals. The animals may have been dead in body, but their souls lived on. They were still vital within that *Sawu'erdeng* dance like the shadows trailing the women. As expected, after the *Sawu'erdeng* dance, hordes and hordes of beasts appeared upon the Earth. Even eagles would fly overhead to bestow blessings upon the people afflicted by disaster.

Next, some miraculous phenomena transpired. The shadows of the deceased generals and soldiers started to flash in the dance mingled together with those of the cows, sheep, horses, camels and animals. Life forms absorbed one another and mutated. This, indeed, concurred with the doctrines of Buddhism. *Life is never ending. It does not diminish, rather it increases. Sawu'erdeng* gives one the sense that God resides within one's body. When several dozen maidens dance en masse, it makes people feel that thousands and thousands of lives are accompanying them. When confronting disasters, the Torghut people retained their calm ferocity. The twelve dances commenced with the eagle dance. The eagles in the heavens swung over when they heard the tune. Following the eagles were large hunks of cloud. The texture of the clouds inspired the basic decorative patterns the nomadic peoples emblazoned upon their dresses and tents. This was the symbol of heaven. The clouds accompanied the eagles just like the white flocks of sheep accompanied the nomads. This again served to confirm that there must be grassland in the heavens.

Upon arriving at the River Ili Valley, their *Sawu'erdeng* dance had attained a high degree of perfection. To the manoeuvring of the men and animals were added the waves of *Sawu'erdeng* sleeves and *Sawu'erdeng* silk scarves. All of them typified feminine beauty. *Sawu'erdeng* formed a style different from styles past. It miraculously combined ferocity with tenderness, swiftness with ease, and wildness with tranquillity. The results were deep, bleak, sad and majestic.

Take the clean spring water,
Wash my clothes;
Washing my clothes,
I bring to mind mama.
Take the bitter spring water,
Wash my hands;
Washing my hands,
I bring to mind mama.

When the song was sung, the white clouds overhead dissipated. Only a forlorn eagle was left. While the man was still singing, the eagle remained motionless in the sky. Among the hundreds of birds, the eagle was the lone king who could stay aloft motionless. The eagle approached closer to the proud, lonely and unyielding heart. The heavens and the earth held their breath. Great flocks of white swans winged over from the belly of the Tianshan Mountains. The Torghut maidens started to dance like they were transfixed by a charm. The dozen *Sawu'erdeng* dances could not satisfy the bidding of the maidens or of the swan. At the sound of the song, the maidens became light, gentle, elegant, mild and peaceful. They became the incarnations of the white swans.

That day, swans were everywhere up in the sky and everywhere on the ground below. Such a delightful human spectacle had never been seen before in the River Ili Valley. The most charming maiden, *Sawu'erdeng*, appeared. The swan is a symbol of love. The eastern route of return represents the route via which suffering is overcome. The Ili Grassland is the sole beginning. The Torghut people continued to travel to the east.

In Daban, which formed the boundary between the River Ili Valley and the Youdoulusi Basin at the Tianshan Mountains, there sprouted large patches of snow lotuses. August was the flowering season for this plant. The snow lotuses all grew at more than 3,000 metres above sea level. As the survivors of a catastrophe, the Torghut people thought that these were the white swans which had fallen from the sky. On that day, the maidens who had created *Sawu'erdeng* all turned into swans and snow lotuses. From then on, the Torghut ladies bore a new name, "Golden Flower". Even now, Oirat Mongolian girls like to name themselves "Golden Flower", just as many Uyghur girls call themselves "Guli". The name Golden Flower was bestowed by God.

Uncle Zhou Zhijie learned about the migration history of the Torghut people long ago. After he entered university, he started to collect materials pertaining to the Oirat Mongolians. He elected to go to Hejing County, which was largely populated by these people, to conduct his field teaching practice. In addition, he had the intention of pursuing his field investigations there. Golden Flower, who was then a high school student, entered his life at this point and later became his wife. Many years hence, after Uncle Zhou travelled along the return road of the Torghut people and reached home, he looked at his spouse Golden Flower differently. Auntie Golden Flower felt peculiar and asked him whether or not he had changed his eyes during the time he was out there. He embraced his wife and whispered in her ears as though he was drunk. He simply repeated two expressions again and again: "Snow lotus, golden flower, golden flower, snow lotus … "

Golden Flower smiled: "After we've given birth to so many kids, did you only just realise that the golden flower is the snow lotus and the snow lotus is the golden flower?"

In fact, Auntie Golden Flower only gave birth to a son, Zhou Batu. The ex-wife had borne a daughter, Zhou Jingjing. Golden Flower conveyed to people the impression that she had a brood of kids. The pupils in the school and the children in the dance classes in the Cultural Palace all became her offspring.[ah] She genuinely took them as her own. Even when she punished pupils, the parents of the children raised no objection. When the kids went back home they always talked about "Teacher Golden Flower". The smaller ones all called her "Mother Golden Flower", making their real mother sound like a stepmother. When they glimpsed Golden Flower and her family on the street from afar, they would shout "Batu's mummy" and "Jingjing's mummy". They jumped and screeched as if they were hailing their own mother.

It was only rational that Golden Flower should tell her husband that she had raised a brood of kids. What is more, she informed her husband that the small houses to be found among the snow lotuses constituted his own hometown. Whenever he travelled with the eagle to the west of the Tianshan Mountains, he would have a hometown there. Hence, such a situation arose. Whenever Uncle Zhou Zhijie came back from his hometown in the Zhou Plateau or from his workplace in low spirits, Auntie Golden Flower would greet him with *Sawu'erdeng*. The two delighted kids would also respond lustily. The wife indicated to her husband with her eyes that *Sawu'erdeng* is not only the home strain of the people of the grassland, but his home too. The husband would then take a breather in the midst of *Sawu'erdeng* and break into *My Mother* like an authentic native of the grassland. That would be the most heartbreaking time for his wife. What is harder for a man than to have to seek out a home in his hometown? What causes more suffering for a man than to have just left his mother and to now be looking for his true mother?

One can imagine how Auntie Golden Flower dances *Sawu'erdeng* to perfection. Although Auntie Golden Flower has become the mother of all the kids under the sun, she still retains the charm and the glamour of a grassland maiden. Zhang Haiyan was arrested by her true beauty the first time she caught sight of Auntie Golden Flower. A long time after having left Uncle's home, she told Zhou Jian: "Who could believe that she is already a mother? She is still a maiden from head to toe. A woman in such an ideal state is surely the happiest kind of woman. How could she attain such an ideal state?" Zhou Jian only knows that Auntie Golden Flower loves to dance: "I dance as well. I started to dance when I was six. My university teacher has been dancing for dozens of years. She once even won the national championship. Comparing her with Auntie Golden Flower though is like setting mud alongside a cloud." Zhang Haiyan then took Auntie Golden Flower as her dance impresario. While learning to dance, she also enquires about the secret of *Sawu'erdeng*. Auntie Golden Flower instructs Zhang Haiyan: "Love what you love." It is so simple.

Auntie Golden Flower and Zhang Haiyan have hit it off. Apart from dance, they exchange women's talk from the bottom of their hearts. Even Zhou Jian does not know what they are discussing.

When Zhang Haiyan is happy she tells Zhou Jian: "Auntie Golden Flower says that the men of the Zhou family love to marry either women from the grassland or women from the city. They cannot get along well with women from the countryside."

Zhang Haiyan is very clever. Before Zhou Jian chases her for an answer she informs him: "The lives of the people of the grassland are closer to modern civilisation. Does 'modern civilisation' mean the civilisation of the city? Both the people from the grassland and the people from the city pay greater attention to their spiritual home."

Zhou Jian is dumbfounded by this and Zhang Haiyan continues: "The spiritual home is to be found in your heart and in your brain. You carry it around with you all the time. In this way, everywhere on the Earth is your home. There is no need for you to catch the busy Spring Festival train or attend the New Year's Eve reunion meal."

Zhou Jian's eyes have already moistened. Zhang Haiyan shakes him by the shoulder: "Don't be like this. I don't want to ruin your hometown and your home. Uncle thought that only he was a stranger in his hometown. He regards you as a lucky guy. Auntie has already perceived that you will be reduced to the situation of your uncle. She is teaching me how to dance *Sawu'erdeng* emphatically. This is by way of giving you a preventative inoculation."

Zhou Jian then says repeatedly that he is OK. Zhang Haiyan

turns Zhou Jian's head and gazes into his eyes: "Don't you pretend." Neither Zhou Jian's voice nor his eyes are trying to deceive Zhang Haiyan.

Zhou Jian tells Zhang Haiyan: "Auntie Golden Flower has been in our family for so many years. Today I understand how much she has suffered."

"She loves your uncle. A woman's love can encompass the sky and the Earth. The trivial matters in your family are nothing."

Zhou Jian was only two or three years old when his uncle went to Xinjiang to try and make a living. He had no impression of this business. As he began to form an understanding of things, all he heard about was his legendary uncle. Uncle came to visit his hometown when he enrolled at university. Zhou Jian was at that time about to matriculate from primary school. Their uncle held his small nephew in his arms and declared to the public: "The Zhou family will have another university student." All the members of the family looked at Zhou Jian differently. His uncle was the first university student to have come from the Zhou family. He was sure to set an example for all the kids. The most glorious point for his uncle was that he had returned home in honour with his newlywed bride Tian Xiaolei. Despite only staying in his hometown for one week, his dream had come to fruition: "Going to university, becoming an employee of the government, and taking a city girl for his wife."

Later on, uncle's career slumped. Far away in a small town in the western borderlands, life did not proceed as he would have wished. Thus, he never came back to his hometown. His friends and relatives gradually forgot him. Only Zhou Jian often thought about his uncle. When his uncle was transferred to the province where his hometown was located and his career flatlined, his wife left him and his friends and relatives jeered at him and mocked him. It was Zhou Jian who stepped forward bravely to defend him. He always ran back and forth doing uncle's errands. Auntie Golden Flower married his uncle and soon grew fond of Zhou Jian. She told her husband that this child was the most honest person in the Zhou family. On account of her grassland simplicity and honesty, Golden Flower often found herself made fun of by friends and relatives in her mother-in-law's home. Zhou Jian sided with her and he alone complained that his kinsfolk were dishonest and mean.

Thus, the members of the family would curse him by saying that he would achieve nothing, just like his Uncle Zhou Zhijie. Zhou Jian would launch a counterattack: "If I could achieve the same position as my younger uncle that would be my good fortune. If you want to live for one day like my uncle you and the next eight generations of your family will have to burn incense as thick as the grinding stone!"

His tough words elicited laughter: "Stupid boy! A good steamed bun consumes more vegetables. A handsome wife consumes the husband. Do you admire your young uncle's good luck? You have not seen the lean life your young uncle is living."

They even treated beautiful love as a burden. They were no better than dogs and pigs.

The high school student Zhou Jian displayed great contempt towards these people. He had already found his beloved Zhang Haiyan, although they had not communicated in close quarters, instead just exchanging greetings and nodding heads. When people made fun of his Uncle Zhou Zhijie and his Auntie Golden Flower and lumped him together with them, their tough words became a form of praise for him. Zhou Jian was elated. Golden Flower praised him for his honesty. He then regarded honesty as the most valuable quality a person could possess. After graduating from university, Zhou Jian did various jobs and lived a rather hard life. All of this had something to do with his honesty. This fatigue continues to this day and has already placed him in dire peril.

It was reasonable that Golden Flower should enjoin him like this. When he entered university, there was already no government sponsorship. His uncle and auntie supported him to finish his university studies. They never issued the same invitation to the other kids in the Zhou family, even though they supported some of them to study in high school and some in college. After all, it was Zhou Jian who embraced willingly and straightforwardly his auntie's requirement to be an upright person.

Whilst talking with his uncle, Zhou Jian realised how people from the grassland cherish their language. They never tell lies, nor are they slippery-tongued. They don't employ clever talk and their manner is not deliberately ingratiating. They dislike opportunism to the point of hatred. Most of the time, Golden Flower whether she was in the village or in her work unit, remained silent. When an expression of surprise came across her face, it must be because she had run into something that was beyond her imagination or fell below the baseline of human decency. If it were too far from the baseline, Auntie Golden Flower could not tolerate it.

The Zhou Plateau was the original site of the Western Zhou Dynasty. It has a long history and rich seams of traditional culture. As a result, there arose a regal climate in which good news was reported but not bad. The ordinary folk followed suit. No matter how greatly an individual suffered or was wronged, nobody dare speak out. If the information was leaked to others everyone would look down on that person and try by all means to bully them. So, when people returned from outside, they each kept up the pretence that they were leading a lucky and harmonious life. In the days of the small-scale peasant economy, this was not such a serious matter, but in these days of the market economy when the whole country is conducting business, one can imagine how much employees are made to suffer when working in private enterprises or in businesses operated by the township. The bosses never worry about this. They know what the result will be if their employees speak out. The bosses only adhere to one bottom line, namely that not one life should be lost and that bother should never be brought to the police station.

One of the child workers from Zhou's family could not bear this anymore. When he came back to the village he could still swallow his suffering and say "hello" to everyone with a forced smile. When he met his mother, he could no longer put up with it. After all, he was just a child. He cried and told his mother the truth. For thousands of years, the people of the Zhou Plateau have tried to keep unspeakable truths hidden away because they would sooner suffer than lose face. His mother shed tears together with her child and comforted him with soothing words. Golden Flower happened to be in the village. She had come over to visit the senior members of the family. Only the child's mother and Auntie Golden Flower were inside the house; nobody else. Everybody was trying to conceal the truth. How could Golden Flower tolerate this? She pulled the child over and probed about everything in detail. The child was fourteen or fifteen, the proper age to be studying in high school. In this day and age so many children in the countryside quit school. As a high school teacher, Golden Flower could only take care of the child that was in front of her.

Auntie Golden Flower did not write a report letter to the government. She went directly to the news agency, that is to say the *Weibei Morning Post*, where I – Hong Ke – was working. I had previously interviewed Golden Flower and compiled a report about her training class for the *Sawu'erdeng* dance. I was willing to conduct a covert operation into the unlicensed factories. I acted as a plant. Of course, it was essential to protect the identity of the child informant. The newspaper could not release a published report. Rather it was featured in the restricted reference and only circulated among the senior cadres. The factory was penalised severely and compelled to make improvements. The child's anonymity was not compromised. The working conditions were improved greatly. The biggest change was that the factory became sanitary and clean. They even invited a professor from the School of Literature at Weibei University to deliver lectures about *Tending the Roots of Wisdom*, *The Zhu Family Admonitions*, and *Pupils' Rules and Disciplines*[ai] to all the employees and the bosses both junior and senior. He presented them with mottoes like: "Be a good son at home and an obedient young man abroad"; "Be friendly and kind to all, draw near to people who are good"; and "If we try to rule others by force, we will never win over their hearts, and if we lead them with principles, then they won't feel oppressed and abused". This new pattern of management was introduced by the Fengqing Construction Materials Company Ltd in Weibei City, yet when it came to the remote villages atop the plateau the principles were only adopted loosely. The so-called "entrepreneurial culture" was a coating upon the Buddha akin to golden leaf.

The child worker did not cry anymore. Nonetheless, he became pale and thin and fell into a state of chronic exhaustion. He never spoke a word when either his mother or Auntie Golden Flower asked him. Auntie Golden Flower was at a loss. Her mother-in-law had instructed her in the essence of traditional culture. Her mother-in-law was unfamiliar with the Classics. She did not even know about the basic materials for enlightenment like *The Three-Character Canon* or *The Thousand Word Primer*.[aj] She rendered these topics into the colloquialisms of ordinary people: "If you screw a ghost, don't let the ghost cry out." The surface meaning of these words was clear, though the hidden connotations were hard for Golden Flower to comprehend. At last, she found a more academic way of expressing this: "The tortured should forfeit their right to groan. Oh, my God!"

When Zhou Jian returned to Weibei City, after repeated consideration Auntie Golden Flower ultimately chose the Fengqing Construction Materials Company Ltd. After having studied and worked inland for so many years, Auntie Golden Flower understood the simple truth that bigger cities were more civilised and fair. One should at least stay in a prefecture-level city like Weibei City. Once one moves to a county town or a township it will be a different story.

Auntie Golden Flower is now quite satisfied with Zhou Jian's current situation, particularly since Zhou Jian has a girlfriend like Zhang Haiyan. The prospect of a happy life lies ahead of them. "Your life in the future will be much better than ours." Zhang Haiyan's face is as red as if it had been bleeding. However, she reveals what is in her heart: "We all admire the life you and my uncle lead. I would die from happiness if I had something approaching that life."

Auntie Golden Flower sighs: "You are right. We are happy. I am a daughter of the grassland. I have what is inborn in the blood of the people of the grassland – to live by chasing after water and grass. Even if we go to the moon, we can raise a tent and build a bonfire to barbecue the stars on. Your uncle has the experience of roving all over the world, though he always has his hometown in his heart. However, when he came back to his hometown even he felt like a stranger here. He came back to his hometown, but his heart could not settle here. You are much better off. You were born, grew up and now work in your hometown. Once you have settled down your heart will be settled too."

Auntie Golden Flower doesn't feel in the slightest the crisis the killing mixer has brought to Zhou Jian. She perceives Zhou Jian and Zhang Haiyan's inner malaise. She misconstrues this as coming from some barrier that has arisen within Zhang Haiyan's family. This is something quite predictable. It is not easy to marry a city girl. Auntie Golden Flower asks Zhou Jian to talk about his plans for the future in front of Zhang Haiyan. Obviously, under the guidance of Golden Flower, in Zhou Jian's grand blueprint he will take two or three years to gain practical workplace experience. He will then try to obtain certification as a structural engineer. Thereafter he will be in a position to strive after a middle-ranking management post. If he fails to get this post, he will still be able to hop into a better company. These things should come to pass after several years. The present danger is posed by the mixer. It is a time-bomb, which can be decommissioned after one or two years. After one or two years, he will have a better network of contacts. Then that cold machine will turn into a hot stove. Before it turns into a hot stove, it will remain a bomb. It is hard to explain this submerged bomb phenomenon to their auntie. Auntie Golden Flower is obviously unfamiliar with the complicated pattern of life and the network of contacts in inland areas. There have been so many misunderstandings and so many jokes that this grassland woman has had it tough.

According to Haiyan's plan, the danger of the mixer will soon be banished. It seems it has already been banished. This needs to be emphasised. Next week Zhou Jian will mount the plateau and attend a birthday banquet for Liu Jun's grandmother. This is like introducing a flame to the stove. Liu Jun genuinely takes Zhou Jian as his good brother. The way of the world as displayed in *Tending the Roots of Wisdom*, *The Zhu Family Admonitions* and *Pupils' Rules and Disciplines* is starting to be revealed. Once in a blue moon, Zhou Jian's face becomes serene and quiet. As the saying goes: "The expression on the face is nurtured by the heart." These prove to be the most relaxed days of Zhou Jian's life. Auntie Golden Flower reflects: "Zhou Jian is an honest child. An honest person is sure to live a good life."

There is something in Auntie Golden Flower's words.

The child worker from the Zhou family suffered several ups and downs. Auntie Golden Flower could no longer assist him. On the streets of Weibei City, as a famous journalist at the *Weibei Morning Post*, I talked with Golden Flower about the unfortunate child. He is not the type to read books. He can only work in unlicensed factories. I know what he is like. I went to the Zhou Plateau and used my personal contact network to have him transferred to work in a more distant town. When leaving that primitive workshop enterprise in the village, the child and I put on a show. My friend from the county TV station shouldered a camcorder and drew the child and me into focus. Although the child was still young, he knew about the ways of the world. He talked a lot about how good the factory is and how pleasant the bosses are. His words even made the bosses who were present feel embarrassed. It was the modern equivalent of 'The Song of the Immortals'[ak]. *The heaven was good and the earth was good, I am good and you are good, everything is good. Then life is good.* The child was tasked with lighter duties in another enterprise in the town. One can imagine how shocked Auntie Golden Flower felt when she saw the photographs and feature on the child in the newspaper. She immediately called my news agency. I told her: "There are many ways to interpret *Tending the Roots of Wisdom*, *The Zhu Family Admonitions* and *Pupils' Rules and Disciplines*. My interpretation is more pragmatic. We have only one purpose. That is for the child not to suffer and to have a good life." I heard the long sigh of Golden Flower from the other end of the receiver. I could not face the scepticism of this beautiful woman, nor could I put down the receiver the moment I ran out of things to say. That was the most helpless and broken-hearted sigh that I ever heard from a woman. Until she gently hung-up, it was like the death of a swan. The graceful wings gradually drooped down. From then on, I could no longer enjoy the cello tune *The Dying Swan* by Camille Saint-Saëns and could not enjoy the classic ballet danced by Pavlova.

A number of years ago, the seniors of the Zhou family enlightened Auntie Golden Flower. The annual birthday banquet held for the oldest grandma of the Zhou family was not only a big gathering for all the clan, but also a prime chance to offer instruction to the grandchildren. The old grandma was ninety years old and remained compos mentis, healthy, ate and drank well and could even play mahjong. She really was the old lucky star of the Zhou family. All the clan thrived under her fortunate charisma. She showed equal concern to each of the younger generation whether they were her blood kin or not. Most of her grandchildren had by then started paid employment. When they wanted to exhibit their filial piety to their grandma, they acted differently from their parents. They tried to win her over by means of soft tactics. The senior grandma had her own secret source of joy. The grandchildren had unique stratagems for offering birthday gifts. The majority of them presented nutritious and health-maintaining items. Zhou Jian persisted in giving American ginseng and deep-sea fish lecithin. The old grandma beamed at these gifts and then put them away. She would enjoy them later after the banquet was over.

Only one grandchild gave her local flavours each year. This year it might be a bowl of soft tofu soup, next year it might be soft tofu soup with bread-cake. One year he offered a plate of fried oat-flour jelly. He served this in a stainless steel pail so it would retain its heat. He lifted the cover far away. It steamed and smelt moreish. While running towards the grandma, he shouted: "Granny, granny, your grandson is fetching you hot oat-flour jelly." His manner was like that of a soldier dashing towards the mountain top with a live hand grenade. The old grandma's heart detonated within her. Even the walnut-like wrinkles on her face grinned. The year after that somebody aped his example, though the result was not so great. The old grandma sampled a mouthful then passed it to others.

Only that grandchild was both charming and clever. His gift was ingenious and his tongue glib. The down-to-earth method was futile for touching the heart of a nonagenarian. The climax of the banquet was her speech. She would declare earnestly who was her lone filial grandchild. Her praise had never fallen on Zhou Jian. Each time Zhou Jian would observe Auntie Golden Flower raising her thumb to him among the crowd. Once the old grandma saw this, the elderly woman became a child for the second time. Thus, she praised the youngster who had offered her wheat-flour noodles more highly. She boasted wildly about the one-yuan Qishan cold noodles. She lauded them as being like a species of 100-year-old ginseng from the Changbei Mountains. Actually, among the other gifts there was a box of 100-year-old ginseng from the Changbei Mountains purchased by her offspring for a pretty penny.

Uncle Zhou Zhijie saw through all of these tactics. He taught Auntie Golden Flower a lesson: "In the *Analects* of Confucius it states of a true gentleman that 'inside the family he serves his father, outside the family he serves his lord'.[a] Now there are no actual lords. The lords have been reconstituted into big or small leaders. The oldest grandma is letting her grandkids in on the secret of how to slip beneath the big leader's quilt."

"Isn't this trying to lasso a wolf with an empty hand?" Auntie Golden Flower became agitated.

Uncle Zhou Zhijie told her: "The way for us to survive is to focus on conquering the reality with a void, turning the heavy into the light, making half a kilo tip the scales at 1,000 and having the minority conquer the majority. Those who do nothing are better off than those who work hard, who work desperately, and are working themselves to death."

For Auntie Golden Flower, the truth started to sink in: "Zhou Zhijie, dare you behave like this for once? I'll maim you."

If you ignore the advice of the old, you will come to grief untold.

Zhou Jian was bound to come to serious grief.

That clever grandchild became an assistant to a general manager only a few years after graduating from vocational school. He did nothing except repeat relentlessly the small tricks he had rehearsed on his grandma.

Auntie Golden Flower's eyes are now becoming numb. She rubs them and opens them again. This time they stretch to their widest. This year, Uncle Zhou Zhijie's cousin's lot has slumped to an all-time low. Just like Zhijie when he found himself in the pit, the pernicious harm flows from his own kin.

That cousin was the first to operate a manual workshop in the village. He worked hard and tried to expand his business to the township. When he was about to make this move, however, he came a cropper and lost almost all of his money. He now cannot face returning to see his parents and fellow villagers. He chooses instead to hide outside and does not even dare come home during Spring Festival. Auntie Golden Flower witnesses the whole horrible spectacle. It is horrible in her eyes, though a common occurrence in the local area.

During this time, all of the friends, relatives and villagers are preoccupied with only one matter, namely greeting the homecoming loser back from the city. While preparing for the New Year festivities, everybody is also preparing their method of helping the guy who had once commanded the wind and the clouds. At first, Golden Flower finds herself greatly moved. A series of words betokening mercy, concern, warmth, honesty and friendship between kinsmen, between villagers and between family members, flashes through her mind. Golden Flower is certain to prepare a lavish gift too.

Golden Flower and her mother-in-law are just like mother and daughter. Her mother tells her the bald truth: "Everybody is bracing themselves to watch the fun. If he comes back in a decent and dignified way, everyone will come over and say 'hello'. If he returns like a beggar or a dog with a wagging tail, all the people in the street will flood over to ask how he is and how he's doing. The first few times he came back in high spirits; showing grace under pressure. He had the machismo of the Zhou family. His hair was combed smooth, his clothes were ironed and pressed, and his leather shoes shone like a raven's wings. He offered everybody he met a cigarette. Spring Festival is on the way, so it'll be harder and harder for him to keep this up. Somebody says they saw him sloshed in the county town. His face was rotten. I'm sure that he'll come back home in a day or too, looking just as bad. Everybody is bursting to see his suffering."

Golden Flower is choked, becoming speechless with shock. The mother-in-law tells the daughter-in-law that the principle of survival is never self-evident on the grassland, but is plain to see here further inland. People here hate being born rather than hate dying. The daughter of the grassland half understands. Her Han mother-in-law is being candid: "Everybody wishes that others will not die and not prosper in life either."

The daughter of the grassland at last heaves out a breath: "Is it still a life if one does not prosper?"

"My child, we have to live like this. A good death is no match for a wretched existence. Living like a shameless dog doesn't mean that you live like a tiger or a leopard or an eagle or a horse."

However, the mother-in-law is still greatly influenced by this daughter from the grassland. She now has those images of the eagles and steeds in her mind. Furthermore, she can substitute these animals for the fierce hawk and the burly cart-pulling horse of the loess plateau.

The mother-in-law then goes to comfort the spouse of the peasant-entrepreneur. The members of the cousin's wife's family have been waiting for the opportunity to take advantage of him. They have witnessed this ordinary farmer force five passes and slay six generals and become a peasant-entrepreneur with glamour. In fact, this entrepreneur is exceedingly honest and low-key in his manner, yet his imposing spirit showed itself. His power was even distinguishable in his calm. He is a big shot now. He is somebody now. How can he go on living like this? How can others live their lives?

From ancient times, the relationship between a son-in-law and his father-in-law has always been an instance of when one person falls, the other rises up. These days, when the peasant-entrepreneur has plumbed the bottom of his life, his wife takes good care of her mother-in-law and the child. Moreover, she takes care of her husband when he comes home. Still, she never shows warmth or candour and is calculating in how flawlessly she operates. Her maternal relatives are fully prepared and wait only for the wind and the last straw that will break the camel's back. The son-in-law has plunged into deep water, becoming breathless. The whites of his eyes are visible as well. They will wait for a while; wait until his belly is engorged with water and he rises to the surface, his stomach pointing upwards just as a dead pig that lacks even one last shred of dignity. They will then drag him to the bank and perform mouth-to-mouth resuscitation. Bringing him back from the brink of death will prove a smart trick. Their chance is now at hand.

Golden Flower escorts her mother-in-law to visit the spouse of the peasant-entrepreneur. She is the wife of her mother-in-law's nephew. Her mother-in-law carries on directly and frankly: "Child, go to the town and get your husband back. Get a haircut, take a shower and buy a set of decent clothes from the shop. Prepare all of the things necessary for Spring Festival and hire a car. We should have our grace under all this pressure. Come back home for New Year in a decent manner."

Her nephew's wife says: "He has never lost his grace. He is always decent in manner. The county town is not America or Germany. How can we catch a taxi and get home so soon? I have to wait on the old and the young in the family. I have no time to go."

The courtyard is jammed with people. Some are even peeping through the window. The mother-in-law continues to try and persuade the woman. She even mentions something she shouldn't: "Child, the one who will be with you until you are old is your man, not your mother's family. You should weigh the words your mother's family tells you. Listening to everything they say can make you eat but never shit."

The woman counters with: "My mother's family has never caused him pain. Did my mother's family block his way to eating shit?"

The words of her nephew's wife stab her in the heart and seize her by the throat. She clutches her chest and falls mute.

Golden Flower charges forward and grabs the woman's collar, her voice as loud as the thunder in the sky: "Your man's body has one more piece of meat than yours does. Without this piece of meat, you are just a lump of stone. If a man loses his dignity, you – his wife – are no better than a dog. Even if you became a whore nobody would make a move on you."

Golden Flower holds onto her mother-in-law and stalks through the crowd with a brave look. There is no need to think about the outcome. The famous words of Auntie Golden Flower spread all over the Zhou Plateau. All the people in uncle and auntie's work unit in Weibei City know about this. *How great it is that man has one more piece of meat than a woman.* The words strike like an exploding atom bomb.

Somebody makes a pithy remark: "Women who are willing to protect a man's dignity like this have almost become an extinct species."

Fashionable culture tends to reduce a great man into a petty one. They will rather make a man into a hooligan or a rascal than a dauntless hero with a bloody-minded character. Whenever uncle argues vehemently with his colleagues or graduate students about issues in the historical field, Auntie Golden Flower, who is waiting on the sidelines with tea and water, will slip in one or two comments which leave everybody dumbfounded. Golden Flower will compare Wu Zetian[am] – the idol of new women – with Empress Zhangsun, Empress Xiao Wen and Empress Xiaozhuang.[an] The success of Wu Zetian brought about a collective decline in the stock of Chinese women after the Song Dynasty. Auntie Golden Flower will juxtapose the Dowager Empress Cixi with Yuan Shikai and Sun Yat-sen.[ao] They acted from the inside in co-ordination with forces from the outside and brought about the end of the Qing Dynasty.

A female colleague comes back from Kangding and shows off a picture of her taken with a Tibetan man who looks like a Tibetan mastiff. She even spreads the news on the grapevine that some European and American women have come to China from thousands and thousands of miles away. Their purpose is to stay with a Tibetan man and to produce a fine seed. There is no need for Auntie Golden Flower to go to Kangding. She tells her female colleague about the lifestyle of the men on the grasslands: "It is a man's business to ride, to wrestle and to sing and dance. Cooking, washing clothes, mopping the floor and bringing up kids would chisel away the bravado of a man. That would cause a man to be nagging and womanly."

Golden Flower even cracks jokes about the police: "The best way to reform a criminal is to let him do housework. The best job for him is as a tailor."

Auntie Golden Flower laughs at her female colleagues: "On the one hand, they are grabbing their man's balls and wanting to make him into a eunuch. On the other hand, they are carried away by the Kangba men who looked like the Tibetan mastiff and a lion. They are destined to lead restless lives, to become hysterical and develop a split personality."

Her female colleagues follow the fashion of gazing at the sky in the belief that this can make a woman beautiful. Auntie Golden Flower tells them that if they gaze at the sky for long enough their eyes will become empty, lost and desolate. If you gaze at your beloved, your eyes will become passionate, bright and warm.

In her spare time, Golden Flower's great joy is to sit under the platform and listen to Zhou Zhijie's academic lectures with fascination. Every day when going to or from work, or taking the kids to or from school, the couple gaze at each other until the shadow of the lover or the beloved is out of sight. That is the habit of the people of the grassland. Their eyesight is trained to scan further and further by their beloved, merging together with the eternal sky and the earth.

Acknowledgements

"Blowing Smoke" and "Hometown" were translated by Professor Hu Zongfeng (Northwest University); "The Tears of the Trees" by Hu Zongfeng and Xu Lin (both of Northwest University); "The Howl of the Wolf" by Dr Wan Bing (Hunan Normal University); "Sweetness Setting In" by Dr Su Rui (Northwest University); "Passing the Winter" by Dr Robin Gilbank and Su Rui (Northwest University); "Golden Altay" by He Longping (Changsha Normal University); and "Snowbird" by Dr Zhang Min (Northwest University). Robin Gilbank cooperated closely in the editing and preparation of each text.

The authors and translators wish to thank Jamie McGarry, Jo Haywood and all at Valley Press for bringing this publication to fruition. Financial support was provided by the Centre for Chinese Literary Criticism at Northwest University. Thanks are also due to Dr J Graham Jones for his assistance in proofreading.

Endnotes

Xinjiang (meaning "New Frontier" or "New Borderland") has been the name used since the nineteenth century to refer to the northwestern region of China which has land borders with present-day Russia, India, Pakistan, Afghanistan, Mongolia, Kazakhstan, Kyrgyzstan and Tajikistan. It is ethnically, linguistically and geographically diverse with a history chequered with bloodshed and disputes over its political status.

Its strategic importance was recognised during the Han Dynasty. Then known by names including the "Western Regions" (*Xiyu*), the transnational Silk Road crossed the territory from the east to the northwest. Natural resources, such as Hetian jade, also came to be prized. Subsequent centuries saw significant Islamisation, with the effect that the Turkic Ugyhur people gradually dominated the Tarim Basin to the south of the Tianshan Mountains.

After the founding of the People's Republic of China in 1949, the People's Liberation Army entered Xinjiang and Chairman Mao reasserted that the heterogeneous borderlands should form one province annexed to the Chinese state, only governed according to special concerns. The incorporation of the Xinjiang Uyghur Autonomous Region was declared in 1955, by which time the Xinjiang Production and Construction Corps (abbreviated as XPCC or *Bingtuan* in Chinese) had been established. "Golden Altay" and, more tangentially, "Snowbird" give accounts of how brigades of the XPCC (famously commanded by Wang Zhen, with Zhang Zhonghan among his Political Instructors) enacted the aim of developing the agriculture and economy of the frontier while simultaneously defending the borders and quelling internal dissent.

By the time Hong Ke moved to Xinjiang in the 1980s, the Corps had already been disbanded and its duties largely transferred to the provincial government. However, the legacy of that period was still felt. The demographics had shifted so that while Uyghurs still formed a plurality of the population and were the principal ethnic group in the south, Han Chinese proliferated in the newly-prosperous Dzungar Basin (including the cities of Karamay, Kuitun and Shihezi) in the north. Today, Xinjiang is still home to substantial communities of Kazakhs, Hui, Kirghiz, Mongols and other minorities, with a total of 43 languages spoken.

a **rubabs** and **dobros** are both wooden-bodied stringed instruments from Central Asia. The former is similar to a lute, whereas the latter is more like a guitar.

b The custom **"a man sets greatest store by the left while a woman favours the right"** has infiltrated all aspects of Chinese people's daily lives. For example, men's washrooms stand on the left and ladies' on the right. A man wears his marriage ring on his left hand and the woman the right. In wedding photographs or on occasions a couple attend together, they also maintain this protocol. Should a pair change places, they may become objects of mockery or derision.

c In many parts of China, it is commonplace to refer to the spouse of a close male friend as **"sister-in-law"** to emphasise one's fraternal bond.

d **The God of the Earth** refers to *Tudi* (known alternatively as *Tudigong* – Lord of the Soil and Ground – or *Tudishen* – God of the Soil and Ground), one of the deities in Chinese folklore. Shrines to him are common in the countryside, where farmers and their families bestow offerings and praise in expectation of, or out of gratitude for, a bountiful harvest. He may be referred to as "grandfather" (*yeye*), so in this passage the master's exclamation is slightly profane, invoking a figure of seniority in a coarse way.

e **Zhen** sounds like the word "shocked" in Chinese.

f   **Osman Batyr** (1899-1951) was a Kazakh resistance fighter. During the Soviet-backed Ili Rebellion, which began in 1944, he was one of the leaders of the forces which resisted the rule of the Chinese Nationalist Party over Xinjiang. However, he later switched sides and opposed the Communists. Captured in Hami, he was executed in Urümqi. Many of his supporters were airlifted to safety, though some remained as guerillas in Xinjiang.

g   **Douglas Mackiernan** (1913-50) is now chiefly remembered as the first CIA agent to be killed in the line of duty. Originally posted to Xinjiang (then known as East Turkestan) in 1943, in June 1947 he was sent to intervene between Uyghur and Kazakh forces (including those headed by Batyr) who were fighting against the Outer Mongols and Soviet Union. His main remit appears to have been gathering nuclear intelligence. Following the withdrawal of the US Consulate from Tihwa two years later, Mackiernan was supposed to remain behind and destroy files and documents to prevent them from falling into Communist hands. The last months of his life saw him trekking vast distances on horseback across the Taklimakan Desert, assisted by Kazakh allies such as Batyr. In the end, he was killed not by the Communists but by Tibetan guards who had been ordered to shoot any foreigners who tried to enter Tibet. It is likely they mistook him for a Kazakh because he was wearing their traditional dress.

h   **Temüjin** was the birth name of Genghis Khan.

i   **The Yang Pass** was first established in the Western Han Dynasty (202BC-9AD) to the northwest of present-day Dunhuang City, Gansu Province. It was the land route for ancient China to carry out diplomatic activities and an unavoidable pass on the southern branch of the Silk Road. It gained its name because it stood to the south (*yang*) of the Yumen Pass. The two passes were originally both doors to the Western Regions. From the Song Dynasty (960-1279AD) onwards, the Yang Pass was gradually deserted because of a decline in communications with the West.

j **Hu Zongnan** (1896-1962) was Chiang Kai-shek's most trusted general. In 1947, he attacked and occupied Yan'an, the capital city of the CPC, and became the famous, though ephemeral "King of the Northwest".

k **Cat's eye gems**, more commonly known as "tiger's eye" in English, are a form of metamorphic quartz with parallel bands which resemble feline markings.

l **Altai** is a city in western Mongolia, not to be confused with the Altay Mountains.

m The **Upper Cave** in Beijing is part of the Zhoukoudian cave complex where the remains of the *homo erectus* Peking Man (possibly up to 750,000 years old) was discovered in 1921. The Upper Cave was subject to much later habitation and contains the remains of *homo sapiens* from 10,000 to 20,000 years ago.

n The **Jinggang Mountains** lie in Jiangxi Province and are regarded as the birthplace of the Red Army. In the autumn of 1927, following an unsuccessful uprising against the Nationalist Party, Mao Zedong and his 1,000 remaining men found refuge for months in the mountains. Eventually, they joined forces with the troops under the command of Zhu De and the Fourth Army was formed. It was from Jiangxi that the Communists embarked on the Long March in 1934.

o **Yan'an** is a city in Northern Shaanxi, lying around 250 kilometres to the north of Xi'an. An arid place of low fertility, it achieved legendary status as the end-point of the Long March and the base of the Communist Party for twelve years (1936-48). While living in dwellings adapted from the local style of cave house (*yaodong*), Mao and his supporters further formulated their revolutionary politics, military tactics and concept of socialist aesthetics.

p   These lines are quoted from the long poem *Merciful Voyage* written by the Qinghai poet Changyao.

q   The legend of **Kuafu** in its various forms is a myth ubiquitously known across China. Very much like Icarus, it has come to serve as a warning to ambitious individuals who are inclined to overstretch themselves.

r   The **cultural instructor** (*wenhua jiaoyuan*) was attached to military units and taught lessons in literature and other cultural subjects to the troops, who often lacked formal education. In the period in which the story is set, his role also served to enforce a revolutionary understanding of the arts.

s   The observation that a **beauty is plump** harks back to periods in Chinese history, most notably the Tang Dynasty (618-907 AD), when the feminine ideal emphasised rounded hips and a broad bosom, thought to be indicative of a pampered, elite lifestyle.

t   "**Such a tender girl can't handle the fire.**" This is intended as a sexual metaphor. The fire denotes male passion, so Old Nana is insinuating that her visitor is possibly frigid or a virgin.

u   In parts of China, especially the northwest, **big front teeth** are taken as a sign of masculine good looks.

v   **Women who entered the water risked becoming infertile.** According to traditional Chinese medicine, women should avoid contact with cold water, especially when they are menstruating or have just given birth. It was believed that a chill caught in these vulnerable stages could easily pass into the bones and imperil reproductive health and physical wellbeing in general.

w **Tuxing Sun** is a character in *The Legend of Deification* (*Fengshen Yanyi*) by Xu Zhonglin (1560-1630AD). The story features immortals who follow the strategist Zhang Ziya and have superhuman gifts. Tuxing Sun was a dwarf who feared the sunlight and had the special ability to burrow underground. He is said to have served in the army of the Duke Wen of Zhou (11th century BC), whose origins lay on the Zhou Plateau.

x **Savoury noodles with seasoned pork** (*saozi mian*) is a staple countryside dish, originating in Qishan County. It is prepared by frying minced pork with vinegar and chilli. It is then served with boiled wheat flour noodles and sliced tree ear mushrooms, shredded tofu, eggs (symbolising wealth), red carrots (prosperity) and garlic sprouts (vitality). The whole lot is usually mixed together while piping hot with extra vinegar and chilli.

y The **Oirat Mongols** are a tribal people, currently numbering around 680,000 and spread between China, Mongolia and Russia.

z The **Household Registration Card** (*Hukou*) was implemented after 1949, though versions of the scheme operated in earlier eras. It details each citizen's background and birth, assigning them as either a countryside or urban resident. Part of the original rationale was to curb an influx of rural workers to the cities, thereby creating demographic stability. However, for many in the countryside, this became a bone of contention since in reality it limited their economic mobility. As time has gone on, restrictions have loosened so that rural residents who gain more qualifications (especially through higher education) can now apply to alter their registration status.

aa The reference to formulating a **Twelfth "Five-Year Plan"** is slightly tongue-in-cheek. As part of shaping and managing the planned socialist economy, every five years since 1953 the Chinese government has laid out a fresh (or modified) set of guidelines and initiatives. Ordinary people may semi-seriously refer to having their own "Five-Year Plan". The twelfth of these denotes economic activities in the period 2010-15.

ab **Su Qin and Zhang Yi of the State of Qin** were military strategists active in the 4th century BC. Prior to the reign of the First Emperor Qin Shihuang (220-210BC) much of the territory of China was divided into warring states, the largest of which were Qin, Qi, Chu, Yan, Han, Zhao and Wei. In order to consolidate the strength of the Qin, Su Qin tried to broker concord between the other six (known as the "Vertical Alliance") in a bid to stop them feuding and possibly imploding. His successor, Zhang Yi, had the same objective but advocated an alternative strategy (known as the "Horizontal Alliance"), encouraging the other states to ally with the Qin to avoid decimation.

ac The **dragon throne** was the lavish seat reserved for the Chinese emperor as he presided over his court.

ad The **Ubashi Khan** (1744-74; reigned 1761-71) was the last Khan of the Kalmyk Khanate. After this episode, Catherine the Great dissolved the Khanate and transferred its power to the Governor of Astrakhan, retaining the leading Kalmyk prince as the Vice-Khan. In other words, authority over the tribes was lost to the Tsarist regime. The above account of the story does not make clear that Ubashi made scrupulous preparations for the journey, even consulting the Dalai Lama for a propitious date for their return. In the end, weak ice on one side of the river prevented thousands of his people from joining the crossing.

ae **Ayuka Khan** (reigned 1669-1724) was the great-grandfather of Ubashi Khan. **Tseren Donduk Khan** (reigned 1724-35) managed to wrest the leadership of the Kalmyks from several rivals after the death of Ayuka. He was succeeded by **Donduk Ombo Khan** (reigned 1735-41) and **Donduk Dashi Khan** (reigned 1741-61).

af This episode in history is described by the English writer Thomas De Quincey (1785-1859) in *Revolt of the Tartars*, first published in *Blackwood's Magazine* in 1837. De Quincey took most of his information from Benjamin Bergmann's *Versuch zur Geschichte des Kalmükenflucht von der Volga* ("Essay on the History of the Flight of the Kalmucks from the Volga").

ag **Zhang Qian** (164-113BC) was the envoy from the Court of the Emperor Wu of Han, who was instrumental in opening up links between the Chinese Empire and the regions of Central Asia. He is closely associated with the development of the Silk Road and with stimulating Chinese interest in colonising what is now Xinjiang.

ah Despite its rather ostentatious name, the **Cultural Palace** (*Wenhuangong*) is a fixture of many urban districts in China. Copying a Soviet archetype, these buildings are a venue for recreational and cultural activities to stimulate urban citizens.

ai **Tending the Roots of Wisdom** (*Caigentan*) is a compilation of maxims and aphorisms edited by Hong Zicheng (fl. 1572-1620). It draws wisdom from Zen Buddhism, Taoism and Confucianism. The philosopher Zhu Xi had a saying to the effect that "whoever has survived on root vegetables can achieve anything". Roots or root vegetables were then perceived as famine food, so Hong's book emphasises how hardship is ultimately character-building. **The Zhu Family Admonitions** (*Zhu Xi Zhijiageyan*) was compiled by Zhu

Bailu (1617-88) in the early Qing Dynasty. It contains many admonitions or aphorisms about personal conduct, especially about the household. These include: "Get up at barely daybreak to sprinkle water in the courtyard and then sweep it" and "Even though it is only a bowl of porridge or rice, we should bear in mind how difficult it was to obtain; although it is only half a length of string or thread, we should always remember how hard it was to produce". **Pupils' Rules and Disciplines** (*Diziqui*) was compiled by Li Yuxiu (1647-1729) and later revised by Jia Cunren. It is a 1,080-character text for schoolchildren that emulates the style of *The Three-Character Canon*.

aj **The Three-Character Canon** or *Three-Character Classic* (*Sanzijing*) is an elementary literacy aid, variously attributed to Wang Yinglin (1223-96AD) and Ou Shizi (1234-1324). Every clause contains just three characters to make them easy for children to memorise and the content covers aspects of history and culture, while emphasising common virtues like filial piety. **The Thousand Word Primer** (*Qianziwen*) dates from the 6th century and serves a similar function, often taught in conjunction with the former. It consists of 250 lines of four characters each, which are grouped into rhyming stanzas of four. Children are encouraged to sing it out loud.

ak "**The Song of the Immortals**" is taken from *The Dream of Red Mansions* (*Hong Lou Meng*), attributed to Cao Yueqin (1715 or 1724-1763 or 1764).

al This saying from Confucius is one of the cornerstones in enforcing the virtue of filial piety in Chinese culture.

am **Wu Zetian** (lived 624-705AD) was the first and only Empress Regnant in Chinese history. She was concubine to the Emperor Taizong of Tang and, after his death, married his ninth son Gaozong, who also ascended to the throne. After

Gaozong suffered a debilitating stroke in 660AD, she assumed ever greater power in court. In 690AD, several years after being widowed, she took the extraordinary step of founding her own Dynasty (the Zhou) with herself as emperor. Wu was generally viewed harshly by Confucian and misogynistic historians, who maligned her rise to power as bloody.

an **Empress Zhangsun** (or Changsun) was the wife of the Emperor Taizong and the mother of Gaozong. Her formal title Wendeshunsheng ("the civil, virtuous, serene and holy empress"), together with anecdotes about her dutiful nature (she threatened suicide if her husband were to die from a bout of illness), suggest she was of starkly different temperament to the ambitious Wu Zetian. **Empress Xiao Wen** (died 936AD) was married to the Emperor Taizong of Liao (reigned 927-47AD). Such was her devotion to her husband that she accompanied him on hunts and military campaigns. **Empress Xiaozhuang** (1613-88) was the wife of the Emperor Hong Taiji of Qing (reigned 1636-43) and Dowager Empress during the reigns of her son, Shunzi, and grandson, Kangxi. Like Auntie Golden Flower, she was an ethnic Mongol, though from the same clan as Genghis Khan.

ao **The Dowager Empress Cixi** (1835-1908) became imperial concubine to the Emperor Xianfeng in her youth and bore him a son and successor, the short-lived Emperor Tongzhi. Contrary to the Qing rules of succession, she installed her nephew Guangxu as the Emperor, so she was the de facto ruler of China for more than forty years until her death. Despite recent attempts at rehabilitation (notably Jung Chang's biography *The Dowager Empress Cixi: The Concubine who Launched Modern China*, 2013), historians have judged her a despot whose resistance to political and economic reforms paved the way for the demise of the Qing Empire. **Yuan Shikai** (1859-1916) was a statesman and military leader, largely responsible for the defence of Beijing at the end of the

Qing Dynasty. He was a sometime ally of Cixi and sworn enemy of Guangxu, who persuaded the Dowager Empress to enact limited reforms such as overhauling the education system. After Cixi and Guangxu died within 24 hours of each other, the infant Puyi was installed as the new emperor. Yuan eventually brokered the terms of the boy ruler's abdication and (following the brief presidency of Sun Yat-sen) became the President of the new Republic of China. In mainland China, Yuan Shikai's military and political prowess have come to be overshadowed by the treachery of his later days, when he fell out with other reformers and moved to restore the monarchy and declare Puyi and then himself Emperor.

Sun Yat-sen (1866-1925) is regarded as the founding father of the Republic of China. Although his government proved fragile and depended on regional warlords to impose order, he is remembered as a skilled conciliator who brought together nationalist and communist tendencies and formulated the Three Principles of the People (*Sanmin Zhuyi*) democratic philosophy: People's Rule (*Minzu Zhuyi*), People's Democracy (*Minquan Zhuyi*) and People's Livelihood (*Minsheng Zhuyi*).

Lightning Source UK Ltd.
Milton Keynes UK
UKHW010615261019
352350UK00001B/51/P